THE GARDEN

part one

MURDERS UNDER THE SUN
SEASON TWO; INTRO

MOLLY: Welcome to *Murders Under the Sun*, a podcast that explores a series of unusual crimes that have occurred in sunny Southern California.

I'm Molly Shure, your host. For the past five years I've worked as a journalist at a local news outlet. Stories of murder and mayhem come across my desk weekly, if not daily. However, one day I noticed something startling.

There seemed to be a connection between several crimes that transpired over a five-year period—seven crimes to be precise. What connected them? Location for one. They all took place within a twenty-mile radius of each other, but that alone wasn't significant.

The thing that pinged in my brain was that many of the people at the center of these crimes knew each other. Not the criminals, which would be an obvious thread, but the victims. I know, I know, six degrees of separation. Didn't I already say the crimes took place in a twenty-mile radius? But we're not talking six degrees here. It's more like one degree.

You'll see if you stick with me for all seven seasons of the show, the crimes circle back around. The people you meet in the first season play a role in Season Seven's story.

Am I imagining things? Is the connection real? Is there one mastermind behind the crimes? Or are they linked by some kind of social, psychological or even spiritual force? I'm afraid that's something you'll have to decide for yourself.

Each season, I'll do a deep dive into just one

of these stories. You'll hear from the people who were victimized, journal, memoir, letters, and transcript entries from others who were involved—sometimes the criminals themselves—and behind-the-scenes information you can't get anywhere else.

So, get out your sunglasses. We're pulling back the curtains and letting the light shine on some of Orange County's darkest mysteries.

part two

MURDERS UNDER THE SUN
SEASON TWO; EPISODE ONE

MOLLY: The crimes we are about to explore are very different from those in Season One, *The Cliff House*. In the first season, we watched a heartless narcissist bent on getting what he wanted at any cost, even if he had to commit murder to do it.

The motivation for the crimes in Season Two is almost a polar opposite. I won't tell you what it is, though. No spoilers here.

You'll experience this story as the people involved experienced it. You'll be confused and frustrated when they are confused and frustrated, and your questions will be answered as theirs are.

In *The Cliff House,* we met Olivia Richards and Brian McKibben, a single mother and her son. It's their lives we're going to dig into in *The Garden*.

The majority of the entries I'll be sharing with you come from Olivia's point of view. I've done my best to tell her story as she related it to me.

There will also be diary entries that were written in the 1990s by a character who will remain a mystery until the second episode. Why wait? Because that's when Olivia learns who she is.

I attempted to interview the diary-writer's sister, but she refused, claiming it was too painful to rehash old events. Instead, she handed over the diary.

As in the last season, I won't be reading the

entire book, just the passages I believe will
help you understand what happened and why.

Some mysteries are whodunnits. I think you'll
find this crime is more of a *whydunnit*. But
enough of me, let's hear from Olivia.

Was it him? An old panic rose in Olivia's chest. The man's head was
bowed over a sheet of paper as he walked across the parking lot of the
Mission Viejo Civic Center. His gait caught her eye first. Proctor had
walked like that, bowlegged and slightly pigeon-toed.

The man's hair was cropped close to his head and threaded with
gray. Proctor's had been brown and had hung in greasy locks to his
shoulders. This man was shorter, not as imposing as the man of her
memories. But, of course, she'd only been a child when she'd known
Proctor.

He glanced up from his reading, and her throat constricted. The
eyes. They were the washed-out color of old denim, cold and predatory.
Could two men have those same eyes?

Olivia stayed in the car and watched him pass. She didn't think he'd
recognize her. It had been so many years. She was an adult now, not a
girl. But, still, the idea of those eyes fixing on her made her skin crawl.

She waited until he disappeared into the library before exiting her
car. It might have been her imagination, but when she stepped out into
the warm evening, she could've sworn she smelled the familiar scent of
him—cigarettes and stale sweat mixed with the mineral odor of chalk.
She'd never forgotten it.

She was ten minutes early for her parenting class, but even if she'd
been late, she would have waited until he was safely inside the library.
Allowing him to pass only feet from her without some kind of protection, a barrier between them... She couldn't have done it. Not even
twenty-two years later.

Olivia hurried across the tarmac feeling exposed and vulnerable, and
ducked into City Hall. Why would he come here? Her mother had

released another book recently. He was a parasite, a man who lived off the fat of other people's land. But why now? Sarah Richards's name had been in the media for years.

Maybe it was just a horrible coincidence. Tumbleweeds went wherever the wind blew, and it often blew west. Since its Gold Rush days, California had drawn drifters and opportunists. Proctor had been both.

Regina, the instructor, beamed at Olivia when she entered the community room where the class was held. Olivia walked to the third row and slid into a seat next to Nanette.

Nanette snapped shut the laptop she'd been working on and glanced up. She was a single mother, a CPA with a busy client load, and had no time for frivolity, but she and Olivia had bonded over their similar circumstances. Her smile of greeting withered when she saw Olivia's face. "Are you okay?"

Olivia was still in a state of shock, and it must have shown. "Yeah, I'm fine."

"You don't look fine. Brian okay?"

"Brian's great." Nanette looked at Olivia over the top of her glasses with doubt in her intelligent, brown eyes.

"I thought I saw somebody I hadn't seen in years. That's all," Olivia said.

"Must be a real charmer."

Regina called the room to order and began taking attendance. But Olivia's thoughts remained with the man in the parking lot. His walk, his eyes, they were what she'd remembered Proctor's to be. But those were the perceptions of a young girl, filtered and blurred by twenty-two long years. The idea that he would show up here, now, or that she would recognize him if he did, seemed more and more unlikely. Reality was, the man she saw had triggered memories, some very bad memories, but he probably wasn't Proctor.

If dreams didn't come true, and in her experience they didn't, she had to believe the same rules applied to nightmares.

2.1.2

ON MONDAY AFTERNOON, Olivia took time off work to accompany Brian's class to the San Juan Capistrano Mission. Every autumn, St. Barnabas's fourth grade classes began their study of California history with a field trip to the Jewel of the Missions. Olivia's attendance was the kind of thing CPS liked to see, but she'd wanted to go. The place was so steeped in history, just being there put her own life into perspective. She loved the architecture, the gardens, and the crumbling ruins of the Great Stone Church. The church had fallen in an 1812 earthquake killing forty-two worshippers, which proved the point: doing the right thing held no guarantees.

Olivia wandered into Father Serra Chapel. Its walls wrapped around her like a cocoon, muting the voices of the children and the rumble of a distant train. She'd come in for a moment of peace. A statue of Father Serra saluted her from his recess in the gold leaf altar as if to bestow a blessing on her decision. But she sat in a pew close to the door anyway. She was nervous about leaving Brian.

The cool air was redolent with frankincense and myrrh—the oils of life and death. She couldn't remember where, maybe *National Geographic*, but she'd read that physicians in ancient times prescribed frankincense as frequently as modern doctors do antibiotics. Sweet smelling myrrh was used for embalming. The word made her shudder.

Stop it. She was being morbid. Fearful. There were plenty of adults outside tasked with watching the students. They'd had nearly six weeks to learn Brian's routines and needs. She could take a minute for herself. *But there were a lot of students to watch.* The saints in the retablo's niches and nooks seemed to condemn her through painted eyes. She didn't know their stories, how they'd managed to achieve sainthood. They couldn't have put more effort into it than she had, she knew that. There was a chill in the air of the small chapel. Olivia left, hurrying out into the fading heat of the day.

Brian's class had been let loose on the central courtyard. Their teacher, Mrs. Margolis, and the two parents who should have been on duty were gossiping in the shade of the portico. The days were growing shorter. The mid-October sun hung low in the sky and reflected off the old stone and stucco walls into Olivia's eyes. She shaded them with a hand and scanned the area for her son.

All she could see were silhouettes, nothing more. But she knew Brian's outline, the curve of his hyper-extended knees, and the funny way he hitched up his shoulders when he ran. She knew the exact spot his cowlick shot up off his head and the pitch of his ski slope nose.

She knew all these things, and she didn't see them.

She strode across the grass to the closest group of boys. She recognized one of Brian's classmates, Noah Wilson. "Hey."

Noah looked up, guilt on his face. He was at that age when all discussions with adults started with trepidation whether he was doing anything wrong or not.

"Have you seen Brian?"

Noah looked at the other boys. They all shrugged in unison. Even if they knew where Brian had gone, betraying him if there was any possibility it would get him in trouble was out of the question. Frustrated, Olivia wound her way toward Mrs. Margolis and the attendant mothers.

Olivia felt the familiar burn in her gut. Brian hadn't wanted her to chaperone the field trip. Mrs. Margolis, a newlywed with no children of her own, had assured her he was in good hands. Olivia had come anyway. She acknowledged her tendency to hover. She had reason to. Brian wandered.

As soon as he'd learned to use his chubby little legs, he'd wandered out the front door and to the neighborhood park. Alone. He'd been on the run ever since.

And now Brian was a brain-damaged wanderer. Since his accident, he'd become impulsive, easily distracted and had memory lapses he filled in with bits of dreams and recollections from other days. The doctor called it "confabulation."

Parents of normal children didn't understand. They made fun of mothers who leashed their toddlers, even though children were arguably more important than family pets. They invented derogatory names, like helicopter parents, for those who kept close tabs on their children's whereabouts. Olivia didn't care. She leashed and hovered proudly. The last time Brian wandered; she'd almost lost him forever.

"Mrs. Margolis. I hate to interrupt..." This wasn't true. Olivia didn't hate to interrupt. The teacher should have been minding her flock.

Annoyance furrowed the woman's usually unlined brow. "Yes?"

"Do you know where Brian is?"

"Isn't he with the other boys?"

"No." *Would I have asked you if he was?* Olivia thought but didn't say.

Mrs. Margolis adjusted her face into more pleasant lines. "He's probably in the gift shop."

He wouldn't be in the gift shop. As far as Brian was concerned, shopping was right up there with broccoli and long division. But that heavy, desperate feeling that accompanied motherhood these days thudded onto Olivia's chest, reason fled, and she ran across the central courtyard toward the museum gift store.

She wanted to scream. Mrs. Margolis knew Olivia was on probation with CPS. Oh, they didn't call it probation, they called it a "Safety Plan," but it was probation. The County of Orange had given her six months to get her act together and prove she deserved to keep Brian. That six months had ballooned into a year because of Brian's health problems.

Olivia not only had to prove she wasn't neglectful, but she also had to prove she was a model of conscientiousness if she were to be deemed a fit parent for a child with Brian's needs. But he'd been doing so well, Fred, her caseworker, was sure the doctors would sign off at the end of the year.

Having Brian under the watchful eyes of a responsible adult at all times was a part of the Safety Plan she was so close to being released from. Mrs. Margolis knew that. Why hadn't a parent accompanied the children to the shop? Yes, stone walls encircled the Mission, but the shop was next to the exit. The exit that led to downtown, busy streets, train tracks.

It took a moment for her eyes to adjust to the dim light in the museum store. When they did, she could see he wasn't inside. She trotted through the aisles of books, rosaries, and all the items adorned with miniature missions anyway. When the panic was on her, standing still was impossible.

Back outside, she searched the grounds with her eyes and tried to calm the wind whipping up horrible scenarios in her mind. Where would he have gone? Please, God, not out the exit. She walked toward the museum, struggling to let intuition guide her. Brian liked the living history exhibits. He might have returned to the rooms decorated with period furniture.

She darted in and out of the Padre's dining room, bedroom, and living quarters. She didn't see him, and there was nowhere for an eleven-year-old to hide in the ascetic furnishings. Outside, near the chapel again, a sob rose in her throat. A prayer, to Mary, to God, to anybody who'd listen, formed with it.

She wasn't Catholic. She'd been raised by an Earth Momma in true ecumenical hippie fashion, but she'd heard Mary's story. Mary, she'd thought, would understand both the joy of having her son returned from the dead and the crushing responsibility it brought.

No answer came. No heavenly finger pointed the way. But she saw the marker for the cemetery. Brian had become fascinated by cemeteries after visiting Disneyland's Haunted Mansion last year.

Olivia followed the signs into the graveyard. It was small, and she searched it quickly. He wasn't there, in front, or behind the one large tombstone. Turning right, she took the path that led to the Sacred Garden and the Bell Wall. If she couldn't find him here, she'd go straight to the administration office and demand they close the exits. If they thought she was an overprotective, hysterical mother, so be it. Better to be labeled overprotective than neglectful. She'd learned neglect had terrible ramifications.

She drew closer to the arched entrance and saw movement. A flit of navy blue against the beiges and browns. She ran.

Through the archway, next to a barred window in the wall of the Serra Gate, stood her son. Her relief was so extreme, her thighs grew weak. She slowed and sidled up to Brian a foot at a time like someone might approach a runaway colt. No sudden movements. No rushing forward and throwing her arms around him. "Hey, buddy. What're you doing?" Her voice sounded falsely cheerful even to her own ears.

Brian didn't seem to notice. "I saw somebody walking around over here. I thought maybe there was another room—like where the Native Americans used to live."

Olivia placed a hand on his shoulder. "You know you're not supposed to take off."

"I couldn't find you." His voice grew sulky. "You're not supposed to take off either."

"I only went into the chapel for a minute. Mrs. Margolis and the other mothers were right there." Or they should have been.

Brian turned and walked toward the cemetery. "Can we get ice cream? Some of the kids are going to get ice cream after."

Olivia thought about saying no. Disobedience ought to have consequences. Wandering deserved punishment, not rewards. But she said, "Sure."

Since she and Davy, Brian's father, had divorced three years ago, she'd been thrust into the role of enforcer. Davy was the yes-man, the fun guy, Mr. Party. She made sure homework was done, teeth were brushed, rooms were cleaned and, most important, Safety Plans were followed.

She'd wanted today to be fun. She'd wanted her turn to spoil her son. "We're going to have to talk about this," she said, and Brian looked at his feet. "But not now. Tonight."

Olivia glanced over her shoulder as they left the Sacred Garden. Movement, a flutter of white, a large bird maybe, disappeared behind the Bell Wall. They walked past the entrance to the graveyard in silence.

"So, what was in the window?" she said when they reached the courtyard.

"It was all black. I couldn't see anything." Brian sounded relieved to change the subject, then darted ahead to join his classmates who were lining up to leave.

"In the gift shop then?" Mrs. Margolis said with a smug smile.

Olivia tried to suppress the anger in her voice. "In the graveyard." She was pleased to see the complacent expression slide off Mrs. Margolis's face.

2.1.3

MIRACLE OF MIRACLES, the next day Olivia pulled into the soccer field parking lot, and Brian was jogging straight toward her car—backpack flapping behind him, cleats in hand. She was so shocked to see her son where he was supposed to be at the time he was supposed to be there, it took her a moment to recognize the tall form behind him.

She lifted her hand to wave to Tom, St. Barnabas's math teacher and assistant soccer coach, but Brian opened the passenger side door and thrust his gear into her waiting arms. "Let's go."

Olivia had thought about Tom a surprising number of times since she'd met him last month. He seemed nice and responsible, and she was pretty sure he was flirting with her whenever she saw him at school or on the field. But all at once the car filled with hurried, sweaty boy, commotion, and confusion, and any thought of Tom fled from her mind. Olivia shifted Brian's things into the rear seat before he sat on them and helped him untangle the seat belt that caught on his gym bag.

By the time she turned to look out the windshield for Tom, he was gone. The disappointment she felt was unexpected. Romance had been the last thing on her mind for a very long time. She should probably keep it that way.

She started the engine and put the car into reverse. Before she could leave her spot, a hand dropped into her open window. Olivia jumped.

"Hi," Tom said.

"You startled me."

"I have that effect on women." He smiled a one-dimpled smile. "I wanted to make sure your wanderer made it into the car."

Olivia put a hand on Brian's thigh but kept her eyes on Tom. "He's right here. Safe and sound."

"I was kind of hard on him today." Tom leaned down and looked past Olivia at Brian. "Sorry, buddy. Just helping out your mom."

Tom's face was so close to hers, she could see the faint stubble of afternoon beard, smell his cologne. She'd never noticed how green his eyes were before. "Whether Brian appreciates it or not, I do," she said.

"I know you guys have been having a tough time." He patted her car like it was a dog he was fond of. "I'd better let you get going."

Olivia thanked him again and pulled out of her space. Before she turned onto the street, she looked into her rear-view mirror. Tom stood where she'd left him, watching her drive away.

"He's mean." Brian's voice was grim.

Olivia glanced at her son, and the happy sunbeam she'd been basking in disappeared into the cloud cover on his face. Tears rimmed his brown eyes.

"What's the matter, Brian?"

"Mr. Hartman."

"Tom Hartman?" Olivia had grown used to Brian suffering under the hands of the other kids on the team, or at school. Kids were mean to those who were different, but teachers and coaches were usually supportive. "What happened?"

"For the whole practice, he was like, right by me telling me what to do. 'Brian, kick like this. Brian, pay attention to me. Brian, watch the game.' Everybody was looking at me."

"Maybe he was trying to help you?"

"That's what Coach said."

"You talked to Coach about it?" Olivia was surprised. Brian's feelings were like the dirty socks he shoved into his gym bag. They didn't come out until the smell overwhelmed him.

"No. He could tell I was mad." Brian pulled on the hem of his shorts with grubby hands. "Everybody could tell."

They rode in silence for a while. Olivia didn't want to minimize her son's embarrassment, but she was pretty sure she knew what had happened. Brian's mind wandered even when his body didn't. He wanted to be treated like all the other kids on the team, but he wasn't like all the other kids on the team. Not yet.

"I'll talk to Mr. Hartman next time I see him. I think he was trying to do a good thing, and he got carried away."

"He's mean."

"Honey. Why would he be mean to you? What reason could he have?"

"He doesn't like me."

Brian's words sliced into Olivia. Before the accident, he'd been such a confident and happy kid. Now paranoia haunted him. The doctors said difficulty interpreting social cues was normal for someone with the kind of head injuries he'd suffered, but that didn't make it any easier. It didn't make the pain any less. She hurt when he hurt, and he hurt a lot these days.

"I'm sure that's not true. I think he likes you a lot, that's why he was paying so much attention to you. If he didn't like you, he'd just ignore you."

Another block went by. Brian said, "I wish he didn't like me."

2.1.4

OLIVIA PULLED up to the curb in front of her home and turned off the ignition. As soon as the engine stopped, Brian threw open the car door. "Dad."

Davy, Olivia's ex, leaned on his car. He was early. He'd called yesterday, said he was planning to take Brian to dinner, and mentioned he wanted to talk to her. He had news.

Brian charged into his father's arms. Davy gave him a bear hug and kissed the top of his head. "Hey, buddy."

"You're early," Olivia said.

"Yeah. I had a job interview nearby."

A job interview. Maybe that was his news? Olivia rejected the thought. A job was news, not an interview.

"I beat you, Dad. I passed level five in *Iron Kingdom*. That means I get a burger at Five Guys, right?" Brian's face was shining, all storm clouds gone.

"No way. How'd you do it?" Davy ruffled his son's brown hair.

The boys talked game strategy while Olivia retrieved the mail and unlocked the door. Brian dropped his bags in the middle of the hall. "I'll show you," he said, excitement punctuating his words.

"Brian—" Olivia was going to tell him to pick up his stuff. To take a shower. Get ready to go. Davy cut her off.

"Hey, what's this?" He pointed at Brian's mess. "Does your mother live here?"

Brian grinned. "Yeah."

Davy struck his forehead with the palm of his hand. "That's right. Well, pick up anyway."

"I want to show you how I beat the level." A hint of whine crept into Brian's voice.

"We have all night. I want to talk to your mom for a minute, okay?"

"Okay," Brian said, and hefted his gym bag over his shoulder.

"As long as you're cleaning stuff up, take a shower. You're pretty ripe. I can smell your feet from here." Davy had a way of concealing commands inside jokes. His methods worked with Brian. Their son headed to his bedroom without an argument.

When Olivia corrected Brian, he resisted, obfuscated, and disappeared. Davy came blowing into his life once a month or so, as free and unpredictable as a summer breeze, and Brian responded like a kite in the hands of a master.

"What do you want to talk to me about?" Olivia sounded brisker than she'd intended.

"Are you going to offer me a cup of coffee?" Davy said.

This was different. They didn't usually socialize. When Davy showed up for his visits, if he showed up, the conversation between them was as brief as possible: Where are you going? Make sure he's home by nine. Don't forget he has school tomorrow. They never chatted over cups of coffee.

Davy sat at the outdated, white tiled counter that separated the kitchen and living room while Olivia busied herself with coffee making.

"I'm not sure how to start this conversation," Davy said, after taking a slug from the mug she deposited on the counter in front of him.

Olivia waited.

"I need to apologize for all the ways I've hurt you and Brian—"

Something between a cough and a laugh escaped through Olivia's lips. She covered her mouth with a hand. "Sorry, go on."

"I know. I don't blame you for being skeptical. I've been... neglectful, selfish. I'm sure you could come up with a longer list of negative adjectives."

Olivia could think of others--like unreliable, irresponsible--but she didn't say anything.

"Anyway, I'm asking for a chance to make it up to you and Brian."

"Davy, I've learned not to expect anything from you, so I'm not disappointed."

"It's different this time."

"Why?"

"I've been dry for almost six months. I'm going to stay that way."

"Dry? Really? You don't mean you're only drinking beer? Or you're only drinking on weekends?"

"No. Dry. I haven't even used mouthwash. When the court gave your mom temporary custody of Brian instead of me, that hit me hard."

Olivia examined his face. He looked healthy, healthier than he had in years. He was clean-shaven. His light brown hair had been recently cut. His blue eyes were clear and pleading. She wanted to believe him, but she'd been down this road before. It always ended in a swamp.

Davy stared into his coffee cup. "I'm not trying to do it alone this time. I know I can't. I'm in a Celebrate Recovery group. I have account-ability. It's different."

"So, this is what, step eight where you have to ask for forgiveness?"

"Nobody's making me ask."

"Tell you what," Olivia crossed her arms over her chest. "Come talk to me when you've been clean for six more months." She needed to see him make it through the holidays before she would even think about trusting him again. Christmas and New Year's were high temptations for social drinkers, and Davy was a social drinker.

"That's fair. We'll revisit the forgiveness thing next year." His jaw hardened.

"Okay," Olivia said.

"There's something else I want to say. I know I've been hit or miss with Brian in the past, but that's over. Tuesday and Thursday nights and every other weekend, I'm on. I'll be here."

"I'm not sure this is the best time for you to turn over a new leaf." Olivia had rearranged her and Brian's lives so she never had to depend on him.

"Why not?"

"CPS. I'm nearly done with the process. If nothing goes wrong, the doctors will sign Brian off in January, and I get my son and my life back."

"That's just as important to me as it is to you." A look of pain crossed Davy's face. He closed his eyes. "When I think about that night... I'm more ashamed than I can say."

He was referring to the night Brian was hit by the truck. No one could find Davy to tell him what had happened until the next morning because he was too drunk to answer the phone. Olivia didn't know if she'd ever be able to forgive him for that. She tried not to think about it. Dwelling on the memory was like swimming in a stormy sea with wrath-filled waves crashing around her. She could drown there.

"I didn't realize what he meant to me until we almost lost him, Liv. It's what's turned me around. I need to show him, prove it to him."

"Honestly, Davy, I only care about what Brian needs, and what he needs right now is people who do what they say they're going to do— every time. I need responsible adult eyes on him twenty-four seven."

"Let me help."

"If you pull the crap you used to pull, I could lose everything I'm working for." Davy had broken so many promises since their divorce, it had almost shattered Olivia. She'd given up hope she'd ever have a fulfilling career. How could she when she was constantly making last minute phone calls to her mother and Davy's father, calling in sick to work, or worrying over inexperienced babysitters? She had a new job now. A job she loved. A job with a future. She wasn't about to jeopardize it.

"I won't."

Olivia crossed her small kitchen in two long strides. "Here. Here is the schedule." She pointed to a chalkboard hanging next to the refrigerator. "Every hour of every day is accounted for: Mondays and Wednesdays, Mom gets him from school at 3:00 and keeps him until I get off at nine. Tuesdays and Thursdays, he goes straight to soccer practice after school. I leave work early, so I can pick him up by four-thirty. Every other Friday I have to close the studio, so your father picks him up from school. On alternate Saturdays, I take him to work with me, and he goes to childcare there. If any one of these things goes wrong, I'm screwed. I don't have time to create backup plans."

Davy pointed at the wall. "Put me down for Tuesdays and Thursdays. I'll pick him up here, or from soccer. You choose. And I'll take the weekends you work."

Olivia crossed her arms. "I can't chance it. Not now. Not when I'm this close."

Davy looked at the ceiling, took a deep breath and let it out slowly. "You don't have a choice." An icy finger trailed along Olivia's spine. "Don't make me play hardball. The courts made you the custodial parent, and I didn't fight it. But only because I have visitation rights. I get Tuesday and Thursday nights and every other weekend. That's what we agreed to."

"But ...but ...that was before." Anger and fear made her words come in sputters. "Before you stopped showing up. Before the accident. Before the stupid Safety Plan."

"I know. It's not fair. I get it. But it's the way it is. It's time I start being a parent."

"You've waited this long, why can't you wait until next year?"

"Because I think we have a better chance of being released from the plan if both Brian's parents are involved in his life."

"Not if one of them is completely irresponsible." The words exploded from her.

"Irresponsible, neglectful, those are labels we get to disprove." Davy pushed himself away from the counter and called out. "Brian, you ready? There's a burger with your name on it at Five Guys." He turned to Olivia. "I know you don't believe me, but I'm not going to let you down."

She hoped it was true, but her hope was thin and frayed, a fragile lifeline.

2.1.5

"YOU LEFT THE FRONT DOOR OPEN," Olivia called through the car window on Wednesday morning. Brian, who'd emerged from their condo, brown paper bag in hand, shot a glance over his shoulder like he didn't believe her. *Focus, baby, focus.*

Brian already had two tardy marks. One more, and he'd have to stay after school. Maybe Olivia shouldn't worry about these things. After all, some mothers had to deal with drugs, online porn, or video game addictions. He was on full scholarship at St. Barnabas Lutheran School, a good private school in the prestigious Dana Point community, a school she'd fought to get him into, and that he'd been suspended from last school year.

A suspension that had led to him being unsupervised for a few hours while Olivia went to work. Hours when he left the house and was hit by a truck, causing him to be in a coma for almost a week. He was still suffering from head trauma. When the truth about the circumstances came out, he was forgiven by the school board. But Olivia wanted to keep them happy. At least until she could afford the tuition on her own.

Rather than waiting in the long drop-off line at the school, Olivia parked on a side street. She might get him there on time if they walked. He'd definitely be late if they fought the traffic jam.

"You don't have to come with me," Brian said.

"I want to." She knew he was embarrassed by her presence. But she had no confidence he wouldn't get distracted by an interesting leaf, or a bug, or a cloud that resembled a leaf or a bug and never make it to class on time.

Brian picked up his pace. His feet, too large for his slender body and made even bigger by the Vans she'd bought a half-size too big for frugality's sake, slapped the sidewalk. He kept his eyes lowered, looking anywhere but at her. Olivia lengthened her stride to keep up. She wasn't going to let him out of her sight until he was safely on school grounds. He was just going to have to deal with it.

When they came to the school parking lot, Brian mumbled something that might have been "Goodbye," and took off running toward the building. Olivia watched him until he walked through the glass front doors.

As she turned to leave, a minivan pulled into one of the staff parking spaces. Art Bishop, the school principal, unfolded his long frame from the driver side. Three kids erupted from the other doors and ran, just like Brian had, to get to their classrooms before the bell rang.

"Olivia. Just the person I wanted to see." She watched Art cross the blacktop toward her. He was six-foot-four, broad-shouldered and muscular and boxed for exercise. He ought to be frightening, but gentle was the first word that came to her mind when describing him.

Art had gone through some marriage problems last February, and Olivia had allowed herself to indulge in a small fantasy about a future with him. Since then, he and Gwen, his wife, seemed to have worked out their differences. Olivia had gotten to know Gwen, and the crush had died an appropriate death.

"Why is that?"

"Gwen has been after me to find out how the job is going."

"It's going well, in fact, I was going to call her. I have news. Fiona asked if I wanted to earn my way into an ownership position in the business. I'm putting in some unpaid hours, and she's giving me a share of the retail profits. I'm going to be part owner of the Fishbowl."

"That's great." A slow smile spread across Art's face.

"I'm still pinching myself."

"Call Gwen. She'd love to hear the details."

Gwen was responsible for Olivia's career change. After Brian's accident, Olivia had to leave her waitressing job and find something with more flexible hours. One of Gwen's past real estate clients had opened a Pilates studio in Dana Point. The Fishbowl was named for the panoramic ocean views visible from every room. Knowing Olivia had a business degree, and that she needed a fresh start, Gwen had put in a good word for her, and she'd gotten the job.

"I will."

Art's forehead creased into concerned lines. "How's Brian doing?"

"Slowly improving. Davy wants to be part of his life. He's in an alcohol recovery group. Says he's not drinking anymore, but I don't know. If he disappoints Brian again, especially now..." Her words trailed off.

Art looked at the sky for a moment, then at her. "It's no secret Gwen and I had troubles earlier this year. I made a decision to forgive her for the sake of the kids. She was their mother, and they needed her. It hasn't always been easy. It's a day-by-day thing. And, she had to forgive me too. My priorities were pretty skewed. It was the right decision for our family. It also began the healing of our marriage."

"I can't see Davy and me—"

"I'm not saying that. But healing comes in a lot of different forms." Art touched her arm. "Sorry if I'm sticking my nose in where it doesn't belong."

Olivia gave a small shake of her head. "You're not. I brought it up, but I do have to get to work." His words chafed. She didn't know everything that had happened between him and Gwen, but she was pretty sure it didn't include substance abuse and abandonment.

They said goodbye, and Olivia headed up the sidewalk to her car. She couldn't stay annoyed at Art. His friendship, and Gwen's, was one of the greatest blessings in her life. They'd done so much for her.

Olivia reached her vehicle and unlocked it with a chirp. As she climbed into her car, she turned to see a young woman walking toward her. Their eyes met and Olivia was struck by how unusual hers were—

deep set, brown and flecked with gold. Olivia smiled, but the woman jerked her gaze away and hurried on in the direction she'd been headed. Olivia felt oddly embarrassed, as if she'd been inappropriate. But her day was too busy to worry about the attitudes of strangers. She put it out of her mind.

2.1.6

THE REST of the day flew by. Olivia had gone to work at noon after running errands, and now it was almost time for the 5:30 barre class. The studio was a bright spot in her life. Her schedule was hectic. She worried about Brian's health all the time. CPS was a thundercloud over her head. Davy was a thorn in her flesh. But peace reigned at the Fishbowl.

She counted four drops of lavender oil as they fell into a diffuser. She recapped the bottle, then added mandarin, Roman chamomile, and vetiver oils. Hope and healing had been working their way into her heart since she'd taken this job. Small things, like tiny drops of oil bursting with the fragrance of future possibilities. She was building something here, something for herself and for Brian.

She thought about the Fishbowl all the time. She mused about ways to market their inventory while she grocery shopped. She jotted ideas for new product lines while she sat at red lights. She read everything she could find on essential oils after Brian went to bed. For the past three weeks, she'd been trying out different recipes with varying results.

"That smells yummy." Yasmin Madani, one of the studio's instructors, put her yoga mat under her arm so she could use both hands to wave the mist into her face. "What's in it?"

Olivia handed her a card with the recipe. "I call it, Pay Attention."

"I'll take it."

Olivia rang up the order as the barre class attendees wandered in. Eight women and one man, all different ages, shapes, and sizes, waved hello as they made their way through the lobby into the studio. Yasmin greeted them all by name, asked about their families, jobs, injuries, pets, whatever the topic of interest was for each. She was wonderful with the clients, several of whom commented on the new scent in the air as they passed through the lobby.

In her studies, Olivia had learned essential oils were much more than a healthier alternative to room spray. They were the pharmaceuticals of the past. Many a doctor, monk, or village medicine woman treated their neighbors with products from the garden until more potent antibiotics and drugs became available. Lately, she'd been researching the different herbs that affected the brain hoping to find something to help her son.

She busied herself with studio bookkeeping during the class. If things stayed quiet, she planned to sneak into the 7:00 mat class, then close up shop when it ended. Brian was at her mother's and would fall asleep on the couch if she ran late. Soon the soft strains of a flute were replaced by the murmur of voices. The class was wrapping up. Minutes later, students entered the lobby singly or in pairs. Some stopped by the computer to register for another class or change their schedule. Some browsed the books, candles, exercise clothes, and oils for sale. Olivia found the rhythm of her work comforting.

By 7:15 the lobby had emptied out. She kicked off her shoes, grabbed a mat and sneaked into the class already in progress. Yasmin walked between rows of students adjusting their form with a touch or a word. Olivia dropped next to a portly man whose face had turned an alarming shade of crimson since she'd last seen him. He was framed by the blackness of the far wall.

When the sun set, Olivia disliked this room's windows almost as much as she loved them during the day. At night they became black mirrors that reflected the interior space in the cold gray tones of a horror movie. The heavy breathing and pained moans from the students around her only added to the effect.

Yasmin squatted beside her and put a hand on her stomach. "Belly button to your spine." Olivia brought her attention back to her body. She worked hard for another half hour then scooted out so she could be at her desk when the class ended.

After the students left the studio, Yasmin slung her gym bag over her shoulder. "Ready?"

"Almost, but don't wait for me," Olivia said. "I have to finish up an order."

"Can't you do it tomorrow?"

"No, it has to be in today."

"I hate to leave you," Yasmin said, but she was already halfway out the door.

Forty minutes later, Olivia turned off the computer. The hum cut short with a beep and silence engulfed the studio. She walked into the exercise room. She stowed her things in a closet at its far end. She grabbed her purse and sweater, flicked off the closet light, turned toward the ebony wall, and came face to face with her own ghost.

Her shoulders tightened. Vulnerable. The word came to her like a whisper. She was on display. An upside-down world like the one Alice discovered inside the looking glass seemed suddenly more real than the ocean she saw during the day. Inhuman creatures peering through the windows into the brightly lit room jeered in her imagination. At her.

She rushed across the wood floor. Her flip flops echoing in the empty space, calling even more attention to herself. *Stop it. There's no one listening, no one watching.* But she hurried just the same and felt better when she switched off the overhead lights.

When she locked the studio door behind her, a fresh spasm of anxiety gripped her. She'd stayed too late. All the other businesses in the center were already closed. Most nights the jewelry repair store and the liquor store still had customers when she was leaving. Tonight, they were dark and still.

With no light coming from their windows, she had to make her way across the landing and down the stairs in the dim glow of the street-lights. Even the parking lot was deserted except for two cars; hers and a small sedan at the far end. She strode toward her Explorer with more confidence than she felt. Keys. She shouldn't have dropped her keys into her purse after locking up.

When Olivia was learning to drive, her mother had shown her how to stagger the car keys between her fingers like a set of makeshift brass knuckles for those occasions when she was out, alone, after dark. Olivia had laughed. Fat lot of good a bunch of keys would do against a man with a gun or a knife. Now she wished she had them.

She rummaged through her bag as she walked, her gaze flickering around the lot, every shadow seemed menacing. Her hands closed on cold metal. From across the lot, she hit the button on her electronic key. Her car beeped. The sound was reassuring.

She hurried to her vehicle and grabbed the handle. The door wouldn't budge. A moment of panic passed before she realized she'd hit lock instead of unlock. Her thumb found the buttons again. She pressed one then the other. All four doors opened.

Then two things happened at once: She dropped her keys. The headlights on the lone car across the lot popped on. Blinded and frantic, she bent to retrieve her keys. Her fingers scrabbled on the blacktop. The car's engine revved. Olivia dropped to her knees, both palms out, searching. The sedan pulled from its parking space. She patted the ground in frenzied circles. It moved closer.

There, behind her front tire. Soft leather. Her key chain. In less than ten seconds, she was inside her vehicle, slamming and locking doors, heart pounding. The small sedan turned right and pulled out of the lot, onto the highway.

She leaned her head on the headrest, closed her eyes and took several breaths to slow her racing pulse. What was wrong with her? The car probably belonged to one of the business owners who was leaving late, like she was.

She wasn't the hysterical type. Yes, she worried more than she should about Brian, but that was it. She'd been a single parent for three years. She was the one who soothed fears, who hugged away the nightmares. She wasn't the one who needed soothing.

When her hands stopped quivering, she started the car. She'd let her imagination run away with her in the empty studio, that's all. It was those black windows, and it was the man in the Civic Center parking lot. Seeing him had transported her to the past the way a familiar scent brings back the time and place it once occupied.

By the time she pulled onto her mother's street, she'd pulled herself together. She was exhausted. That was her problem. Worry woke her almost every night and last night was no exception. Disembodied voices in her dreams scolded her for being a neglectful mother. Visions of Fred, pulling a screaming Brian from her arms had danced through her drowsy head at three in the morning.

An uncomfortable thought entered her mind now. What if the sedan in the parking lot belonged to someone from Child Protective Services? She'd been so preoccupied thinking about Proctor and the past, she hadn't thought of that. What if a deranged CPS worker was following her, spying on her?

She barked a dry laugh. No, she was over-tired, over-whelmed, and over-paranoid. People were watching her but not through windows, or in dark parking lots. They used appointments and classes and endless rules and reams of paperwork. Fred kept telling her she couldn't do it all on her own. She had to rely on her support system—Brian's grandparents, close friends. That wasn't easy for her. As she left the shelter of her Explorer and stepped onto the dark street, uneasiness enveloped her again.

MOLLY: At first blush, Olivia seems to be struggling with paranoia. Yes, there was the strange man in the parking lot, and the car that seemed to be waiting for her when she left work. But that man may have just resembled the man from her past, and the car she thought was following her might not have been. She has nothing solid to hang her fears on.

We also have to take into consideration that she's suffered a lot of emotional blows leading up to this moment. Her anxiety might have been caused by Brian's accident, the disintegration of her marriage, or even a

```
childhood    trauma    that's    come    back    to
haunt her.
```

```
     Then again, maybe someone is actually following
her. You know the old chestnut: Just because I'm
paranoid  doesn't  mean  people  aren't  out  to
get me.
```

```
     You'll have tc wait for the next episode to
learn more. But before I leave you, I'd like to
read the first of the diary entries I told you
about in the intro to the show. It may seem this
entry is entirely unconnected to Olivia's story,
but stick with me. The two stories merge about
twenty years down the road.
```

***

Saturday, June 6th, 1992

I blotted my lips on a Kleenex and sent an air kiss to my reflection in the mirror. Not bad for a woman approaching middle age. I felt pretty tonight.

"Mom, I want to watch *Dr. Quinn* but Tomas says we have to watch *Young Indiana Jones*. I don't like *that*. It's scary." Lily, my daughter, leaned against the bathroom doorframe.

"I rented some movies from Blockbuster. Pick one of those." I pushed a strand of black hair behind my ear, surveyed the effect then pulled it out again.

"I want to watch *Dr. Quinn*." Lily's chin dropped to her chest for dramatic effect.

"Chiquita, this is a special night for your father and me. Can't you get along? Just for one night?"

"Tell that to Tomas." Lily ran a skinny, bare toe along a grout line in the white floor tile.

"I will, but right now I'm telling you." I put a finger under my daughter's chin and lifted her heart-shaped face, so much like my own at that age. "Be a good girl for me, okay?"

"What movies did you get?"

"Go look. I picked up *The Addams Family*. You both wanted to see that."

Lily, *Dr. Quinn* forgotten, skipped along the hall shouting, "Tomas, Mom says we have to watch a movie, and I get to pick it."

I walked to the bedroom and opened the jewelry box on my dresser. I found the black velvet bag all the way at the bottom and lifted it out. Doug had bought the emeralds for me on our tenth anniversary. He'd said they brought out the green in my eyes. I didn't wear them often. Not that I didn't love them. I did. It's just that they were more fancy than my life. But tonight, on our fifteenth anniversary I wanted to please him and bring out the green in my eyes.

The doorbell rang. Would he ring the bell? That morning he'd called me from work and asked if he could come by at 6:30. He'd said it like we didn't live in the same house. Like we weren't married. Like he was asking me out on our first date. My smile tightened my cheeks when I imagined him standing at the front door of his own home, flowers in hand, pretending to be my beau. I picked up my purse.

"Pizza." Tomas's voice was certain.

"I've got it," Stacey said. I'd given the babysitter twenty dollars for the pizza thinking Doug and I would be gone before it arrived. I looked at my watch; 6:50. An uneasy butterfly batted its wings in my stomach.

I had no control over time. It was forever sneaking up on me while I was thinking about other things. The more I needed it to cooperate, the more it ran amok. But Doug had no problem with it. He ran time like a drill sergeant.

The kids were in the kitchen. Stacey pulled a cheesy slice of pizza from the box while Tomas positioned a paper plate to best catch the strings.

"Me too." Lily danced from one foot to another.

"Grab a plate," Stacey said.

I poured a half a glass of wine from an open bottle on the counter. Maybe it would calm my wayward nerves. It wasn't like Doug and I were really on a first date. We were an old married couple. But there was something about the pretending that made my belly flutter.

"Don't you have a reservation?" Stacey said.

"I don't know. I'm not supposed to know, remember?"

"Oh, whoops." Stacey smiled. "I didn't say anything."

I finished my wine in the time it took for Tomas to eat two slices of pizza and Lily two bites. It was now 7:15. He was forty-five minutes late. Worry injected a bit more adrenaline into my bloodstream. Just as I was pondering a second half glass of wine the doorbell rang again.

Tomas started to rise from his seat at the table, but I put a hand on his shoulder. "I'll get it," I said. I pressed the wrinkles from my skirt and walked to the front door.

I wouldn't be surprised if making me wait was part of Doug's plan all along. His philosophy about romance was that it didn't happen in ruts. People cheated because they were looking for excitement. He liked to keep me a little off balance. He called it anti-affair insurance. I rubbed my lips together to smooth my lipstick, assumed my sexiest smile and opened the door. On the stoop were two uniformed policemen.

Doug and I never celebrated our fifteenth anniversary, or our sixteenth, or any other after that.

MOLLY: On that disturbing note, I'll say goodbye. If you aren't a member of the *Murders Under the Sun* Facebook group, I suggest you join. The link is in the show notes. Every week I ask a question there to get you thinking. We had some pretty hot debates in Season One.

This week's question is: Do you think Olivia is paranoid? Or is someone stalking her? Let's get the conversation going.

(**cue music**)

VO: If you enjoyed this episode, please leave

us a five-star review on your favorite podcast service—it really helps. *Murders Under the Sun* is edited by Jim Wilbourne, theme music is by Eclectic Blends, and I'm your host, Molly Shure.

part three

MURDERS UNDER THE SUN
SEASON TWO; EPISODE TWO

MOLLY: Welcome back to *The Garden*, Season Two of *Murders Under the Sun*. I'm Molly Shure, your host.

Before we get into this week's episode, I want to talk about an issue that has carried over from last season. Perhaps unwisely, I told the listening audience how I got into crime reporting. The story, in brief, is that my college roommate and bestie went out to a bar one night and never came home. Melissa Shilling was a sweet and wonderful friend whose disappearance changed the trajectory of my life.

During the season break, a man emailed me. He'd heard what I'd shared on the show from a friend. He wrote that his cousin, Ariana Blackstone, also a CSU-Fullerton student, disappeared in the 2005-2006 school year.

While this is all very strange, I have to believe that the police must know about it. I admit, I did not. I didn't come across that name even when I was actively trying to find out what happened to Mel, but why would the cops tell me anything? I was just a college kid.

One of the detectives told me to stop snooping around, that it might be dangerous. Honestly, that scared me, and I gave up on it. Gave up on Melissa. I still feel bad about that, but my role today is to report on crimes, not to solve them. As devastated as I know the friends and family of Ariana are—and I do know—there isn't anything I can do about this case.

I can tell people about the details of Olivia Richard's story, however. And maybe, hopefully, someone listening will be safer for it. So, let's get into the episode.

Last week, we got to visit with a few of the people from Season One. Art, Gwen, and Fiona each play a small role in *The Garden*. Remember, I mentioned all of these stories are linked by the victims. What this means is one of the questions we'll be asking ourselves every season of the show is: What does this relationship signify?

We also met most of the key players of the current season. Olivia, her son Brian, her ex, Davy, and Brian's coach, Tom. Based on your comments, many of you think Olivia is a little off her rocker. However, as others of you pointed out: Why would I be doing a true crime podcast about a woman nothing happened to? Good point.

This story unfolds a little more slowly than last season's, but trust me, it will twist like a climbing vine as it goes along. At this point, we're still laying the groundwork. Turning the soil, so to speak. Are you sick of the garden metaphors, yet? I'll try to control myself.

Today, we'll be getting into the burgeoning relationship between Olivia and Tom. Will the romance be an important piece of the puzzle or is it a red herring? Will Olivia's past prove to be the inciting incident in these crimes or is it only the events of the present that matter? We'll get a few more clues in this episode.

And today, as promised, we'll learn who our mystery woman is as Olivia does. Of course, Olivia never read the diary entries you're hearing until recently. I sent her a copy when we were in the interview process. I won't tell you her reaction, however. It would be a spoiler.

Let's get into the episode.

2.2.2

ON THURSDAY, Olivia jogged up the steps of St. Barnabas and through the glass front doors. She had fifteen minutes to run Brian's lunch to his classroom and get to the Fishbowl. The studio was an eleven-minute drive from here. Which meant she had four minutes to deliver the lunch Brian had left on the kitchen counter and get to her car. It was the second time this month—and October wasn't even half over—that Brian had forgotten it.

If she had more income. Correction. *When* she had more income. Things were going well at work. She'd crunched the numbers. When the Fishbowl grew from a small success to a thriving enterprise—when she was flush—she was going to splurge on school lunches for Brian. This running back and forth was getting old.

"Olivia." A voice snapped her around. A tall man in a soft plaid button-down shirt and chinos loped toward her. It was Tom. It took her a moment to recognize him without the red soccer shirt and black gym shorts. He looked great. "I've been hoping I'd bump into you," he said.

Olivia had mixed feelings but smiled.

"I was going to call, but I decided I wanted to talk to you face to face. Do you have a minute?"

"I don't," she said. "I have to be to work in..." she looked at her watch, "twelve minutes. I'm dropping off Brian's lunch."

"Let me do that for you." Tom reached for the paper sack.

Olivia hesitated. She hadn't heard anything about Coach Tom, positive or negative, since Tuesday. She assumed Brian's opinion hadn't changed in two days, so he wouldn't be thrilled to have his lunch delivered by the man.

"Hey." His face grew serious. "That's what I want to talk to you about. I didn't know about Brian's accident, Olivia. I didn't mean to..."

He looked so repentant; Olivia handed him the lunch. "I get it. It's okay."

"No. No, it's not okay. I'd like to talk. Are you free tonight? After soccer?"

"I have to get Brian home, fed, homework. You know."

"I understand. You better get going. Don't be late."

Olivia turned to go, then had a thought. "You know, tomorrow night I get off at eight, and I don't have to pick up Brian from his grandfather's until nine. It's not long, but I'd have time for a quick glass of wine."

His face brightened. She wasn't sure why she'd agreed to meet him. Her life was complicated enough without involving someone else. Maybe it was because he seemed so concerned about Brian. The adage must be true: a way to a woman's heart is through her children.

"Livvie, I have someone I want you to meet." Fiona glided to the counter followed by a tall woman. "This is Sage. I told you about her. She's a wealth of information on herbs, a real medicine woman."

Sage looked like what Olivia thought a medicine woman ought to look like. She had strong, handsome features, an olive complexion, and thick hair that must have once been glossy black but was now touched with gray. Laugh lines etched her eyes, but otherwise, her skin was clear and glowing.

"I hear you're a student of natural medicine," Sage said in a low, melodious voice.

"Not really. I mean, I'm studying, but I don't know much..." Olivia let her words dwindle.

"There's a lot to learn." Sage nodded.

"And she's doing great," Fiona beamed at Olivia as though she were a clever toddler. "We can't keep enough oils in stock."

"You'll have to educate me. I've never worked much with essential oils. They're hard to make well at home, and I use what I grow. I focus more on tinctures, teas, lotions, things like that," Sage said.

"I'd love to see your garden," Olivia said.

Sage smiled. "You're officially invited."

"Olivia," a woman with a blond bob held up an oil diffuser. "Can I get your advice on creating a beginner's kit?"

Olivia excused herself and went to help. By the time she'd rung up the diffuser and a bag of oils, Sage had left.

"Isn't she lovely?" Fiona looked up from the computer where she'd been working. Olivia knew she meant Sage.

"She is."

"I don't know how old she is, but I know it's much older than she looks. I've heard she makes magical skin cream."

"Does she sell it?"

"Oh, I like the way you think." Fiona's eyes brightened. "Ask her. Her face is great advertising."

"You don't have anything to worry about. Your skin is beautiful." Olivia walked to her side of the desk and logged into the studio's management program. She had some client schedule changes to make before she left for the day.

"Glowing?" Fiona's eyebrows rose and hid behind her bangs.

Olivia inspected her friend's face. Fiona had a light sprinkle of freckles across her nose and the pale skin of a redhead, but her cheeks did seem to be more pink than usual. "Okay. Glowing. A new makeup brand?"

"No. I think it's attributed to increased blood flow and hormone changes." Her tone was matter of fact, disinterested even. She turned her eyes to the computer screen as she spoke.

It took Olivia a moment to interpret the act. "What're you saying?"

Fiona shrugged one shoulder.

"Are you pregnant?"

She nodded and a wide smile shot across her face. Olivia reached across the desk and hugged her. "Congratulations. I'm so happy for you and Devon."

"Me too. I'm happy for us too."

Fiona and her husband had been trying to conceive for close to a year, and although Fiona said the trying part was fun, the lack of success had been discouraging.

"When?" Olivia said.

"The end of April. I just passed week twelve. I didn't want to tell anyone until after the first trimester." Olivia hugged her again.

"You don't know how relieved I am you decided to become a partner in the business. I need you now more than ever. I can get the girls to take my classes and my clients, but they can't run the studio."

"It's a win win," Olivia said.

Fiona shut down her computer. "I'm afraid I'm going to be relying on you more and more, what with doctor's appointments and all."

Olivia didn't answer. As happy as she was for Fiona, the idea of added responsibility fell like a weight across her shoulders. She was barely keeping up with her schedule as it was.

"Devon moved his office into the garage. We decided to paint the walls buttercream. It's neutral, but still says nursery. I saw the cutest wallpaper border with lions and tigers and giraffes that would go great with the color. A jungle theme works for either sex, right?" She didn't wait for Olivia to respond. "But Dev wants to do a cowboy motif—kind of a *Toy Story* thing. I said that wouldn't work for a girl. He said we could do Jesse, you know she's the cowgirl doll, but..."

Olivia stopped listening. Her thoughts turned to the past, when she and Davy had decorated Brian's room. It was before they knew he was Brian, not Caitlin. They'd papered with teddy bears and balloons, some pink, some blue. They'd been so happy.

Davy was the only one who'd been able to get Olivia out of the black moods that descended on her from time to time. As opposite as their personalities were, she'd believed they were soulmates. She was Yin to his Yang. She centered him, and he made her more adventurous. She helped him take life a bit more seriously, and he helped her see the humor in things. Until he lost his job.

At first, he wasn't too worried when the tech company he worked for went bankrupt. He'd been a successful salesman and was sure he'd be attractive to the competition. But so many companies left California for states with friendlier business environments in those years, private sector jobs were scarce.

Olivia was working part-time for her mother as her publicist and marketing manager. She'd loved the work. She had planned to gain experience with her mother's book sales, then build her own promotion company focused on authors. But that would have taken years, and they needed income right away. She went to work as a server and took as many hours as she could get at Enzo's Sports Bar, while Davy job hunted and watched Brian.

It might have been boredom, his ego, or a combination of both, but Davy started drinking then. He never did anything by halves. When he worked, he was the highest earning salesman in the company. When he drank, he became a class-A drunk. She threw him out a year after he lost his job.

"Dev wants to know the sex of the baby as soon as we can, but I don't know. I kind of like the idea of being surprised. What do you think? Did you know Brian was a boy before he was born?" Fiona's question jerked Olivia back to the present.

"Ah, no. We didn't know. We were surprised."

"See." Fiona's eyes widened. "That's what I say. I'm going to have to get that man of mine in line."

Olivia found herself wishing she had a man to get in line. It would be wonderful to have a husband to share the burdens she'd been carrying—a father for Brian. Fiona seemed to intuit her thoughts. "When are you going to start dating again?"

Olivia shrugged. "I'm getting a glass of wine with a teacher from Brian's school tomorrow night, but we're going out to talk about Brian."

"If you want to discuss a student—not that I'm an expert yet—my understanding is you call a parent-teacher meeting. You don't ask the kid's mother out."

"A glass of wine isn't a declaration of undying love." Olivia started packing up her tote bag. It was almost time for Brian's pick up.

"No, but if you have enough of them it can lead to one."

"Not if Brian has anything to say about it. He doesn't like Coach Tom." She wondered if that was a permanent situation, however, because she was pretty sure she did like Coach Tom.

2.2.3

THE FAMILIAR SCENTS of Turk's—grilled food, stale beer, and mild dockside mildew—welcomed Olivia as she opened the door. It was one of the few harbor hangouts that hadn't succumbed to the new upscale, tourist image the city of Dana Point was trying to project these days. Decorated in 1990s faux sailing vessel, it looked more like part of the *Pirates of the Caribbean* ride at Disneyland than an eating establishment.

Nothing had been touched since Turk Varteresian, a muscle man from Hollywood's Golden Age, had cut its red ribbon. Black and white pictures of old film stars and the big man himself in Neptune and gladiator costumes still adorned the walls. Olivia loved it.

When she'd left the parking lot at the Fishbowl, a Honda sedan had pulled out after her and trailed her along the Coast Highway as far as the harbor. When she turned onto Golden Lantern, it had continued south. It might have been a coincidence, but it looked a lot like the car that had given her the willies on Tuesday night.

Voices were raised to combat other raised voices. Mama Cass crooned about dreaming little dreams. Olivia had forgotten how loud Turk's was, or maybe she'd never noticed. A nervous tingle slid along her arms. This might not have been the best place to have a serious conversation about her son's problems with the new soccer coach. She'd only picked it because it was in her comfort zone, a home base. And it was close to work.

Before she could turn around, go outside and text Tom about changing locations, she saw him. He sat in a booth by the darkened windows, a beer in one hand, a menu in the other. He glanced up and smiled.

She squeezed past two men at the bar who looked like aging surfers and slid in across from him. "Maybe this isn't the best spot—"

Tom interrupted her with a wave of his hand. "Turk's is great. I'm from San Juan, so I always went to Swallows Inn. This is pretty much the same, only without the underwear."

"Underwear?"

"Yeah, Swallows is a little more upscale. They hang bras from the ceiling. I'll have to take you there sometime."

"Thanks, it sounds interesting," Olivia said, feeling better about her choice of venues.

A waitress with tired eyes stopped by the table to take their order. When she walked away, Tom took a long draught from his beer, set the glass down and looked Olivia in the eye. "I'm sorry," he said.

"For what?" Olivia said.

"I shouldn't have been so hard on Brian that day at practice. I don't know what I was thinking. I guess I felt bad for you. You seem so stressed. I wanted to help."

"It's okay—"

"No. It's not okay. I have this hero complex. I'm working on it, but when I see a pretty woman with a problem, I can't help myself. I'm like a retriever with a tennis ball."

A hangdog expression crossed his face, and this time Olivia did laugh. "I forgive you. And I get it. Brian is smart, but he comes across like he doesn't care. That can be infuriating."

"Right. All I could think was this kid needs to get a grip. He's hurting himself, and he's hurting his mother. So, I sat on him. Next practice, Don—Coach Parker—takes me aside and tells me about the accident. I felt like a jerk. So, again, I'm sorry."

"Again, I forgive you."

"How long was he in a coma?" Tom flinched as soon as the words left his lips. "Is it okay to talk about it?"

"Yeah. It's fine. They kept him in a medically induced coma for nearly a week, until the swelling went down in his brain."

"It must have been nerve-wracking waiting for him to come out of it."

"It was the worst five and a half days of my life. He looked okay. I mean, bruised and bandaged, but I knew all that would heal. The scary thing was they couldn't tell me what condition his brain was in."

"How long ago was that?"

"Last February, so eight months ago."

"But he's good? Mostly, right? He has some trouble with attention, but other than that he seems good."

"Yes," Olivia said the word slowly. How much should she reveal to this man? He seemed genuine, concerned, but she knew from experience when words like brain damage were used, people got nervous. "The attention thing is a bit of a problem, though."

"His grades?"

"Grades are lower, but not too bad. He's just really impulsive. It's hard to predict what he's going to do."

"The disappearing act? Coach Parker warned me about that the first week of soccer."

"He's always done that," Olivia said. "I could tell you stories that would scare you into male-pattern baldness."

"Please don't." Tom put a hand on his thick, black hair. "It's my only redeeming feature."

Olivia grinned. She liked the self-deprecating humor. She decided to test the waters. If Brian's problems were going to scare him away, it was better to know up front. "Brian's always been a dreamer. But now, he has a harder time distinguishing between imagination and reality. The doctor calls it confabulation. He invents memories or grabs them from other times to fill in gaps. It seems like he's lying, but he's not. He believes what he's saying is true."

"Is it like schizophrenia?" Tom's brows knit together in concern.

"No. No. Nothing like that. It's mostly little things, like..." She searched her mind for a good example. "Okay, every morning I put his lunch on the kitchen counter in a bag and remind him that it's there. At least once a week, he'll leave it home."

"Kids forget their lunch all the time." Tom shrugged.

"Right, but they realize they forgot it when they open their backpack, and it's not there. Brian remembers putting his lunch into his backpack the days he leaves it home as clearly as he does on the days he brings it. The first time it happened, he accused a classmate of stealing the bag. He was so sure he'd brought it with him."

"We all do things like that when we have a lot on our minds, don't we? There are times I could swear I shaved until I run my hand over my chin."

"True. People get confused when they're preoccupied or tired, but Brian confabulates when he's neither. And sometimes it's not just little things like forgetting lunch; sometimes he believes his dreams, or daydreams actually happened. I don't want to make it sound worse than it is. The doctors believe it will resolve itself as he gets older. But meanwhile, I have to be vigilant. Speaking of which..."

"You need to go? Already?" Tom looked disappointed.

"I do." Olivia waved at the waitress. "I'm sorry." Mike hadn't been able to take Brian tonight, so Sarah was doing double duty. She'd had him Monday, Wednesday, and now Friday this week. Olivia didn't want to be late.

Outside, in the damp, salty air, Tom fell in beside her as she walked to her car. "I wish I could help, Olivia. You bring out that hero thing in me."

Her throat tightened. It had been a long time since anyone wanted to be her hero. "An extra pair of eyes when he's away from me would be great."

"I can do that."

"Only..." She hesitated. She didn't want to insult him after his kind offer, but she knew Tom wasn't Brian's favorite person.

"Don't worry." Tom stopped and turned to face her. "I know what you're going to say. But I can be subtle. I used to be an undercover KGB agent. Bet you had no idea."

"No." She laughed.

"See how subtle I am?" He took her arm, and they continued toward the parking lot. "There are lots of things you don't know about me because of my incredible subtlety."

Olivia was glad Tom was walking her to her car. He was funny and charming, and she was still a bit nervous because of the sedan that had followed her earlier.

"I'm also a master chef." Tom was still talking. "I make a mean chicken curry."

It had been too dark to see the car clearly, and it was a common body type.

"It's a coconut curry."

It might not have been the same vehicle.

"I prefer Thai to Indian."

Honestly, she didn't know if the car was following her, or if it just happened to be headed in the same direction.

"How about dinner tomorrow night?"

"Dinner?" She forgot all about the car. Dinner was definitely a date.

"Yeah, dinner. At my place. I'll cook."

"Is that allowed? I mean with you being a teacher at St. Barnabas? I thought teachers and parents weren't supposed to fraternize."

"I'm not Brian's teacher."

"But you're his coach."

"Assistant coach."

"I don't want to get you in any trouble." She didn't want to get in any trouble either. She wasn't about to risk Brian's scholarship for chicken curry, no matter how handsome the chef was.

"I checked the Employee Handbook before I asked you. It's fine, but if you'd rather not..."

"No. It's not that. Dinner sounds wonderful." It was Davy's first weekend, so she didn't need to worry about Brian.

"Around seven then?" He sounded hopeful.

Davy. Just thinking about him made her angry and frustrated and something else. Something else she didn't want to think about. "Great. I'll be there."

Olivia's cheeks hurt from smiling. She'd had a stupid grin plastered on her face for at least three of the seven miles between Turk's and her mother's. Then she remembered the car. The car that probably wasn't following her.

She didn't like how jumpy she'd become since she'd seen the man who may, or may not, have been Proctor. She only wished she knew. If it weren't him, she could return to fretting over valid things like Brian's health and CPS and Davy and the Safety Plan. As adept as she was at the fine art of worry, even she could only juggle so many concerns at once.

Before she turned onto her mother's street, Olivia made a decision. She'd talk to Sarah about it. She'd have to tread carefully. Proctor was a sensitive subject. But her mother was still in touch with some people from that time in their lives. People who might know his whereabouts.

Sarah was deep in writing mode when Olivia entered her house. "He's on the couch." She waved a hand toward the living room without looking away from the laptop that sat on the dining room table in front of her. One of her books about Brian the Bloodhound, named for Olivia's Brian, had won a Caldecott Medal. They were beloved by many, especially their inspiration.

Grandmother and grandson were close, much closer than Olivia and her mother had ever been. The stories created a special bond between them. They shared a world Olivia wasn't a part of.

The house was warm and quiet and smelled like lavender and cinnamon, a combination of scents that always evoked in her a bittersweet sense of longing. Instead of going directly into the living room to collect Brian, she leaned on the white molding lining the dining room's entryway and watched her mother work. After several silent seconds she said, "Mom, can I talk to you?"

Sarah turned her head. She looked lovely against the pale blue-gray paint of the wall behind her. Her face was etched with warmth and intelligence, but a distracted expression hung on it like a "do not disturb" sign.

"Just for a minute," Olivia said.

Sarah blinked like a swimmer clearing her eyes. "Sure."

"It's probably nothing, but I can't get it off my mind."

Sarah gave her laptop a last, wistful glance, and pivoted toward Olivia. "What's up?"

"I saw a man. A man who looked like Proctor."

Sarah's cheek twitched. "Proctor?"

"Yes. Have you heard from him? Do you know if he's in California?"

"No. No, of course not. I've completely lost touch with the man."

"But you know people who know him."

"I guess... Winnie and Drew, they run in the same artistic circles. But we never talk about him."

"Could you ask them?"

"Liv." Sarah opened her eyes wide in appeal. "Why would you want to dredge up old trash? Even if it was him you saw, who cares?"

Olivia pushed off the wall. "I care, Mom. If he's in California, I want to know."

"Why?"

"If a rattlesnake might be in your front yard, wouldn't you want to know?" Olivia's voice rose.

"Mom?" Brian appeared in the hall behind her rubbing his eyes.

"Hi, pumpkin." Olivia hugged him.

"Are we going home now?"

"Yeah. Go get your backpack." When he disappeared, she locked eyes with her mother. "Will you ask?"

Brian returned, and Sarah rose from her chair. "See you next week, sweetheart." She kissed his brown tangles.

"Please." Olivia mouthed the word over the top of her son's head.

Sarah closed her eyes for a moment, opened them and said, "I'll make a couple of calls."

That was the best Olivia was going to get from her mother tonight, so she let it go. Next week she'd ask again if there was no news. She'd learned to be persistent when it came to Sarah Richards.

2.2.4

OLIVIA WIGGLED a plastic container of quinoa salad into the bottom of her too-small thermal bag and put a can of unsweetened, flavored soda water on top. She'd been trying to eat better, kick the diet soda habit. Her studies about essential oils had opened a door into the brave new world of holistic health and alternative medicine. She was horrified by some of the things she'd learned about the average American diet. Change wasn't easy, but she saw the necessity. Brian sulked when she replaced his fluorescent orange chips with organic corn chips, and she still struggled from sugar withdrawals, but they were going to get healthy if it killed her.

The doorbell rang. Davy was on time for his first full weekend with his son in at least a year. She heard the slide of Brian's stocking feet on wood and the slam of his hands on the front door. "Dad." The single word sang with joy and excitement. Olivia's shoulders tightened. Davy had better stick with his new resolutions. She couldn't bear to see Brian's heart broken like it had been so many times in the past.

"Hey, champ." Davy filled the hall. Davy always filled a room. Not with his size, he was average height and slender of build, but with personality. It was one of the things that first attracted her to him. She'd become painfully shy and reclusive after what had happened on the farm when she was a kid. Davy had changed her. Going out with him was like going out with a celebrity. Everyone seemed to know him, and everyone who knew him liked him. He'd made the world feel like a friendlier place. He'd given her courage.

"Let's go." Brian threw the strap of his duffel bag over his shoulder and beamed at his father. Davy had promised a trip on Sunday to one of his favorite places on the planet, the San Diego Zoo. It was all Brian had talked about since Tuesday.

"I hear it hurts if an elephant steps on your foot when you're not wearing shoes," Davy said. "Better bring some."

Brian looked at his socks, dropped his bag and skated to his room.

"Okay, here are Brian's meds and his supplements." Olivia handed Davy a baggie filled with pill bottles. "I put a note inside to explain what he gets when. Also, I'm trying to keep him off gluten, sugar, and processed foods—they're linked with impulsive behavior in children. Here's a list of what he can't eat." She held out a typed sheet of paper.

"It's best if he's restricted to an hour of computer time a day. I know he loves playing games with you, but he gets hyper if he stays on too long, and you'll have a terrible time getting him down for the night."

Davy's eyes narrowed, and he nodded. She continued, "Sticking to the schedule is essential. Get him to bed by nine, nine-thirty, no later. He likes to read before he goes to sleep. It helps him shut down his brain. He has a book. He can read alone, of course, but he still likes to be read to, in fact—"

Olivia," Davy interrupted her. "He's my son. I can do this."

Olivia pulled a hand through her hair. "You'll keep a close eye at the zoo tomorrow?" Taking Brian to a large public place filled with interesting and distracting things was like piloting a small, leaky boat through a storm. But she had to admit, if there was anyone with sailing skills, it was Davy. Before he started drinking, he'd had a sixth sense about his son. When Brian disappeared, Davy was inevitably the one to find him.

"You know I will," Davy said. "I, ah, I got that job I interviewed for on Tuesday." He looked at the floor, like he was too nervous to watch her reaction.

"Good for you," Olivia said.

"It's a good job. Best I've had since Shuffly." He shifted his gaze to her face. "It's a public relations company. Not a lot of money to start, but room for growth. I'm excited about it."

Olivia didn't know what he wanted her to say. His charm often got him in the door; the question was could he stay inside? Brian jogged in at that moment and saved her from having to respond. "I'm ready."

"See you Sunday." Davy kept his gaze fixed on her. She gave him a curt nod.

"You got a new car." Brian's voice rang through the open door.

Davy followed him outside. "Yeah. I wanted to surprise you. It's not new, new, but it's new to me."

"Sweet." Brian ran around to the passenger side and opened the door to inspect the interior.

The car was a dark gray Honda Civic. It looked about three years old, certainly newer than Olivia's old Ford Explorer. How could he afford it? His credit was shot. He must have had to shell out a hefty down payment to qualify for a loan.

If he had that much cash, he should contribute more toward Brian's needs. Davy had made all his child support payments for the past three months, plus extra. He said he planned to gradually make up all he'd missed over the past two years. He even gave her a spreadsheet with the numbers. But the car bothered her.

He glanced over his shoulder, and as if he was reading her mind he said, "My dad cosigned on the loan. There are times I have to drive out to meet clients. One of the stipulations of this job was that I have a presentable car. It's a means to an end."

Somewhat mollified, Olivia waved goodbye and walked into the house to finish getting ready for work. She'd be busy at the studio until three, then home to wash her hair, redo her makeup, and get to Tom's by seven.

Wrapping her head around the fact that she had a date wasn't easy. She'd only had two boyfriends in her life, Craig Caldwell—high school math class nerd—and Davy. She'd never gone out more than once or twice with anyone other than her husband on the far side of high school —never wanted to.

She and Davy had met her junior year at Cal State-Fullerton. It wasn't love at first sight. They were such opposites; she'd found him annoying but seemed to be the only person in the world who did.

Because Olivia was an introvert, never having more than a few close friends at any one time and Davy attracted a crowd, she'd thought him shallow and superficial at first. She soon realized he genuinely enjoyed people. She didn't remember the exact moment she succumbed to his charms, but by the end of the term she'd fallen hopelessly in love.

They'd married right out of college and had Brian three years later. The first nine years of marriage were good ones. Olivia had been content and filled with dreams of a happy future. Davy's drinking had drowned most of those dreams. The ones that survived the divorce had been hit by the truck along with Brian. Since she'd been at the Fishbowl, some of them were waking from their coma. And now she had a date.

2.2.5

OLIVIA HELD up a hand to knock on Tom's front door but hesitated. Knock, or ring the bell? A knock was informal, friendly. People selling solar panels rang doorbells. But maybe a knock was too casual? She and Tom didn't know each other that well. She stared at the door for several more seconds. Salesmen rang, friends knocked. She was overthinking this. She knocked.

Tom looked good in Saturday casual—leather flip flops, jeans, and a bright white t-shirt that echoed a smile made brilliant by his warm skin. He leaned over and kissed her cheek after closing the door behind her. "Come keep me company. I'm still cooking." He led the way through a living room that looked like a page out of *Architectural Digest* into the kitchen.

Olivia perched on a stool next to a granite island. He poured her a glass of wine, then returned to the cutting board he'd obviously abandoned to answer the door. "Just have to finish the salad, and we can go sit outside."

"Take your time," Olivia said. "I like watching other people work."

"Cooking isn't work. Teaching is work. Cooking is relaxation."

"Not for me, but I don't know what I'm doing in the kitchen."

"You don't fix meals for Brian?" His voice registered surprise.

"Oh, yeah. I mean, I can do the basics, mac and cheese, burgers, steamed veggies. That's about all Brian will eat—minus the veggies, of course. Those are for me."

"Won't eat his vegetables, eh?" Tom whacked a carrot into a hundred uniform slices.

"Not without a fight. I'm trying though. I've been learning about how important nutrition is for brain functioning."

"It sure is. I can tell which of my kids aren't eating well at home. They're tired, have a hard time focusing. It's not just the financially strapped families either. Sometimes it's kids from wealthy homes. Mom is so busy with her tennis club; she sticks a box of sugar cereal or toaster pastries on the table and lets the kids help themselves."

Olivia squirmed. She'd done exactly that many times, but it wasn't so she could run off to play tennis. It was to get to work on time.

While Tom sliced and diced, she let her eyes wander around the room. Stainless steel appliances gleamed between mahogany cupboards. The counters were gold-veined black granite. Copper bottom pans hung from a stainless semi-circular pot rack. This room had been carefully designed and no expense spared.

A pot on the stove belched out fragrant steam. Her stomach growled. She hadn't eaten much that day—too nervous—but the delicious scents and the half glass of wine she'd already drunk were working their magic. She was hungry.

"Ready to go outside?" Tom dried his hands on a dishtowel and picked up the bottle of wine.

Around the perimeter of the small, enclosed courtyard were clay pots filled with foliage. Not foliage wilted from October's heat wave like the plants on Olivia's balcony were, but thriving, green vegetation. In its center was a glass-topped table and four chairs. A fountain splashed against the far wall.

Tom placed the wine on the table and disappeared through French doors into the kitchen. The garden was lovely and well-manicured. It was... neat. That was the perfect word for it, and not the 1960s cool, groovy version of the word. It was neat in a line-everything-up-according-to-size-and-color kind of way. She sat in one of the chairs, sipped her wine, and looked around her. There were three, exactly three, sizes of clay pots arranged in identical groupings in the four corners of the space. The largest pots all held small trees: citrus, what looked like an avocado, and one she couldn't identify. The medium sized pots held bushes: a rosemary, a gardenia, a lavender, and some kind of sage. The smallest pots held herbs.

Tom reemerged with a bowl of hummus and a basket of crackers. "Hungry?"

"Your garden is so... orderly," Olivia said. "All I have is a tiny patio and it's a mess." She gestured toward one of the groupings. "My plants are half dead. I can never remember to water the poor things."

"I find order calming." Tom sat next to her. "Kids are so disorganized, I guess I need an oasis. A place to refuel."

Olivia nodded. She wasn't sure what to say. She felt like she ought to find it relaxing too. It had all the right elements, very *feng shui*. But there was something surrealistic about it. It almost looked staged, like a picture from a magazine, like his living room. There wasn't one brown leaf, one misshapen branch. All the trees and bushes were pruned to the exact shape and size of their counterparts. The herbs trailed over the edges of their pots artistically. It was a bit too perfect.

"So, tell me more about your nutritional studies." Tom dipped a cracker into the hummus.

"I'm researching essential oils for work, but most of the websites I end up on are about health in general. I've grown obsessed with alternative medicine."

"It's a powerful tool." Tom's face grew serious.

"It's amazing to me how most of the medical community poohpoohs it. If you can't buy it from a pharmacy, doctors don't give it any credibility."

"It sounds like you've had a bad experience?" Tom studied her face. He was a good listener, but Olivia wasn't sure how much she wanted to say. She didn't want Tom to think Brian was worse than he was, but Tom was a teacher and a coach. He worked with kids all day long. More importantly, he worked with Brian. He could be a good resource.

"The doctor wants to put Brian on ADHD drugs." The words came in a rush. "But I don't want to. It's speed, pure and simple. I know the new studies say kids who take those are no more likely than anyone else to abuse drugs as adults, but who pays for those studies?"

"It's a hard decision. I've seen it benefit some kids, but doctors prescribe it like they are giving out candy these days."

"I know, right? I want to try everything else first. If we have to go that way, we have to go that way, but not yet."

"So, what have you tried?"

"Well, as I said it's a battle, but I've changed his diet quite a bit. I've switched to mostly organic fruits and veggies, gotten rid of the processed crap, and I'm weaning him off gluten." Tom nodded as if agreeing with her decisions. "I've also put a diffuser in his room and I'm trying different oil recipes while he sleeps."

"How about supplements?"

"Yeah, he's on a bunch of them."

"Are they working?"

"That's the sixty-four-thousand-dollar question. It's hard to tell. Brian doesn't have ADHD. He had brain damage. Things seem to be getting better, but his brain may be healing on its own. Maybe what I'm doing is helping, maybe not. I'm not sure."

"Are you free tomorrow?" Tom said.

Olivia, startled by the abrupt change of subject, didn't answer right away.

Tom grimaced and shook his head. "That didn't come out right. I'm not trying to get you to spend the night or monopolize your whole weekend. But there's someone I'd like you to meet."

"Who?"

"You'll see. If you can come."

"Brian gets home around four. I have chores..."

"Could I steal you away in the morning?"

Reluctance tightened around her. Even moving slowly into a relationship was a stretch for her, and he was moving fast. Besides, if she didn't get the vacuuming and dusting done on Sunday, when would she do it? Her weeks were so busy. And she'd planned to go to the farmer's market in San Clemente to pick up some produce.

"Just for an hour or two? I think you'll enjoy yourself," Tom said.

Why shouldn't she go? Did the idea of doing something for herself, something not directly related to Brian's welfare, make her feel guilty?

Her mother would say that was unhealthy, for her and for Brian. Her mother was right. "Okay. What time?" she said.

The ring of a kitchen timer traveled through the open glass doors.

"Dinner." He stood. Olivia pushed her chair back to join him.

"No, stay. I'll bring everything out. It's such a nice evening."

It was. The heat of the day had tapered off. Olivia was comfortable in a sleeveless dress. She poured herself a bit more wine and relaxed. So, this is what it felt like to be waited on. She couldn't remember the last time she'd sat still while someone else bustled around putting a meal together. It was nice, peaceful. A soft breeze brushed the hair from her forehead.

As she sat and sipped, she felt the tension and worry that had been her constant companions since Brian's accident slipping from her shoulders. Maybe having a man in her life would be good for her, and for Brian. If Mama was happy, everybody was happy. Wasn't that how the saying went? While she waited for him to return, her mind took tentative steps into an imaginary world where Tom was that man. His garden was growing on her.

2.2.6

"ARE you going to tell me where we're going now?" Olivia asked as she settled into the passenger seat of Tom's Honda the next morning.

"Nope." He flashed a grin at her and pulled away from the curb.

"I hope I'm dressed appropriately. If I embarrass you in public, it's your fault."

"You look great." His voice deepened as he said the words.

Olivia flushed and resisted the temptation to check her hair in the mirror on the sun visor. She didn't think about her appearance often these days. She hoped it wasn't obvious.

Ten minutes later Tom exited the freeway onto Ortega Highway and followed the signs toward downtown San Juan Capistrano. They passed the Mission and made a right to enter the Historic Los Rios district.

Olivia loved this area of town. It was small, only three or four blocks of old houses that cozied up to the train tracks. Some were still residences, but the section closest to the train depot had been converted into boutiques, art galleries, and cafes.

To her surprise, Tom turned onto Los Rios. Although it was a through street, there were no parking spaces, or sidewalks and pedestrians strolled in the middle of the road oblivious to traffic. He navigated around a family of tourists taking photos, an older Hispanic woman pushing a shopping cart full of bags, and a young couple walking a German Shepherd.

"You know you can park behind the Adobe," Olivia said. They were passing the little museum housed in one of the original adobe homes. Behind it was a dirt parking lot.

"I know the area."

At the end of Los Rios, in the front yard of a home camouflaged by trees and bushes, sat a weathered statue of St. Francis. His beatific face welcomed Olivia to the district. His arms were open, his palms upturned in invitation. Lichen and moss softened his stone robes.

The day was clear and warm. Weather predictions promised a hot afternoon, but the morning was lovely. She glanced at Tom. His face was handsome in profile. Last night he'd been nothing but charming and supportive. They'd talked about her work, his work, all safe topics. He'd given her a demure kiss on the cheek when she'd left. Her fears about moving too fast seemed unfounded.

He made a right, and then another right up a long dirt driveway. An old farmhouse hid beneath a stand of oaks at its top. They exited the car. A breath of wind caught Olivia's hair and whisked it into her face. It carried the unique combination of scents she associated with the district, sage and creosote laced with the bitter tang of horse manure. It was a warm, smoky smell that made her hungry for hot chili and cornbread.

"Where are we?" she said.

"This is my mother's house."

She looked at him with questioning eyes. They'd only been on one date. It was much too soon to bring her home to mother.

"That's why I didn't tell you where we were going." He reached around and squeezed her shoulders. "I think you're wonderful, but don't worry, I'm not proposing. You'll like my mom. She's into herbs."

A pale-yellow house squatted on dry grass. A broad enclosed porch stretched across its matronly hips like a skirt. The temperature dropped several degrees as Olivia walked under the oaks. The shade was so dense it was like entering a darkened room. She followed Tom up three peeling wooden steps, through a screen door and into the porch.

Tom strode across gray painted floorboards to the front door and threw it open without knocking. "Mama," he called.

"In here." An alto voice echoed from somewhere deeper inside.

"I brought company." Tom walked along a central hall toward an open door at the rear of the house. Olivia caught glimpses of worn furniture, dark woods, and primary colors—reds, blues, yellows, greens glowed in the dim light.

She blinked as they entered the kitchen. Sunshine slanted through an open door and poured through a wall of windows. Bunches of hanging herbs made strange shadows on the floor. A pungent aroma, familiar but she couldn't name it, hung in the air.

At the stove stood a tall woman with long, thick, salt and pepper hair hanging down her back like a rug. She stirred something that steamed and bubbled in a large, black canning pot. "I'll make tea." She turned to face her guests, and her eyes widened. "Olivia."

"Sage."

"You two know each other?" Tom said.

"We do," Sage said. "We met at the Fishbowl. I take classes there."

Tom looked crestfallen. "I thought I was going to get to introduce you."

"No, but I'm so glad you brought her for a visit," Sage said.

"Since you know everything and everybody, you probably already know Olivia is into herbs and all that holistic stuff. I thought she'd like to see your garden." Tom kissed his mother on the forehead.

"I would." Olivia smiled. "I've heard it's wonderful."

"You're thoughtful, *mijo*. Tea first, or after?" Sage set her wooden spoon on a trivet and lowered the flame under the pot she'd been stirring.

"How about I make tea while you give Olivia the tour. I'll bring it outside when it's ready." Tom carried the kettle to the sink without waiting for his mother's response.

Sage opened the door and Olivia stepped into a fairyland. "Oh." She had no other words.

The yard was segmented into a patchwork quilt of color by rock borders and narrow paths. Bright blooms sprang from trees and bushes and dotted the dark chocolate soil. Butterflies and bees flitted from plant to plant. Olivia inhaled the sweet smells of lavender, jasmine, and orange blossom.

Sage had been watching her face and looked pleased by Olivia's reaction. She led her down the stoop and across an expanse of grass into the labyrinth. They stopped to pick a leaf, crush it, and release the fragrance, then to examine a rare plant. When Tom emerged several minutes later with mugs in hand, Olivia hadn't yet traversed half the garden. They moved to a wooden picnic table under a pepper tree surrounded by Adirondack chairs.

"The descriptions I've heard didn't do it justice," Olivia said when Tom asked her what she thought.

"I've taken you through the kitchen garden. The rest," Sage gestured to the other half of the maze, "is medicinal. I don't do much with those plants these days—some skin creams, tisanes, and tinctures to fight a winter flu. But my grandmother took care of the whole neighborhood in her day. Many of the herbs here were planted by her or are sown each year from seeds of plants she introduced. See that?" She pointed to a tall tree with feathery foliage. "It's ginkgo biloba—sixty years old. It was only a sapling when she passed. Tea from the leaves is excellent for the memory."

"Mama is modest," Tom said. "When I was a kid, I hardly ever went to the doctor. If my sister or I got sick, she'd mix up a cup of tea or dump us into a hot tub filled with herbs."

"Modern medicine is wonderful for some things, but I prefer the old remedies if the problem isn't serious." Sage lifted her cup and blew on the contents.

"Olivia has been doing research—"

"Essential oils, I know." Sage interrupted, then sipped her brew.

"And herbal medicines." Tom's voice took on an irritated edge. "Her son was in an accident. He has some challenges."

Olivia's cheeks burned. She wished Tom would've let her share Brian's story in her own time. She knew brain damage was a physical problem like a broken leg or sprained ankle and nothing to be ashamed of, but there was a stigma attached to it.

When her grandmother was young, people thought erratic behavior was the work of demons. Those with autism, brain damage, and mental illnesses were called "bad seeds." Children weren't allowed to socialize with them. God forbid if you ever married one. Things hadn't changed that much despite CT scans.

"What kind of challenges?" Sage looked at Olivia.

"Impulsivity, paranoia, false memories," Tom said.

"Confabulations, not false memories." Olivia corrected him, annoyed he'd answered for her. "There's a difference. The whole concept of false memories came out of the 'Satanic Panic' of the eighties and has since been discredited."

"I remember," Sage said. "Everybody and their brother thought they'd been abused in a cult ritual but had blocked out the memories. I think *The Exorcist* and *Rosemary's Baby* started it."

"*The Exorcist* scared the tar out of me," Tom said. "And I only saw the edited for TV version."

"Which you weren't supposed to watch." Sage's lips tightened into a thin smile.

"Always the rebel." He winked at Olivia.

"So, what is confabulation?" Sage said.

"Well, for one thing, it's a legitimate diagnosis." Olivia's words were pointed. She wasn't ready to let Tom off the hook. "It happens when the brain loses track of things and decides to fill it in with something that didn't actually occur—a bit of a dream or a memory from another time."

"The brain is the final frontier of medicine, I think," Sage said. "Doctors can weigh it, measure it, watch electrical impulses travel across it, but it's still a mystery. And mysteries make people nervous."

Olivia nodded. "I'm careful who I share information about Brian with. I've found old prejudices still exist."

They sat without speaking for a long moment, birdsong filling the quiet. Sage broke the silence. "So, what's the prognosis?"

Olivia spoke before Tom could jump in. "They're not sure. They want to drug him, but I think I see improvements without drugs."

Tom looked across the table at his mother, "I thought maybe you could help."

Sage stared into the distance and didn't respond.

"I don't expect... I didn't come here to..." Olivia floundered, wishing

Tom hadn't gotten involved. She didn't want to put Sage on the spot, and she wasn't willing to give Brian an unknown concoction. She couldn't. She could only try holistic remedies that didn't interfere with his current medicines and were approved by his doctor.

Sage patted Olivia's arm. "I'm not sure I can help."

"Of course you can." Tom's voice was tight. "The ginkgo biloba." He waved a hand at the tree. "And I know you have other things in the garden that improve brain function."

He and Sage locked eyes for a long moment. The tension that passed between them was almost palpable. Olivia hated the idea that the discord was because of her, because of Brian. "Please—" she began, but Tom lifted a hand to silence her.

"Let me think about it," Sage said with a sigh. Tom's shoulders relaxed, and he turned to Olivia. "Would you like to see the rest of the garden?"

She would. She wanted to get up and move away from what had become an awkward situation. But she also wanted to know the secrets of medicinal plants more than she'd wanted anything in a long, long, time.

MOLLY: So, Tom is the little Tomas of the diary, and Sage is its writer. This knowledge will help us understand what makes him tick as the season progresses.

Speaking of Tom, there's nothing like a little romance to add spice to a story. What do you all think of him? Seems like a great guy, doesn't he? He's got a nice mother, a good job, and he's neat and clean. That's more than I can say for some of the guys I've dated. Add to that, he can cook, which is the cherry on top of the ice cream sundae in my book. I'd love to have a guy cook for me.

But I digress.

I have another diary entry for you now. If you remember from the last episode, our mystery woman —who we now know is Sage—was waiting for her husband to pick her up for their anniversary, but the cops showed up instead. Turns out her husband was in a car accident. It was pretty tragic. Let's pick up her story from there.

Friday, June 12th, 1992

I sat by Doug's bed breathing in the scent of disinfectant, bedpans, and antiseptic. The lamp on the table near his pillow was unlit. The light from the hallway made odd shadows with his nose and cheekbones turning his face into a moonscape of crags and hollows.

I folded and twisted a tissue around my finger like a wedding ring and waited for him to wake. The doctors had backed off the drugs they'd kept him sedated with for the past three days. The swelling in his brain had gone down, but they couldn't be sure about the extent of the damage until Doug could tell them himself.

I'd spent my anniversary night right here in Mission Hospital. I'd sat in the waiting room counting the dots on the carpet. The doctors had fought to save Doug's life in an operating room. It seemed he'd been hit by a drunk driver on his way home to pick me up for our date. The driver, a thirty-year-old house painter who'd consumed a six-pack or two on the job that day, was fine. What a relief.

Doug stirred and a mumble of sound escaped his lips. I reached out and touched his fingers. I couldn't hold his hand because of the tubes running from it, but I wanted to make contact. "Doug, honey. I'm here." I didn't know if he could hear me, but I kept talking anyway. "You've been in an accident, but the doctors say you'll be fine."

What they'd really said was that they were cautiously optimistic.

They'd put his body back together, wrapped his broken ribs, and stitched up his head and face. But his brain had taken a beating, and the brain was a touchy thing.

"You have broken ribs and some ugly bruises, but nothing that won't heal up in a month or so. You are a pretty lucky guy. Well, as lucky as a guy who gets T-boned by a drunk in a Ford Super Duty can be."

His fingers tightened around mine for a second. A bubble of hope floated into my chest. "It'll stop those girls at the office from chasing you, for a while anyway. I mean, I love you no matter what, but you're no glamour boy right now. I'm trying to prepare you for the mirror."

"Hey." His voice was a rasp of sound.

"Yes, Doug. I'm here, honey." Tears sprang behind my eyes. He knew me. He could speak.

"Shut up."

I stiffened. Shut up? Was he joking? Already? That was a good thing, wasn't it?

"I will. I'll shut up now, and I'll get the doctor." I pulled my fingers from his and ran from the room. A dark-haired, dark-complected man in scrubs leaned on the counter of the nurse's station laughing with two women seated behind it. His name tag read, "Justin." The look on my face must have been shocking, because Justin left off talking mid-sentence.

"My husband's awake," I said. "Dr. Harrington wanted to be notified as soon as he woke up."

Justin pushed off the counter and headed toward Doug's room. I followed. Justin flicked on the long, overhead, light as he entered.

"Good morning." His tone was as jarring as the light. This would be no Lamaze rebirth with ambient lighting and soft music. "How are we feeling, Doug?"

Justin bustled to the machines by the bed and made some notes in the chart that hung there. Then he turned to his patient. He checked I.V.s, catheters, and bandages with the practiced hands of a professional. "What did he do that made you think he was awake?" This was addressed to me.

"He said, 'Shut up.'"

Justin leaned over the bed. "Can you talk to me, Doug?"

Doug's eyes moved behind his lids, but didn't open.

"Sometimes it takes a while for them to fully wake. Call me if he says or does anything else."

As soon as the efficient Justin left the room, I turned off the overhead light. Doug looked less scary in black and white. I sat in the chair I'd only left to shower, eat, go the bathroom and make that one foray to the nurses' station After three days it had become so much a part of me, I had a dream my arms were made of blue vinyl.

"So, you're not talking? Trying to make me look silly?" I said to my husband's inert form.

Doug's fingers picked at the sheets.

"Well, I know how cranky you are before you get your coffee. But I don't think they'll give you any until you talk to someone besides me."

I talked to Doug like I'd always talked to Doug: a light tone, a stream of consciousness, no pretense or forethought. Perhaps if I acted normal and natural, things would become normal and natural. Perhaps this monstrous looking body that smelled of iodine and blood would become my husband again.

I thought about kissing him. That worked in fairy tales. The princess and the frog. Snow White and the prince. A kiss was a transformative thing. But there was no place on that injured landscape I could see to plant one.

Instead, I leaned forward to take his fingers in mine again but stopped. His hand wandered across the blanket as if it was seeking something, investigating. Its movements reminded me of a spider. I hate spiders. I pulled my hand away, sat back and waited for Doug to speak again.

MOLLY: This doesn't bode well. What has happened to Doug's brain? That's what I want to know.

We'll find out more next time, but meanwhile, let's talk about Tom in the Facebook group. What do you think? Is he good for Olivia? Or are

Brian's feelings about him a red flag? Most kids dislike their mother's love interests unless that person is the other parent. So, there's that.

Speaking of the other parent, how do you feel about Davy? Sure, he says he's turned over a new leaf, but Olivia's been down that road before and been disappointed. Let's hear your thoughts.

(cue music)

VO: This episode is brought to you by Sweeter than Honey, Gourmet Cooking Supplies in Laguna Nigel. Transform your dinner into dining! *Murders Under the Sun* is edited by Jim Wilbourne, theme music is by Eclectic Blends, and I'm your host, Molly Shure.

part four

MURDERS UNDER THE SUN
   SEASON TWO; EPISODE THREE

MOLLY: Welcome back to *Murders Under the Sun*, Season Two--*The Garden*. I'm Molly Shure, your host.

Before we get into Episode Three, I have to say, I loved reading all your comments about Tom in the Facebook group. Some of you loved him. Some of you absolutely didn't. He's definitely a mixed bag.

As is Davy. You want to like Olivia's ex—at least I do—but he's done a lot of damage in her life and in Brian's.

On a side note, thank you to Perry and Stephen, who offered to cook for me. I'm hip deep in work at the moment, but I might just take a rain check.

I'd also be remiss if I didn't mention the kerfuffle in the group about the email I received about Ariana Blackstone. Honestly, people, I've told you all I know.

Yes, I do know the police miss things, but they're the professionals here. They have resources I simply don't have. Two missing students in a population of 35,000—that's what the enrollment was in 2005—isn't a significant number. Statistics would dictate a certain number of strange occurrences. I encouraged Ariana's cousin to contact the police if he thinks her disappearance might be related to Melissa's. So, again, people, I'm a reporter, not an investigator.

Now, back to our episode.

I promised you this story would begin to twist

and today is the day that begins. It might just be Olivia isn't as paranoid as we thought. I won't say anymore. Just wanted to throw out that little teaser.

Let's get into it. Here's Olivia.

2.3.2

OLIVIA SAT ON HER LUMPY, green sofa and stared at the eucalyptus tree outside her living room window. The house was still silent except for the sounds of chirping birds and the occasional car passing by on the street. Brian would be home any minute.

She missed him. It was the first weekend they'd been apart since her mother had temporary custody. But time alone was a rare and precious commodity. She soaked in the peace of her remaining moments like a cat on a windowsill soaking up the sun.

She'd just ordered grapefruit, cinnamon, and ginger oils for the studio. Several clients had asked if diffusing essential oils could help them lose weight. Apparently, it could. This combination of scents should suppress the appetite, boost metabolism, and give people more energy without reaching for the chocolate. It would probably be even more effective in a topical lotion, but she didn't feel qualified to create one. Maybe she'd talk to Sage about the idea.

As she sat, she ran through possible names for the solution. "Fat Away" sounded like a cleaning product. "Sniff and Burn" sounded illegal. "Slim Scent." That wasn't bad. She closed her laptop. Whatever she called it, it would sell. Orange County housewives were a vain lot.

"Mom," Brian burst through the front door. He ran across the living room and threw himself into Olivia's arms. She hugged him to herself, hard, grateful he was home. "Can we get a dog?" Brian's eyes were pleading.

"A dog?" Where had that come from? Olivia looked past Brian to Davy, who leaned on the wall in the entryway. He shook his head to let her know it wasn't his idea.

Brian's eyes widened. His cheeks flushed. "At the zoo they use them to help take care of the cheetahs. It's so cool. The cheetahs learn not to be afraid of people because the dogs aren't afraid. It makes them, like, tame."

"That's amazing," Olivia said, smiling at her son's enthusiasm.

"I really want a dog."

"Honey."

"Please, Mom."

Davy walked into the room. "Give your mom a break. Let her think about it, okay?"

"I don't need to think about it." Olivia shouldn't snap at Davy in front of Brian, but she couldn't handle a dog right now. He knew that. She could barely keep up with the responsibilities she already had. She stroked Brian's hair, and softened her voice. "It's not a good time to get a pet, baby. We're never home. It wouldn't be fair. Dogs need a lot of attention."

Brian untangled himself from her arms and paced across the small living room. "I'll drop out of soccer. I'll come right home from school every day. I'll take it for walks. I'll feed it. I swear. You won't have to do anything. I'll take total care of it, Mom. I will."

Olivia could just imagine. With Brian's memory issues the poor dog would be fed two or three times one day and not at all the next. Lord knows where they'd end up if Brian took it for a walk. "No, honey. Maybe in a couple of years."

Brian opened his mouth to protest, but Davy interrupted. "Hey, buddy, why don't you go put your stuff away in your room. I need to talk to your mom."

Brian looked at his dad for a long moment, then walked to the entryway where he'd dropped his duffel bag. "Tell her all that stuff you told me about how dogs are good for people who forget a lot. Okay?"

Davy jerked his head in the direction of Brian's room. Brian, shoulders slumped, headed out.

"What were you thinking?" Olivia said as soon as he was out of earshot. "I can't take care of a dog. I'm starting a business, running Brian everywhere he needs to go, helping with homework, taking care of the house. Some mornings I don't have enough time to brush my hair."

Davy let her rant until she ran out of steam. "You done?"

Olivia glared at him.

"I never said it was a good idea to get a dog. He was mesmerized by the whole cheetah thing. A zookeeper was in the enclosure, playing with the animals and talking to the crowd about the program. I think we spent an hour in that one spot."

"Then when you left, you filled his head with stuff about service dogs. Right? He's not disabled, Davy. He doesn't need a service dog."

"All he wanted to talk about on the way home were dogs—how smart they are. The things people can train them to do. I wasn't suggesting he needed one. It was a conversation. He came up with the idea to ask you for a dog all by himself."

Olivia paused. She'd jumped to conclusions. She was good at that these days, especially when it came to Davy. "I guess all little boys want dogs," she said, sadness overshadowing her annoyance. Family pets were often one more casualty of divorce.

"A dog could be a help. It could be trained to nudge him toward home when he gets a wild hair and decides to take off. It could find him if he does wander away."

Her annoyance returned. "I don't have the time, or the money, to train a dog."

"I'm not saying now is a good time, but we can't follow him around forever. He's getting older. We're going to have to let out the leash a little, no pun intended. A dog might not be a bad idea."

"You're very good at coming up with ideas—what Brian wants, what Brian needs. You can't drop them in my lap anymore, Davy. It's full. You need to take care of your own ideas."

Davy stared at her, a blank expression on his face, then pivoted on his heel and walked toward his son's bedroom. The front door slammed about five minutes later. He left without saying goodbye.

Maybe she'd been too tough on him. He'd said he hadn't meant to put ideas into Brian's head. But, if she was honest with herself, she knew the problem wasn't that Brian wanted a dog. It was seeing Davy as often as she did now. It wore her down. His presence poked holes in the box she'd stuffed her rage, and hurt, and grief into after the divorce, and she didn't like what was spilling out. Vindictiveness wasn't becoming.

2.3.3

A CAR CAME alongside Olivia's and blocked her. She'd been about to pull away from the curb. It was Monday morning, and she'd run late, again. She'd parked down the street from St. Barnabas and walked Brian to the entrance. It saved so much time she was surprised she hadn't thought of it sooner.

Olivia and Fiona had met with a lawyer the previous week to outline a limited partnership agreement. They were signing papers that morning. She wanted to be on time, and she would be if that car would get out of her way.

She glanced over, wondering what the holdup was. It was Tom. He leaned across the passenger seat of his vehicle and gestured for her to lower her window. "I'm sorry," he said as soon as she did.

When he'd dropped her off on Sunday, she'd exited his car without giving him so much as a kiss on the cheek. She wasn't angry at him, exactly, just feeling wary. He meant well, but it had put her in an awkward position. "For what?"

"Springing my mother on you like that. I wanted to surprise you with the garden, but I guess I should have prepared you."

That wasn't the problem. The problem was, he'd taken a lot for granted. She didn't like having her confidences shared without her permission. Her voice frosted over. "No, it was great. I loved the garden."

"Yes, but things got kind of tense there for a bit."

Olivia thought about her next words. She'd always hated confrontation, but Brian's accident had changed her. She'd become bolder. She'd learned to ask for what she needed. If not for herself, for her son. "I wish you wouldn't talk about Brian's problems with other people. It's a sensitive subject for me. I'd rather be the one to decide who I want to tell about it."

After a stretch of dead air, Tom said. "What a dolt. God, I'm sorry. My students are so much a part of my work life, sometimes I forget they're somebody's child. I can be too damn clinical. Can you forgive me?"

He sounded so contrite, she felt herself thawing. "Of course."

"Will you go out with me again? Or did I totally screw things up?"

She smiled. "I'll give you another chance if you behave yourself."

"How about this weekend?"

Too soon. She planned to traverse this road slowly and carefully. She'd already been surprised by one pothole. "How about next? I have Brian this weekend, and I want to do something special with him. Davy took him to the zoo yesterday. He came home all excited about getting a dog. Once again, I'm the bad guy because I said no. I need to come up with something so much fun it'll drive dogs right out of his head."

"There's an event at the Mission on Sunday. They're doing basket weaving and a Native American storyteller is coming. Doesn't Brian love all that living history stuff?"

"He does, and he loves the Mission."

"My mother is on the board. I can get you in for free."

"You don't have to--"

"I want to. I'll even bring a picnic lunch." A car horn sounded behind them. "I'll pick you both up at ten. The program starts at 10:30." He shot her his one-dimpled smile and drove off before she could say yes or no. She guessed she'd be seeing Tom this weekend after all. So much for taking things slow.

"Open it." Fiona grinned at Olivia.

"You shouldn't have," Olivia said and stuck a finger under the flap of the envelope Fiona gave her. She pulled out a card depicting a cartoon mother with a harried look on her face holding a squalling infant. On the inside, it read, "Congratulations."

"Shouldn't I be giving this to you?" Olivia said, confused.

"I told her that card was silly," Yasmin said.

"Starting a new business is like having a kid." Fiona's voice was deadpan. "They're a whole lot of trouble. You don't get any sleep, and it takes about thirty years before they pay off. Welcome to the biz."

"You're such an encourager." Olivia, perched on a stability ball in the big exercise room, wobbled as she leaned over to hug her friend. The rest of the Fishbowl's staff had come in after the last class of the day on Monday evening to surprise her. They sat on mats or stability balls around two Pilates boxes they'd shoved together as a makeshift table, the remains of a large order of Indian food and several empty wine glasses in front of them.

"Hey, I'm just telling it like it is," Fiona said.

"Here." Yasmin handed Olivia a big pot of kitchen herbs decoratively planted. "It's from me, Karen, Airi, and Julianne. Julianne is sorry she couldn't be here. She's teaching a class at Peak Pilates tonight."

"We knew you were into herbs and stuff," Airi said.

"Thanks. You guys are going to make me cry." Olivia's tone was light, but she did feel her throat shutting down. She'd only been at the Fishbowl for two months and three weeks, but already it felt like home.

She looked at the group gathered around her. Karen, the Pilates drill sergeant, who'd intimidated the hell out of her when she was first hired. Yasmin, the lithe dancer, whose dizzy behavior made her irritated and laugh in equal measure. Airi, the tiny, tough yoga instructor, who was as precise and organized as Yasmin was flighty. And Fiona who'd become the closest thing to a sister Olivia had ever had. They were her family now.

"Just don't get too important to take classes," Yasmin said.

"She might not have time," Fiona said. "New business. New boyfriend. She's a busy woman now."

"Boyfriend? You're kidding?" Yasmin slapped Olivia's arm so hard she almost toppled off her round perch.

"I wouldn't call him a boyfriend." Olivia felt her cheeks glow. Probably the wine.

"How many dates have you been on?" Airi asked.

"Three, if I count a quick glass of wine at Turk's."

"If he asks you out again, you're officially dating." Airi's tone was definitive.

"Is that some kind of formula? Four dates and you're dating?"

"Yes. I read it in *Cosmo*."

"She's right." Fiona chimed in. "It's the law. Dev says so." Devon, Fiona's husband was a family law attorney.

"Whatever. I'm taking things slow." Olivia reached for her wine glass. She didn't tell them about her plans to go to the Mission on Sunday with Tom.

"Silly woman," Karen said.

At eight-thirty Olivia doled out hugs and thanks, gathered her gifts and cards and headed out to her car. Fiona insisted she leave early and let the rest of them clean up and close. The celebration had been for her, after all. She'd offered to stay and help, but they'd shooed her out the door.

Brian was at her mother's, so she didn't have to rush. But she didn't want to take advantage either. Because Sarah made her own schedule, it was easy to forget that publishing was a business like any other. There were deadlines and appointments to keep.

Olivia reached her car and balanced her pot of herbs on one knee while she fished in her purse for her keys. She clicked the door open. As she leaned inside to deposit her cards and the plant on the passenger seat, she saw a bit of paper stuck under the windshield wiper. She could only make out two words, "Missing Boy," in bold, black letters.

Probably a flier from a desperate family. She reached for the paper. There were two sheets. Not fliers, but printed copies of newspaper articles. One headline read, *Missing Boy Found Dead*, the other, *Boy Killed in Tragic Accident*.

She moved to the hood of her car and spread out the pages. What was this about? Olivia's gaze skittered between the two stories illuminated in the dim light of a streetlamp. They were written about three and a half years apart, one in 2008 and the other in 2012.

They happened in different cities, Boise, Idaho, and Chandler, Arizona. One of the boys was ten, the other nine. One was missing for twenty-four hours, the other was gone for two days before he was found. The first boy, the one from 2008, drowned in a rushing river after a week of rainstorms. The child from 2012 fell to his death while rock climbing on a camping trip.

Why had someone left this for her?

2.3.4

OLIVIA LOOKED UP. Her head snapped right then left, as if she might find the answer to her questions somewhere in the dark parking lot. Apprehension slid over her, cold and damp. She folded the papers, got in the car, and locked the doors. As soon as she put Brian to bed, she'd research the stories from the safety of her couch.

As she drove to her mother's, she wondered if the clippings had anything to do with the car in the parking lot last week. Probably not. The earlier event was most likely paranoia, her imagination. This was a deliberate act. Someone wanted her to know about these boys. But why?

Someone from CPS? That's the only thing that made any sense, and it didn't make much. Maybe an anal-retentive case worker was trying to keep her on her toes by sharing cautionary tales. A shiver ran along her spine. Someone who left cryptic messages on windshields had to be a few tacos short of a combo plate. She stepped on the accelerator and got to her mother's in twelve minutes instead of the usual fifteen.

Sarah answered the door in a long, white cotton nightgown, her gray hair hanging loose, and gave Olivia a sleepy smile. Olivia looked past her and saw Brian dozing on the couch. She exhaled with relief. "You're headed to bed early. Everything go okay?"

"Fine. It was a long day. We fell asleep watching a movie. How was work?"

"It was nice. Fiona and the girls threw a little congratulations party for me."

"Lovely." Sarah covered her yawn with a blue veined hand.

Olivia hushed her voice as she crossed to her sleeping son. "Sorry, I'm late."

"You're actually early. Anyway, I turned in my manuscript yesterday. I'm giving myself a few days off."

"You deserve it." Olivia lifted Brian by his shoulders to a sitting position. His head lolled onto his chest. "He's out."

"You were like that at that age. You'd sleep through anything."

Olivia didn't respond. When she was Brian's age, she'd developed that ability for survival. If she hadn't learned to sleep through the noise, and all the comings and goings of her mother's crazy roommates, she'd have never slept. "Did you find out anything about Proctor?"

"No, not yet. I've been busy."

A question dropped into Olivia's mind, one that hadn't occurred to her before. One that made her heart thud. She propped Brian up on the couch and walked into the dining room. Her mother followed. "Look, I'm sorry, but you know how I am when I'm winding up a book. I get in—"

"Did Proctor ever do anything to any of the boys at the farm?" The question came in a harsh whisper.

"What? Why do you ask?" Her mother's skin paled.

"Just tell me."

"I don't know. I don't think so."

"Would Winnie or Drew know?"

"They've never said anything like that."

"But they wouldn't, would they?" It was better to forget. In those days, her mother's crowd thought laws were for squares, big brother was watching, and the police were pigs. There was an unspoken agreement between them to ignore one another's sins, even Proctor's.

Sarah hugged her arms around herself. "Why do you want to know? Now? After all these years?"

"Please, find out for me." Olivia wasn't ready to tell anyone about the articles until she had some clue as to what they meant, or why they were left for her.

Brian never fully woke, not even when Olivia pulled off his shoes and pants and trundled him into bed. She tucked the covers around him and hurried into the living room.

She took the newspaper articles from her purse, laid them next to her on the lumpy green couch and turned on her laptop. She typed the basic facts from the top article into her search engine: name—Peter Compton, date—April 2008, place—Boise, Idaho. The first thing that popped up was the article she already had. Below were some shorter, less detailed news stories, the funeral announcement, and finally his obituary.

After reading each account, she pieced together a sad story. Peter was the only child of a single mother, Anne Compton. Reading between the lines, Olivia guessed he'd had some issues similar to Brian's. One Tuesday morning he rode his bike to school along the river trail as usual. He arrived on time according to teachers and classmates. He left school at 3:15 and was seen pedaling toward the Boise River, but he never made it home.

Peter was a latchkey kid, and Anne worked late that night so wasn't aware of his absence until she arrived home in the evening. After calling all his friends, her ex-husband, and every relative within ten miles, she called the police. A missing child alert was issued, and search and rescue teams dispersed.

His bike was found on the river trail at midnight. His body wasn't found until the next day when a fisherman saw it snagged up on a felled tree about a mile and a half downstream. They surmised Peter had wandered too close to the edge of the water and had fallen in and drowned—a tragic accident.

A line in his obituary brought tears to Olivia's eyes, "Peter was a sweet and loving child with a curious nature. The great outdoors was his favorite classroom. We'll miss him but are comforted to know he died in the river—the place he loved most on earth."

There was more information about the second boy, Trevor Johnson, because of a lawsuit filed by his mother against a local father-son backpacking club in 2013. Trevor went on a camping trip with the club to a place called Queen Creek Canyon, about forty-five minutes from Phoenix. The club leaders believed he sneaked out of his tent on the second night of the trip, climbed part way up a treacherous rock face, lost his hold and fell to his death. It was two days before a search and rescue team found him.

According to the adults on the trip, Trevor had mentioned rock climbing several times. They'd explained to the boys it was too dangerous without proper training and equipment. The backpacking club's lawyer claimed the boy had ADHD and had left his medication at home. Trevor was survived by his mother, father, stepmother, and younger sister.

Olivia rubbed her neck, stiff from bending over the computer, and looked at the time, 1:13. What a waste. She wasn't any closer to understanding why the news stories were placed under her windshield wiper. Or, who'd done it.

She shut off her laptop and padded to Brian's room. He lay still under a blanket covered in racecars; his face angelic as only a sleeping child's can be. He was the same age as those boys in the articles, the same age she had been when Proctor had come into her life.

When she was ten her mother moved them both to a commune in Vermont. The big farm, with vegetable gardens, sheep, chickens, and a milk cow seemed like a slice of heaven at first. They'd arrived on a beautiful September day. It was the time of year when leaves set fire to the woods, and the air was as crisp as the late apples still hanging from the trees.

They pulled up a long, packed dirt drive and were met by two middle-aged people. Rainy and Edgar, in jeans, work boots and flannel shirts, looked more like siblings than the husband and wife they actually were. Despite the clothes, Olivia could tell by looking at them they were city transplants. They were too round, too friendly, and too androgynous to be austere New Englanders.

Rainy and Edgar took them into a farmhouse kitchen that smelled of lavender, cinnamon, and baking bread and set a cracked mug of cocoa in front of Olivia. In later years, whenever she smelled that combination of scents she would be transported to the warmth and comfort of that room. Distracted though she was by chocolate and cinnamon bun ecstasy, she still caught bits and pieces of the adult conversation.

"We inherited the place from my Great Aunt Ida five years ago." Rainy was talking to Sarah, Olivia's mother. "But we had no idea how to care for it."

Edgar set down his mug and slapped a hand on the worn, oak table. "One day Teach and Patty showed up with the kids. Saved our asses."

"They've been a Godsend." Rainy smiled. "A Godsend."

Kids. Olivia listened more closely.

"You have more people living here now, though, don't you?" her mother said.

"Fifteen adults and five children. Sixteen and six, if you two join us. Teach and Patty invited some friends to work the harvest that first time. They never left. More folks showed up in the spring for planting. Pretty soon stray souls were wandering in like hungry cats," Edgar said.

"Edgar didn't have the heart to shoo them away." Rainy glanced at her husband with so much love, Olivia felt a pang of longing.

Sarah agreed to take on the housecleaning and help whenever they needed her in the gardens. The adults shook on it and Olivia and her mother carried their shabby suitcases up a flight of creaking stairs into a bedroom overlooking a dirt road.

This was the first time in her life Olivia had regular, daily companionship with people of her own age. Teach, the original caretaker, had been a grade school teacher before moving to the farm. He was a tall, thin, gentle man who stroked a bushy beard while he told stories. He taught the six children in residence the basics: reading, writing, and arithmetic.

They followed him around the farm in the mornings for science lessons. That's what he called learning to milk, gather eggs, and tend sheep. To be fair, he did regale them with facts about the nature of plants and animals while they worked. Olivia remembered more from those lessons than she did from the textbooks of her later years.

In the afternoons, they'd gather in a small room of the main house that had been turned into a classroom. There, Teach taught them long division, grammar, and French. After lessons, he'd read them stories about famous people from the past. It was the happiest time of Olivia's young life, until Proctor showed up.

It had never occurred to her before tonight that he might have been a danger to any of the other children. But why wouldn't he have been? He was evil. Evil touched the people around it, wherever it went.

She pushed the bangs from Brian's forehead with one finger and kissed him softly. Her chest ached. Those poor mothers. She knew the pain of thinking your son might not survive the night. She could only imagine how it would feel if he didn't. Excruciating. She straightened and felt strength course through her. Brian wasn't going to be in that kind of danger ever again.

2.3.5

"TV OFF," Olivia said. Brian obeyed, dragged himself off the carpet, yawning, and headed toward the door.

"Shoes." She stopped with her hand on the knob. He gave her a sleepy smile, ran to his room, and reemerged with his Vans in his hand. She hated to rush him after a busy day at school and soccer practice, but she'd agreed to drop him off at Davy's by 5:30.

Davy. He irritated like a splinter. He reminded her of Ferris Bueller, the character from the old 80s movie, who was wildly rewarded for his irresponsibility. Two days into Davy's new job, the company expanded his sales territory because another employee left unexpectedly. He now made more money than she did. He also paid less rent than she did—for a nicer place. He'd even lost his alcohol weight in a couple of months without having to change his eating habits.

She was being petty. She should have been happy for him, but she wasn't. Honestly, she wanted him to suffer, at least a little, for all the ways he'd made her suffer. She wanted him to experience some of the same struggles she'd experienced after he'd started drinking. His charmed life exasperated her.

She drove into Davy's complex through a river rock entrance flanked by palm trees—much more elegant than the suburban side street she lived on. "Stop, Mom." Brian pointed out the window, excitement on his face. Davy stood in a well-landscaped green belt that ran between the banks of buildings. It took a moment for her to see the reason for the emotion in Brian's voice. Davy held a brown leash in his right hand, at its end was a black dog.

She pulled up to the grass, and Brian flew out of the car. "Dad, whose is he?" He dropped to his knees by the animal.

"Yours," Davy said.

Olivia turned off the ignition and got out of the car.

"Mine? Really? Hi, boy. Hi there." The words sputtered from Brian's lips between dog kisses.

"What do you mean, he's Brian's?" Olivia asked.

"I was out running errands yesterday." Davy wore the innocent smile that always drove her crazy. "I passed this pet shop that was having one of those adoption days. There were all these dogs out front, and I stopped to take a look. That was my first mistake." He shrugged. "This big guy comes charging over to me, climbing on my legs, tail going a mile a minute. I couldn't resist."

"I told you I didn't want a dog," Olivia said.

"I know. He's not yours. He's mine. Mine and Brian's."

"I can't believe you." The words edged past Olivia's frozen lips.

Davy's eyes grew wide. "Brian wanted a dog. I think a dog would be good for him. You said yourself I come up with ideas, then expect you to carry them out. I'm taking responsibility for a change. I thought you'd be happy."

"Happy? Happy that you're always the fun guy, and I'm always the heavy? Happy you get to take Brian to the zoo and Disneyland, and I get to take him to school and doctor appointments? Sure. I'm ecstatic." Olivia ran a hand through her hair and turned toward the car. She needed to pull it together. She'd broken her own rule—never fight in front of Brian.

"Olivia, come on. You're being unreasonable." She spun to face him. He held up his hands in supplication. "Call me. I'll take him to the doctor next time. I can come over and do homework with him too."

"I have to get home," she said. He was right, she could ask. The truth was, she didn't want to. She wanted to control Brian's schedule without having to consider Davy. It might be selfish of her, but there it was.

"You needed to be the custodial parent in the beginning, I get that. But we could go fifty-fifty now. I could help more. I want to."

Fifty-fifty. Cold crept over Olivia. Brian was hers. It was bad enough having to drop him off Tuesdays, Thursdays, every other weekend and share holidays. No way would she give up any more of her parental rights

"Here, Dad. You better take him back," Brian said, his face stoic. Davy's eyes bored into Olivia's as he took the leash from his son's extended hand.

"No. No. Brian, honey, I'm sorry. Of course, you and your dad can keep the dog. I'm... I'm just tired. I didn't think about what I was saying." Olivia wished she could snatch back her words, lock them in the black vault they'd escaped from. She kneeled on the grass by her son and hugged him to her. "He's yours. Yours and Dad's, just like Dad said."

"I don't want him if he's going to make you and Dad fight."

"It's not the dog's fault your mom's a nut." She gave him a weak smile. "I didn't mean it. Honey. Really. Look how cute he is." The dog strained toward Olivia.

"He likes you, Mom."

"I like him too," Olivia said. "What's his name?"

"His previous owner called him Crackers." Davy looked at Brian. "But you can name him anything you want to."

"What do you think, Mom?" Brian turned to her; his eyes full of hope. Shame burned on Olivia's cheeks.

"Crackers is cute. Do you like Crackers?"

"It fits. Wait until you see him loose in the apartment. He's a crazy guy," Davy said.

Brian hugged the dog. "Hi, Crackers. Hi, buddy."

Olivia kissed her son and said a terse goodbye to Davy. The chill from his words stayed with her all the way home. He'd wanted more time with their son, and she'd given it. Primarily because she had to, but still, she'd been trying to work with him. It never occurred to her Davy might want to share custody.

He'd cleaned up his act. He'd joined a faith-based recovery group, got a decent job, a nice car and a place to live. He'd look pretty good to a judge right now.

When Davy was drinking, he'd been a disappointment, but never a threat. He couldn't even handle temporary custody when CPS had taken Brian from Olivia, which was why her mother ended up with him. Davy 2.0, the new and improved version, could pose a problem.

Thank god she hadn't told him about the newspaper articles, or her fear that she was being followed. If he knew a danger from her past had possibly resurfaced, it might motivate him to take legal action for Brian's sake. But she didn't need Davy. She could take care of Brian on her own. She'd been doing it for three years.

Good lord. A new thought made her stomach clench. What if he decided to go for full custodial rights? What if he wanted to switch roles with her? Recast her as the part-time parent, and him as the primary caregiver? She needed to figure out who was sending her messages and handle it before anyone else learned of it. Especially Davy.

2.3.6

NOT EVEN THE SOFT MUSIC, sweet smells, and brilliant blue light of the Fishbowl were able to lift Olivia's spirits the next morning. During the early press of classes, she was too busy to worry, but an unnamed anxiety lay heavy across her shoulders. It made her think of those dead-fox stoles women used to wear in the forties. Whenever things quieted down, she imagined it reanimating and whispering its poison in her ear: *You're going to lose him. Lose your son.*

A gentle cough brought Olivia to attention. She looked up from her paperwork to see Sage standing by the desk. "You look busy."

"No. Nothing that can't wait." Olivia forced a smile.

"I brought you something." Sage shuffled through the embroidered Mexican bag hanging on her shoulder and brought out a glass mason jar. "If you don't want to try it, I understand. But after what Tomas said, I thought maybe..."

"What is it?" Olivia took the jar from her hand and held it up. Amber liquid glowed in the light from the window.

"It's a tincture. I made it with organic apple cider vinegar—no alcohol—and herbs from the garden. It's my grandmother's recipe. She used it to treat everything from postpartum depression to hyperactivity in kids."

Olivia didn't know what to say. When Tom had asked his mother to help, Sage seemed uncomfortable. The gift was generous, both because of the time and effort, and because it had seemed to tax her emotionally. But Olivia would need to know more before she gave any to her son. "What's in it?" she asked, hoping she didn't sound unappreciative.

"I thought you'd ask. I know what a researcher you are." Sage dug into the large bag again. "Here." She set a folded sheet of paper on the counter. "The recipe."

"Thank you," Olivia said.

"Good mothers don't give anything to their children without knowing the ingredients, potential side-effects, contraindications, all that." Sage put her hand on top of Olivia's, her fingers cool and dry. "And you're a good mother."

"Does it come with instructions?"

"Motherhood, or the tincture?" Sage grinned.

"If you have motherhood instructions, I'll take those too."

"Wouldn't it be nice if kids came with a manual?" She tapped on the folded page with one finger. "Start slow and build up the amount you give him if he seems to be tolerating it okay, but all that's on the paper. I haven't made it in years." Sage's eyes clouded for an instant. "But it's a good recipe. It's helped a lot of people." She said with a note of defiance in her voice.

"I'm sure it has," Olivia said. "I appreciate it."

"I'd better get into class. Fiona hates it when we're late."

After Sage disappeared down the hall, Olivia unfolded the page and read the ingredient list—St. John's Wort, rosemary, and ginkgo biloba. It sounded safe, but she'd see what she could find out online that evening and call Brian's doctor on Monday.

She put the jar and instructions in her big tote bag under the counter and forced herself to focus on the store bookkeeping. The predictable pattern of debits and credits usually calmed her nerves. She finished as the lobby began to fill with departing students. She waved goodbye to Sage, took care of some scheduling issues, sold an exercise top and a book on essential oils, and shut off the computer before the front door closed for the last time.

"Busy morning." Fiona's voice entered the room before she did. "Let's close up for an hour. I'm starved. Want to get curry? It's all I can think about these days." Olivia hesitated. She wasn't sure she could eat. Her stomach was still in knots. "My treat," Fiona said.

They ordered a couple of bowls of rice topped with tofu and pumpkin curry from a small place on Pacific Coast Highway and took them to an outside table. "So, what's with you?" Fiona settled into her metal chair.

"What do you mean?"

"You're not your usual cheerful self."

"I didn't know it showed."

"Probably didn't to the clients, but I know you."

It had been almost three months since Olivia had started work at the Fishbowl. In that time Fiona had become a good friend, but Olivia didn't have much experience with friendship. Her unsettled childhood, moving so often, had taught her to be a loner. She needed to talk things out with someone objectively to stop the negative cycle in her brain. It was difficult for her though. "Davy got a dog." She blurted out the words.

"So?" Fiona dug into her food.

"Brian's been begging for a dog since Davy took him to the zoo, but I said no. So, of course, Davy goes and gets one."

"Where's the dog going to live?"

"At Davy's." Olivia poked at a cube of tofu with her fork.

"I don't get it. What's the problem?" Fiona's words made Olivia feel small and childish. She tried to explain.

"I feel like he wants to tempt Brian away from me. Make himself and his home more attractive. Make Brian want to go live with him."

Fiona's face softened in sympathy. "If that's what he's doing, it's not going to work. Brian loves you. You're his mom. Dad might be fun, but Mom is Mom."

Olivia hesitated, as if saying the words might make them a reality. "Davy mentioned sharing custody fifty-fifty."

Fiona froze, fork halfway to her mouth, then returned it to her plate, food untouched.

"I couldn't handle that. I dread the weekends he has Brian," Olivia said. "I miss him so much, but it's not just that. It's Davy. I don't trust him. Even before we were divorced, before he started drinking so heavily, he had a wild streak. He would play these elaborate pranks on people."

"Like?"

"There was a man in his old company who was always hitting on the receptionist. She was young, pretty, easily intimidated. Davy signed him up at a revenge website. The guy started getting hundreds of spam emails a day. His inbox blew up. He got hauled into the boss's office for visiting porn sites during the workday. He almost lost his job. It was pretty bad."

Fiona hid a smile with her drink cup. "Sounds like a fitting punishment."

"Fiona," Olivia said, exasperated.

"It was a bit harsh, but I don't think the way he treats an old lech has anything to do with his parenting style."

Olivia shrugged, not willing to let it go.

"How did the custody thing come up? Did he threaten you? Was he testing the waters?"

"No. Not threatening, I guess. I'd blasted him for not taking on the hard work of parenting, for always wanting the fun parts. After that, he said maybe we should share custody."

"Okay," Fiona picked up her fork again. "I think you're borrowing trouble. It sounds like he wants to make up for some lost time, be a parent for a change."

"That's the exact phrase he used." Olivia could hear the doubt in her own voice. "But this dog thing. Brian's going to want to be over there all the time to be with the dog."

"Every kid wants a dog until they have to walk it, pick up its poop, feed it, train it. If Davy is putting on the parent role, he'll make Brian do all that when he's over there. It might be a good thing for him to have chores at Dad's house, not just yours."

Olivia nibbled on a piece of pumpkin. It was true; dogs were a lot of work. That was one of the reasons she didn't want one. Maybe a shared responsibility would be good for Brian and Davy, bond them in a different way. "You think I'm overreacting?"

"Just a little."

"I was wondering if I should talk to Devon? See if there was something I should do to protect myself." As a family law attorney, Devon had handled his fair share of custody cases.

"I don't think you're at that point. But tell you what, I'll fill him in and see what he says."

"Thanks." Olivia's anxiety grew lighter, but only for a moment.

With the dog issue resolved somewhat, her thoughts shifted to the newspaper articles. She'd made a decision not to tell anyone about them, but should Fiona be an exception? Would she have some wisdom that might shine a light into that well of confusion?

No. Olivia didn't want to upset her, especially in her current condition. Fiona hadn't completely recovered from everything she'd been through earlier that year. The past February had been tough on both of them. It was the month Brian's accident occurred. It was also the month a murder was committed in the home Fiona had inherited in Laguna Beach. It had affected her deeply. Besides, she'd tell Olivia to go to the police, and that wasn't something Olivia was ready to do.

"On to happier topics, how are things going with the school-teacher?" Fiona said.

Olivia realized she'd never told Fiona about her trip to Sage's on Sunday. All the excitement over buying into the business had driven it from her mind. "He's Sage's son."

"What?" Fiona's eyes grew large.

"Crazy, huh? He took me to her house on Sunday to see her garden. Seemed disappointed we already knew each other."

"Small world. So, what's he like? Is he tall, dark, and beautiful like Sage?"

"Actually, yes. He looks a lot like her." Olivia suppressed a smile.

"Then I approve." Fiona lifted her iced tea for a toast. They clinked cups. "When are you seeing him again?"

"We're taking Brian to a living history event at the Mission on Sunday."

"Hmmm..." Fiona folded her napkin in half, taking time to press the crease with a fingernail.

"What?" Olivia said.

"Isn't it a bit early to involve Brian?"

"Extenuating circumstances." Olivia waved a hand in the air, dismissing Fiona's concern. "He's Brian's soccer coach. They already know each other."

"Does Davy know?"

"Know what?"

"That you're dating someone who's tall, dark, and beautiful?"

Olivia locked eyes with her friend. "You think that might be why he's making noises about joint custody?"

"He might be feeling insecure. Worried he's going to lose his son."

Olivia pushed her half-eaten food away. "That's not going to happen. No matter how crazy he makes me, Davy is Brian's dad."

"Maybe you should make sure he knows that's how you feel."

Fiona was right, but sharing something like that with Davy wouldn't be easy. It sounded too much like forgiveness, and as much as she thought she should be, Olivia wasn't ready to forgive.

2.3.7

"HERE." Brian held up something that looked like the nest of a demented bird. "It's for you."

"Thank you. It's wonderful." Olivia turned it around in her hands so she could admire it from every angle.

"I thought you could put your keys and stuff in it."

"I could." If she did, she might never see them again. The basket looked carnivorous.

It was a perfect Sunday for an outdoor event. The late October days were beginning to cool, but the sun was still warm enough to release the lovely scents of the Mission's gardens. Salvia and mock orange competed with honeysuckle; pink bougainvillea, brilliant against gray stone walls, shimmered in the morning light.

"Good job," Tom said.

"Thanks." Brian's smile faded when he looked at Tom. He no longer seemed hostile toward him, just tentative. Olivia took that as encouragement.

"I think the storyteller is on in a couple of minutes," she said. "Want to go get a good spot?"

Brian jogged in the direction of the gathering crowd. She started to follow, but Tom put a hand on her arm. "We can see him from here. Give him a little space."

Olivia was irritated by the intrusion, but she stayed where she was.

"I don't know a lot about child psychology," he said. "But one thing I do know is, if you show kids a little trust, they'll usually make an effort to deserve it."

"Maybe. But Brian has issues most kids don't."

She watched her son's brown head bob through the group of children assembled on the grass and drop into a center spot. She relaxed. A little. Tom might be right, but she planned to keep an eye on her son even if it was from a distance.

The storyteller, a beautiful, round-faced woman dressed in a long buckskin dress, walked into the circle. She turned on her microphone and began speaking. Soon the children were lost in the world of the Juaneño Tribe of long ago.

Tom leaned over and spoke into her ear, "You know we've never had a real date."

"What about that lovely dinner you made me? That was a date, wasn't it?"

"I mean a more traditional date. I pick you up at your house with flowers in hand. You get all dressed up in something sexy. I take you out to an overpriced restaurant. That kind of date."

"Are you asking me out?"

"Yeah. Would you go out with me Friday night?"

"Let me check Davy's schedule," she said, and turned to watch the storyteller. Moving slowly with Tom was beginning to look like an impossibility.

Twenty minutes into the hour-long program, the pressure in Olivia's bladder she'd been ignoring for the past half hour grew uncomfortable. She'd waited because she hadn't wanted to leave Brian alone. When he was small, she could take him to the ladies' room with her, but he was too old for that now.

Tom was here, so he wouldn't be alone. And, as Davy said, they had to begin letting out the leash a bit. "Can you watch Brian for a moment?"

"Sure." Tom's eyebrows raised in question.

"Ladies' room," she said.

He nodded.

"It only takes a second for him to disappear." She sounded overprotective, even to herself.

"Olivia," he said her name slowly. "People pay me to supervise their kids for thirty hours a week, thirty-six weeks a year. I think I can handle the five minutes it's going to take you to go to the restroom."

"I'm sorry," she said, but he'd already returned his attention to the action in the central courtyard.

Olivia walked across the grass toward the visitor center. The building was cool and dimly lit after the bright sunshine. She followed signs to the bathroom door. The small, tiled room was clean and empty and smelled of strawberry disinfectant. She walked to one end and closed herself inside a stall. A moment later, she heard the door to the bathroom open and shut, and the click of shoes. Another sound, hair spray maybe. She flushed the toilet.

When she was done, she walked to a sink to wash her hands and glanced into the mirror on the wall to check her hair. Her breath caught. In its reflection she saw B, R, I in large black letters scrawled onto a half-opened stall door.

B, R, I. Her palms slicked. The room was spotless when she'd entered—no graffiti anywhere. She was sure.

She glanced around, looking for the person she'd heard enter, but saw no one. Heart skipping, she moved to the stall and pulled the door shut so she could read all of what was written: *Brian is in danger*.

The paint was still wet. The message was for her. It had to be.

She spun around scanning the stark white room. The other stall doors were closed, and there were no feet visible beneath. Olivia stepped to the closest. She placed a hand against the cold metal and pushed. The door swung open. No one inside. She moved to the next and repeated the process. Empty. There was nowhere else to hide.

Cold fingers crept up Olivia's spine. "Hello." She yelled into the void. "What do you want?" Only an echo returned.

Fury ripped through her. What kind of person would try to scare a mother like this? "Tell me what the hell you want," she screamed to the blank walls.

A sudden need to see her son gripped her. She burst through the bathroom door, ran along the dark hallway and out into the sunshine. The group of students gathered around the storyteller were standing now. Several played rhythm instruments. Some danced in halted steps. Where was Brian?

She scoured the crowd, heart racing. She didn't see him anywhere. A hand gripped her arm. It was Tom.

"Where's Brian? I thought you were going to watch him." Olivia heard the panic in her voice, but didn't care. She only cared about finding her son.

Tom pointed into the circle. A boy covered in a coyote skin cavorted around the storyteller enacting a character from one of her tales. It was Brian. She hadn't recognized him in the costume. "He's having fun, Olivia. You should try it."

She didn't respond. Cool relief washed over her. Tom's face formed a tentative smile, and he led her to the shade of the portico. "You okay?"

Olivia nodded. She couldn't talk. She watched the rest of the program without comprehending; her thoughts in a tangle.

Finding the newspaper articles on her car in the parking lot of the Fishbowl had been upsetting, but this... This was worse. Her place of employment was listed on her records at CPS, school, all kinds of places. It was easy information to come by. But someone would have to be watching her, listening to her conversations to know she was going to be at the Mission today.

She reviewed her week. The only person she'd mentioned the event to was Fiona. Could Brian have told someone he'd be here? He was excited when she'd told him about it earlier that week. He might have talked it up at school.

That thought sent a jolt of adrenaline through her. What if the person wasn't admonishing her to be a more careful mother but threatening her son? *Brian is in danger.* That's what the message on the stall door said. *Brian is in danger.* From whom? From the writer?

Proctor. His name filled her with the claustrophobic fear of a hunted animal. She sidled closer to Tom and threaded an arm through his, suddenly cold despite the warmth of the day. He grinned at her. "Great program, huh?"

She gave him a feeble smile. Standing close to him made her feel safer. She considered telling him about the words on the stall door but decided against it. If she told him about that, she'd have to tell him about the articles, and CPS, and the Safety Plan. Just the thought made her cheeks sting. They didn't know each other well, and probably never would if she became a single mother with baggage.

"I think she's wrapping up." Tom lifted his chin in the direction of the storyteller. Olivia made a move toward the dispersing children. "What's your hurry?"

"We'd better get going." All she could think about was getting her son home where he'd be safe.

"We haven't had lunch." Tom looked hurt.

"I know, but..." She couldn't think of an excuse to leave, not without telling him about the graffiti.

Brian ran toward them, his words singing across the grass. "I got picked to be the coyote. Did you see me?"

"I did. You did a great job," Olivia said and hugged him harder than she intended.

"I wanted to be the coyote because coyotes are dogs. Did you know that? I read all about them in a book Miss Travers gave me."

"Who's Miss Travers?" Olivia released him.

"She works at the library at school. I told her I liked dogs, and she's been giving me books about them. Not giving. I can't keep them. I'm just borrowing them."

"That's nice of her."

"She's nice. She likes dogs and history stuff. I'm starving."

Tom caught Olivia's eye. "I made a peanut butter and jelly sandwich, and some Rice Krispie treats."

"Can we eat now?" Brian's eyes pleaded with her.

"I also made shrimp salad and brought a nice bottle of Sauvignon Blanc." Tom's voice sounded hopeful.

"Let's eat," Brian danced around Olivia.

She'd wanted this weekend to be special, and it still could be if she didn't ruin it now. Brian's life was difficult enough without adding her fears to it. She was the parent. It was her job to shield him from danger, from problems he wasn't equipped to handle. And it wasn't like someone was going to snatch him away right from under her nose. But even as the thought passed through her mind, her gaze traveled over the faces in the crowd looking for cold, blue eyes.

He would do something like this. He got off on the fear of others. Her jaw clenched in anger. If it was him, the last thing she would do was play along, satisfy his sick needs. She would sit under a tree, eat her picnic, relax, or at least appear to, and Proctor would know he hadn't succeeded. "Okay." Olivia let herself be led toward the street where Tom's car was parked.

"I know what I want to be for Halloween." Brian bounced by her side. Every year the decision was left until the last minute and every year it was a tremendous rush to put the costume together. She hoped this one wouldn't be complicated.

"Let me guess. A coyote."

"No. That would be too hard. I want to be a Juaneño. I asked the lady. She said I could wear jeans and a T-shirt. That's what a lot of the men wear now. Then I could make, like, a necklace with shells and put on some fake tattoos. She showed me a picture. Wouldn't that be cool?"

"Very."

"I could get a leather shoelace and string stuff on that. I wish I had a deer hoof. They used to put deer hooves on necklaces. I have Dad's old rabbit's foot. You think I could use that?"

While Brian prattled on about his costume, Olivia scrutinized everyone they passed on the way to the street. She didn't see anyone who looked like the man she'd seen in the parking lot two weeks ago. Was it only two weeks? It seemed like an eternity.

"I thought we could park behind the Adobe," Tom said when Brian finally took a breath. "There are picnic tables there. Then after lunch we could walk over to the pony rides and the petting zoo."

"Petting zoo." Scorn peppered Brian's voice. "Isn't that for little kids?"

"Not just for little kids. I used to go there when I was your age, and it's a lot bigger now. They have all kinds of stuff. You can feed llamas and goats and Guinea pigs."

"Do they have any dogs?"

"I don't think they have dogs, but they have horses."

Olivia listened to the happy banter between Tom and Brian. She hoped they'd become friends. Brian would have to accept someone before she would even consider a relationship with that person. But she did like Tom, and she wasn't going to let graffiti destroy their outing. She'd call her mother that night and see if she'd talked to Winnie and Drew. Meanwhile, she'd do her best to put it out of her mind and keep Brian in her line of vision at all times.

MOLLY: Okay, that was creepy. Olivia heard the person who left the message on the mirror when she was in the bathroom stall at the mission. Realizing they'd been in such close quarters had to be jarring. And how strange were the newspaper articles on the windshield?

Someone is definitely trying to get her attention. For those of you who thought she was paranoid, I'd say maybe not. This seems pretty threatening.

Before I give you the question of the week, however, I've got another installment from Sage's diary for you. It's a difficult section, but crime is a difficult topic.

Friday, June 19th, 1992

I adjusted the pillow behind Doug as he settled onto the chaise lounge on the front porch. My nerves were singing like telephone wires. He'd been quiet, almost sullen, on the ride home from the hospital. I'd been so full of emotion; words wouldn't choke past my larynx. Clarice had talked a streak. My sister could never stand silence.

She'd helped me get Doug into the house, carry in his small bag of clothes and put a pot of coffee on. Then she left, taking the energy of the day with her. The house felt as still and somber as a graveyard.

I should never have sent the kids to my mother's for the weekend. I'd thought it would be better for Doug to have some peace and quiet in his first days at home. But I hadn't thought about being left alone with him.

We hadn't been alone together since his accident. Yes, I'd spent two weeks of days and nights in his hospital room, but the hall was full of people. Distractions walked by the open door every few minutes. Nurses popped in and out with their cheerful, efficient chatter. Now there was just me and this stranger who looked so much like my husband.

"Are you hungry?" I said.

"No." Even his voice, before always on the edge of laughter, wasn't his own. His words came in low, raspy grumbles.

"Thirsty?" I pulled a throw across his legs.

"I'm fine. Stop fussing." He slapped my hand. I pulled it away like it had been burned. Doug, my Doug, wouldn't hit a woman. Although he took the wooden spoon to Tomas on occasion, he'd never so much as patted Lily on the bottom.

As a child, I'd read stories about changelings—creatures left by fairies in place of a mother's true child. Creatures who looked like the child but weren't. Maybe behind those legends were the true stories of babies who had been dropped on their heads or shaken hard enough to cause brain damage. Because that's what I had now—a changeling husband.

I stood for a moment, not wanting to provoke him further but not wanting to leave.

"What are you staring at?" Doug said, his tone edged with rage.

"Nothing." I fled to the bedroom.

An hour later I emerged and tiptoed onto the screened-in porch to check on him. He looked like his childhood pictures as he slept. Short, dark fuzz covered his head where it had been shaved, reminding me of the crew cuts his father had insisted on. His face, too thin and gaunt for a man's, was more like a fast-growing boy's. I reached out a hand to touch him but hesitated, not wanting to wake him.

Barking erupted from the neighboring yard. Doug's eyes flew open. His face pulled into angry lines, shattering the youthful image. "That idiot dog. Why doesn't Paul keep it quiet?"

I walked to the edge of the porch and peered through the screen. The sun was low in the sky. Angel's Trumpet, which only emitted its sweet scent in the evening, wafted up from my garden. "Pepe has treed a squirrel." I kept my tone light, hoping to defuse the tension.

"I don't care what it's done. I want it to shut up."

"Do you want to move into the bedroom? It's quieter."

"No. I don't want to move into the bedroom." He pitched his voice higher in a mockery of mine. "I want to sleep on my own damned porch. I've had enough of dark rooms."

He sounded so much like his father; I examined his face for signs of ghostly possession. Clyde Hartman, dead these past fifteen years, had been a cruel man. The brunt of his anger had been directed at Doug's mother. I'd seen the bruises to prove it. But plenty of pain had slopped over onto Doug and his brothers as they were growing up. Doug worked hard to be gentle, kind, and respectful—in every way his father's opposite. He'd succeeded until now.

"You can't have it both ways." I gentled my voice like I was talking to a petulant child. "Out here you can get fresh air and watch the world go by, but you'll hear the world go by as well."

I loved the sounds of my home. The Los Rios District of San Juan Capistrano was a throwback to another time. It was the oldest neighborhood in California, and many of the homes were settled on good-sized parcels of land. The neighbors were close enough so one felt a part of a community, but not so close you heard all their business. The music that filled my day was made by the chatter of the birds in the garden.

The garden was a masterpiece. I could say that because it wasn't all my handiwork. It was a multi-generational project that spanned more than fifty years. The women in my family were famous in these parts for their skill with both culinary and medicinal herbs. We made teas and tinctures, poultices and pomades.

When I heard about a neighbor with a cold or a bad bee sting, I'd bring over one of my remedies. Some of them were so effective, I'd gained a reputation as a medicine woman of sorts. My great-great-grandmother had been the only healer the Los Rios district had for many years, so I guess I came by it honestly.

Because Doug was still on several prescriptions, I hadn't planned to medicate him myself, but I was rethinking that. I couldn't allow the kids to come home and see their father like this. He would terrify Lily. A little ginkgo biloba and St. John's Wort couldn't hurt, and it might help. I decided to brew some up with black tea to mask the flavor, then pour it over ice.

"I made enchiladas. I know how tired you are of hospital food."

Doug grunted.

It wasn't exactly a joyful or grateful response, but at least it wasn't criticism. "I'll bring you an iced tea then go get dinner ready. We can watch a movie while we eat if you want. I stopped and got a few videos yesterday."

He ignored me and stared out the window like I hadn't spoken.

MOLLY: Apparently, Doug is no longer the man Sage married. The fact that his father was an abuser does make me wonder if the seeds for that dysfunction had been planted long ago. As we discussed in Season One, these things often have a genetic component.

Perhaps the seed was there, lying dormant, then Doug's accident broke its shell, and it began to grow. We'll have to wait and see.

Switching topics, the question of the week is this: Should Davy have gotten the dog? Yes, it's great that Brian has a dog to play with, but does it make Olivia look bad? Is it a form of manipulation on his part, or was he just trying to do something nice for his son? Let me know what you think in the Facebook group.

(cue music)

VO: If you enjoyed this episode, please leave us a five-star review on your favorite podcast service—it really helps. *Murders Under the Sun* is edited by Jim Wilbourne, theme music is by Eclectic Blends, an I'm your host, Molly Shure.

part five

MURDERS UNDER THE SUN
SEASON TWO; EPISODE FOUR

MOLLY: Welcome back to *Murders Under the Sun*. This is Molly Shure, your host.

Before I get into the episode, I just want to say I was happy to see how many dog lovers are in the audience. I have a dog myself. He's a black lab mix like Crackers, but his name is Diesel. He's my main man at the moment.

While I agree, the dog does make Davy more sympathetic, we must remember that David Berkowitz killed eight people supposedly at the orders of a dog. Not everyone who likes dogs is a good person. However, I admit, I do tend to look side-eyed at people who don't like dogs. But I digress.

In the first three episodes of this season, we met Olivia and her son Brian, learned about her difficulties in raising a child who'd experienced brain trauma along with the more typical issues of being a single parent.

But there's something darker happening in Olivia's and Brian's lives. An unknown person is following her and leaving her disturbing messages, and she has no idea why. This would seriously freak me out, people. I'm actually kind of amazed she remained as stable as she did.

Today, she's going to do something many of you thought she should have done sooner. She's going to recruit help. We're also going to learn a bit more about the mystery man from her past, and I can tell you, you're not going to like him. Let's just say he's not a nice guy.

Before I give away the whole episode, let's hear from Olivia.

2.4.2

BRIAN GOT in bed early without an argument. He was tired from the Mission trip and their afternoon tromping around San Juan Capistrano. Olivia tucked him up with a book about dogs and made him promise to turn off the light at nine. Then she went into the kitchen and put the kettle on for a cup of chamomile tea. While she waited for the water to come to a boil, she dialed her mother.

"Hi, Liv." Olivia could tell by the tension in Sarah's voice she hadn't made the calls. "I know why you're calling, and I haven't—"

"Mom. This is important."

There was a long silence. Then Sarah said, "Why? I have to have a reason. I can't ask about Proctor out of the blue, especially when they know how I feel about him."

It was Olivia's turn to be quiet. She poured hot water into a mug, found a tea bag and weighed the pros and cons of telling her mother about the newspaper articles and the message on the stall door.

The comforting scent of chamomile wafted up into her face as she bobbed the bag in the water. Her mother loved Brian as much as she did. If Sarah thought he was in danger, she'd move mountains to keep him safe. "Odd things have been happening since I saw that man who looked like him," she finally said.

"What kind of odd things?"

"Last week, after the party at the studio, I went out to my car, and somebody had left copies of newspaper articles on my windshield. They were about two little boys who died in tragic accidents."

"Boys from around here?"

"No. One was in Idaho. Boise, I think. The other one was in Phoenix." Sarah didn't say anything, so Olivia went on. "Then when we were at the Mission on Sunday, I got another message. Someone wrote 'Brian is in danger' on a stall door while I was in the bathroom."

Olivia heard a sharp intake of breath, then Sarah said, "And you think this has something to do with Proctor?"

"It's a hell of a coincidence. First I see someone that could be Proctor's older brother, then I get these bizarre messages."

"You think he's threatening you? Threatening Brian?" There was a catch in Sarah's voice.

"That, or someone's trying to warn me about him."

There was another long silence on the other end of the phone, then a heavy sigh. "I didn't want you to know. I didn't want to upset you."

Olivia's pulse tripped a beat. "Didn't want me to know what?"

"Proctor is here. He called three weeks ago."

Olivia sat at the kitchen table; her legs weak. It was one thing to think he was here, another to know it. "What does he want?"

"He has pictures..."

"Pictures?"

"Of me. Of him and me. Things that could hurt my career."

"He's blackmailing you?"

"That's not what he called it, but yes. That's what it amounts to. He said he'd sell me the pictures."

"You're not going to give him money." The question exploded into a command. "He'll never leave you alone if you do. You know that. He'll keep coming back for more."

"He said he'd give me the pictures, then he'd go away."

"Right. And as soon as he runs through the money you gave him, he'll find more pictures or remember those were in the cloud. Mom, how bad could they be?"

"Bad. If it was just sex, I could weather the storm. But there are others. We all did drugs back then, Livvie."

"You're an author, not a politician, not a pastor. It wouldn't shock anyone if an author did some recreational drugs in her youth."

"If I wrote adult fiction, it would be one thing, but I don't. I write for children. Pictures like these would tank book sales, I'm telling you."

Whether it was true or not, it was obvious her mother believed it. "We have to go to the police," Olivia said.

"No. If we go to the police, he'll release the pictures to the media." Sarah's voice was emphatic.

"But Brian."

"I won't allow him to hurt Brian. I'll tell him, if he doesn't stop threatening you, the deal is off."

"The deal? You've made a deal with him already?"

"I had no choice."

Olivia stood and began to pace across the linoleum floor of her small kitchen. "You do have a choice, Mom. You can tell the police. He needs to be stopped. What if he killed those boys in the articles? What if he wants to do something to Brian?"

"Let me get the pictures from him. Then we can tell the police about the threats to Brian."

"There's no proof he threatened me or Brian. The only thing we can prove is that he's a blackmailer."

"There's got to be another way." Her mother sounded desperate. "If this comes out, I'm not the only one who'll be hurt. There are other people in the pictures. Drew is a judge now. Rochelle Anderson, from Michigan, is a high school teacher. Not to mention you. Having a mother with a checkered past won't help your cause with CPS."

Olivia leaned her elbows on the kitchen counter and dropped her head into her hands. Her thoughts had become viscous sludge, and her head felt too heavy to hold upright. "Have you given him any money yet?"

"No. I've been moving things around. Selling stocks."

"When?"

"I told him I'd call him when I have it."

"Don't do anything. Okay? I need to think."

Sarah agreed in a reluctant voice, and they hung up. Olivia poured her cold tea into the sink and headed to Brian's bedroom. He lay curled under his blanket of cars, breathing softly. She kissed his forehead and watched him sleep for a long time.

When she left him, she went to her room and lay on her bed on top of the covers, fully dressed. She stared at the ceiling, watching light trails from the occasional passing car cross the white plaster until dawn made them first dim, then invisible.

2.4.3

"READY?" Brian hopped up and down.

"Ready." Olivia had agreed to pick up Brian from Davy's at eight on Thursday night since she was going to be out anyway. When she pulled into guest parking, she saw Brian, Davy, and Crackers waiting under a streetlight. Brian pounced on her car, pulled her out, and dragged her to the greenbelt as soon as she turned off the ignition.

"Hold his eyes shut," Brian said to his father.

Davy turned Crackers so he faced away from Brian and pressed the dog's muzzle into his leg. "I got him."

"Okay." Brian took off at a run across the grass, crossed a small street, and disappeared behind a dark hedge near the community pool. Watching him go made Olivia's nerves jangle.

"Let's wait a minute. I want him to forget about Brian." Davy gave Crackers one end of a knotted rope, and the dog fell into a game of tug-of-war. Cracker's black coat gleamed in the solar lights that rimmed the greenbelt. His teeth flashed white, and a happy growl reverberated in his chest. "Do you have that sock?" Davy disengaged Crackers from the rope and told him to sit.

Olivia fished around her bag for the dirty sock she'd been instructed to bring. It hadn't been hard to find one. Brian's gym bag was always full of them. She handed it to Davy.

Davy gave the sock to Crackers to sniff. "Find."

Crackers pivoted on his feet, nose to the ground, and whined with excitement. This, it seemed, was even more fun than tug-of-war. The dog led Davy in a serpentine path that soon straightened. Olivia followed. They crossed the short street, and Crackers leaped forward nearly pulling Davy into a large privet hedge. A joyful bark, and her son's laugh brought a smile to Olivia's face.

Brian emerged from the hedge with Crackers at his heels. "See how good he is, Mom? I told you he could find me."

"He did. Good boy." Olivia kneeled to hug the dog. His hind end wagged so hard he almost toppled over.

"Give him a treat. He always gets a treat when he finds someone." Brian pulled a fuzzy dog biscuit from his jeans pocket and handed it to her. Crackers nibbled it from her fingers. The lint didn't seem to bother him.

Olivia straightened up. "Who taught him to do that?"

"Mr. Raffle," Brian said. "The man who had Crackers before Dad got him. He was training him to be a search and rescue dog, but he got sick."

"He abandoned the dog?" Olivia found it hard to believe someone would spend so much time and money on an animal and then discard it.

"No. He's on the board of the animal rescue organization we got Crackers from. They agreed to take Crackers to adoption days for him until they found the right owner," Davy said.

"He was very picky, and he picked Dad." Brian beamed at his father.

"And you. I told him all about you." Davy ruffled Brian's hair. "He said if Crackers liked you, he liked you too. Crackers is a smart dog."

"Are you smart? Are you smart, Crackers?" Brian danced backward on the grass with Crackers leaping beside him. Davy and Olivia followed.

"Did you know Crackers had search and rescue training when you got him?" Olivia asked.

"It was one of the first things they told me. I had to sign a paper agreeing to keep up with the training if I wanted him."

Olivia stopped walking. "You did?"

"Yup."

"Why? That's a lot of work."

"I thought it would be good for Brian."

Olivia resumed their trek to the far end of the greenbelt where Brian played with the lab. "What, you think we can send the dog after Brian if he wanders away?" Doubt crept into her voice.

"No. Well, maybe. But that's not why I took Crackers. I think if Brian understands what's involved with finding someone who's lost, if he gets to see the worry and the fear and the effort of the searchers, it might change him. Make him think."

Davy's self-sacrifice surprised her. "You're doing a good job with him." Olivia lowered her voice.

"It hasn't been hard. He is a bright animal," Davy said.

Olivia had meant Brian, but she let it stand. Brian had been more focused since Davy had been in his life on a regular basis. He'd forgotten his lunch yesterday for the first time in two and a half weeks. And when he called to ask her to bring it, he remembered he'd left it on the table by the front door. That might not seem like a victory in some homes, but it was in hers.

Brian's mid-term report card came in yesterday, and almost all his grades had improved too. Only math still hovered at a C minus. Some of the improvement was due to the time, healing, and his new health regime, she was sure. But she knew it was more than that. Brian was happy. He had his dad back.

Davy had decorated a bedroom for Brian in his condo. He worked with him on homework. He'd helped him with his Halloween costume and took him to a harvest event at his church to trick-or-treat. He was doing the kinds of things fathers do. She had to admit; this new Davy seemed to be good for their son.

Brian was quiet on the ride home. As she pulled up to the curb, he broke the silence. "Do you hate Dad?"

Olivia faced him in the dark car. "No. Of course not."

"Sometimes you act like you do."

She thought for a long moment before answering. "Sometimes I get mad at him."

"You mean like when he was drinking beer and stuff?"

"Yes, that made me angry. He stopped coming home, stopped taking care of you."

"But he's better now."

Again, she paused. "It does seem like it."

"Do you think you guys could ever love each other again? That Dad could move home?" Brian's eyes glittered in the lamplight. Olivia chewed her bottom lip. She didn't know what to say. The answer was a definite no, but that wasn't what Brian wanted to hear. Erasing Davy from her heart had been a painful experience, one she never wanted to go through again. "Dad wants to," Brian said.

"Why do you say that?" She hoped Davy hadn't been filling Brian with false hope.

"Just stuff he says."

"Like what?"

"Like he's always going to be there to keep you and me safe. He's never going to leave us again."

Safe? Why bring up safety? "He said that? Said he'd keep us safe?" Olivia said. Brian nodded.

A new suspicion whispered in her mind. Was it possible Davy was the one who left the newspaper articles on her car? Wrote on the stall door at the Mission? Was he trying to scare her, so she'd run to him for protection? Acquiring a search and rescue dog could be part of the plan—planting seeds of fear, then positioning himself as the solution.

No. That was crazy. Davy might be impulsive, a loose cannon at times, but he wouldn't do something like that. "Let's go." She threw open her car door with more force than necessary.

After she tucked Brian in, she made a cup of chamomile tea to quiet her nerves. She'd drink it this time. She wasn't planning on a repeat of last night's sleeplessness. She sat on the green couch cradling the warm mug in her hands, inhaling its floral steam. Her gaze rested on the window, now covered by blinds.

The idea Davy might be behind the recent events revolved in her brain like a car show exhibit on a turntable. Would it drive? She examined the idea it might not be Proctor, but Davy who was trying to spook her. She thought about what Fiona had said about Davy's jealousy toward Tom.

The night after Tom had been rough on Brian at soccer practice, she'd felt she was being watched at work. The articles showed up on her windshield right after she'd gone to Turk's with Tom. The message on the bathroom stall was written while she and Brian were on an outing with Tom. Could Tom be the trigger? And if he was, who else but Davy would care if she spent time with him?

Her eyelids grew heavy. She set her empty mug on the coffee table and pulled a throw blanket over herself. Davy and Tom faced each other in that place between dreams and wakefulness, the tension between them crackled in the air. But she didn't have time to sort them out, she was looking for Brian.

She moved past the men and found herself on a sloping path. She couldn't see him, but she knew Brian was up ahead in the darkening woods. The path twisted and turned, burrowing deeper into the gloaming. Branches reached out spindly arms grabbing at her hair, her clothing, and blinding her to what lay ahead. She could only see the few feet of mossy trail directly in front of her.

Then she heard Brian's voice, piping high, and the frantic barking of a dog. She began to run. But the faster she ran the fainter his voice became, until all she could hear was the hoot of a night owl and the whistle of a distant train. Its sound filled her with the kind of undefined foreboding nightmares are made from.

2.4.4

"MOM." A voice, and a gentle shake of her shoulder hauled Olivia from sleep. "Mom, why are you sleeping on the couch?" She rolled over and pried open her eyes. Her son's face came into focus. "I'm going to be late for school."

The words worked like a shot of espresso. "What time is it?"

"Almost 8:30."

Olivia threw off the throw blanket and ran into her bedroom to pull on a pair of yoga pants, then realized she'd gone to bed without changing into her pajamas twice in two days. Not good, but at least it would save time today. After dragging a comb through her hair, she hustled Brian out to the car.

By the time they got to St. Barnabas, the drop-off line had been reduced to the stragglers who were as late as she was. She left Brian at the curb with promises to bring him something for lunch before noon.

Olivia swung by her favorite coffee shop on the way home. A double latte would hit the spot. She opened the front door and nearly whacked into the woman at the end of a long line. It was bustling inside. Customers' voices rose above the roar of coffee makers, the rumble of grinders, and the banging of grounds canisters against trash cans. She hesitated. Her teeth felt like they were covered with fur, her skin slicked with oil. She didn't want to run into anybody she knew, but the cafe smelled wonderful. The siren call of caffeine won out. She joined the line.

Eight minutes later, she placed her order and went to stand with the crowd gathered at the pickup window. She answered three emails and sent a text to Fiona to let her know she'd be late while she was in line. Now she opened the Fishbowl's Facebook page, trying to make the most of her wait. A deep voice at a table behind her said, "Olivia."

Mike McKibben sat at a table in a corner of the coffee shop with a half empty mug and *The Register* in front of him. She walked closer to her ex-father-in-law. "Mike."

He smiled; Davy's smile. His round face was a plumper version of her ex-husband's. The narrow nose, the kindness in his green-blue eyes, they were all Davy. But instead of light brown hair, his face was framed with hair so white it almost glowed. Olivia smoothed her own hair self-consciously.

"What are you doing here on a Friday morning? I didn't think the Fishbowl could run without you," he said.

"I overslept."

His eyes narrowed as he examined her face. "You feeling okay? I could keep Brian overnight if you need a break." Mike picked Brian up from school on Fridays and kept him at his place until Olivia arrived.

"No. I'm good. Just zonked out on the couch and didn't have my alarm."

"I wish I needed an alarm." He shook his head. "Couldn't wait to retire from the department so I could sleep in. Who knew sleeping in would mean five-fifteen instead of five a.m.?"

"I don't wake up at five, but I don't usually sleep this late. My schedule has been a little off," Olivia said.

"Well, I repeat, if you need a night to yourself, I'd love to spend more time with my grandson."

A barista called out her double latte. "That's me. See you around six." She leaned over and was enveloped by the scents of pine and smoke, his familiar aftershave. She kissed his smooth cheek and left the shop.

When Olivia got home, she went straight to the bathroom and turned on the shower. She spiked the water up as hot as she could handle, stepped in and let the jets do their magic. When she emerged fifteen minutes later, the sweat and the cobwebs of the night had been washed away. She felt refreshed, awake and her mind hummed with caffeine.

She squirted a generous amount of lavender body lotion in her hand, began rubbing it onto her legs, and thought about her day. She decided to stop by Enzo's, her old workplace, and pick up a meatball sandwich for Brian. It was one of his favorites, and she could say hello to Enzo while she was there. He'd been kind to her at the lowest point of her life. She didn't know how she would have made it through the horrible weeks that followed Brian's accident without him. Or Art. Or Mike. They were her heroes.

Mike. She set down the lotion with a thud. Why hadn't she thought of it sooner? Mike would know what to do about Proctor. He'd retired from the Orange County Sheriff's Department three years ago. He had knowledge and connections. More important, he was a free agent now and could be discreet. She was sure he'd help her mother. She'd talk to him when she picked Brian up that evening.

Olivia walked into her bedroom and pulled a fresh pair of leggings and a new yoga top from her dresser. The only hitch was she didn't want Davy to know about the newspaper clippings, or what had happened at the Mission. He and his dad were close now that Davy had turned over a new leaf. She stuck one leg into her exercise pants and stared at the wall.

But why would she have to mention any of that? She wasn't absolutely sure Proctor was behind the threats, or the warnings, whatever they were. Blackmail was sufficient reason to seek help. She continued dressing. No sense in muddying the waters with things she wasn't one-hundred-percent positive were related.

She slid her feet into a pair of slip-on sneakers, fluffed her damp hair with her fingers, and ran out the door. And if they were related, both problems would be resolved with a single solution—getting rid of Proctor. Maybe it was the sleep, maybe the latte, but she felt more optimistic than she had in weeks.

2.4.5

THE WEEKEND HAD BEEN QUIET. Too quiet. Davy picked Brian up at eight o'clock Saturday morning and didn't bring him home until eight o'clock Sunday night. She'd cleaned. Olivia was on the messy end of the neat-messy spectrum and had never understood people who felt a need to sterilize things when they were anxious. But Tom's words about order and peace going hand in hand had rung in her head while she mopped, dusted, and rifled through closets.

Olivia put a stack of library books she'd found under a pile of Brian's dirty clothes into a tote bag. Several were overdue. Davy had signed Crackers up for search and rescue classes, and Brian was obsessed. He'd read every book on the topic that his new best friend, Miss Travers, had found in the school library, then moved on to the Dana Point library. Olivia would return them on her way to the studio. She was closing that evening.

She glanced around her living room making sure she hadn't forgotten anything. It looked a bit naked without the usual clutter, but she liked how organized she felt. Her laptop, planner, and the files she'd been working on were in the tote by the door with the books. The only thing she was missing was the glass jar. She'd left it in the kitchen.

The doctor wasn't enthusiastic about the herbal concoction Sage had given her, but he didn't think it would hurt Brian either. After doing her own research, Olivia decided to try it. Since he'd started taking it, Brian had been right where he was supposed to be every time she picked him up from school or soccer. He'd gotten all his homework done without being nagged, and he hadn't confabulated.

Whether it was the tincture, Davy's presence in his life, the dog, the natural process of healing, or all of the above, she didn't know. But she wasn't going to argue with success. Brian was up to the twelve drops a day recommended for his age, and the jar was empty. She was taking it to Sage after work for a refill.

She picked it up off the dish drainer, swiped it with a towel, and reentered the living room in time to see Tom's dark green Honda pull up to the curb through the front window. He'd offered to take Brian to the soccer team's away game in Santa Ana. She'd said yes. It was Tuesday, so it was Davy's night with Brian, but he'd called yesterday to tell her he had a work conflict.

It was the first time he'd given up an evening with his son since he'd started the new schedule. She wasn't worried, not yet. But it had created a conflict, until Tom came to the rescue.

"Coach Hartman is here," she called out. A moment later, Brian appeared with his gym bag slung over his shoulder.

"Got your cleats?" she said.

"Yup." He opened his bag and showed her the shoes.

"Clean socks?"

He pulled out a pair and waved them at her.

Olivia opened the front door and followed him to the street. He jogged around to the passenger side of Tom's car. She leaned into the driver's side window.

"Hi." Tom's right cheek sprang a dimple.

She reached into her pocket and handed him a folded twenty. "For dinner and gas."

Tom waved the money away. "I got it."

"No. Really. It's so nice of you to—"

Tom's smile faded. "Come on, Olivia."

"I'm just saying..."

"I thought we were past that."

"I don't want to assume." She stammered over her words.

"I wish you would."

"Don't be upset with me." She stuffed the money into her jeans. He sighed and looked at her. "I'm sorry." She bent over and kissed him on the cheek.

A car pulled up behind Tom's. Davy ejected from it. Olivia straightened and felt her face flush.

"What's going on?" Davy said.

"Hi, Dad." Brian waved through the window.

"Hey bud, where're you going?"

"Coach Hartman is taking me to my game. It's in Santa Ana, and Mom has to work."

Davy looked at Olivia through slitted eyes. "It's my night."

"You said you had a business meeting."

"My meeting was canceled."

"How was I supposed to know?"

"I don't think we've met." Tom stuck his hand out of the window. Davy ignored it. "Crackers has a training class tonight. I wanted to take Brian."

"That sounds totally sick. Can I go, Mom? Please?" Brian leaned across Tom to peer at her through the driver side window, his face pleading.

"No, honey. You have a commitment to the team. You need to go to the game."

"It's my night." Davy's voice was tight.

Olivia met his glare for several long seconds. "You guys better get on the road before the traffic hits." She patted Tom's arm.

"Bye, buddy." Davy waved to Brian as the car pulled away, then turned to Olivia. "Really, Olivia?"

"Really?"

"Why wouldn't you ask me to take Brian to his game before sending him off with some strange guy?"

"You said you couldn't make it tonight. And Tom isn't some strange guy. He's Brian's coach."

"I know. I know all about him. Brian told me you were dating one of his coaches, and he doesn't like him."

"We're not really dating. How do you know he doesn't like him?"

"He told me. How do you think? We talk. I'm his dad. Dads and sons talk."

"Of course he's going to tell you he doesn't like Tom. Brian wants us to get back together. Nobody else stands a chance."

"Maybe it's because the guy is a jerk to our kid. Did you ever think of that? Wait, forget I asked." Davy turned from her and strode down the sidewalk like he needed to put distance between them. He spun around. "You didn't think of it, because you're not thinking right now, are you?"

Anger ignited, hot as a torch, inside her chest. She opened her mouth to blast him, but he beat her to it. "If you were thinking, you wouldn't be making out with the man in front of our kid. What if Brian gets attached, and it doesn't work out? It could traumatize him."

His words were like lighter fuel. "Wait, let me get this straight." Sarcasm streamed from her lips. "You're worried about our child being traumatized? The man who stopped coming home, who abandoned us, is worried about traumatizing his kid?"

Davy's face turned scarlet. He raked a hand through his hair. "I blew it, okay. I know that. I've admitted it. I'm trying to do better. But this guy... this guy isn't our kid's father. He doesn't love Brian. In fact, it sounds like he doesn't even like him."

"I don't have time for this right now. I have to get to work." Olivia stomped up the path to her front door.

"What do you know about this man? I mean, really know?" Davy followed her. "Where does he come from? What did he do before he moved here? What kind of person is he?"

She answered over her shoulder. "He grew up here, in San Juan Capistrano. I know his mother. She's a lovely woman. He teaches high school math at St. Barnabas. Anything else?"

"Yeah. Lots. Where did he work before St. Barnabas? Brian says he's new this school year. How come he's never been married? Or has he been? For all you know, he could have a wife and kid in another state."

Olivia crossed the threshold of her apartment and turned to face him, one hand on the doorknob. "You're reaching, Davy. Tom's a nice guy. He's stable and responsible. He has a good job. He's good with kids, and he likes us—Brian and me. He might be around for a while, so you better get used to it."

She closed the door in his face. Her words surprised her. She hadn't realized until that moment that she did want Tom to be around.

She slid behind a window drape where Davy couldn't see her and watched him. She didn't want to leave until he drove away. This was the first fight they'd had since he'd gotten Crackers, and it left her shaken. She'd promised herself she'd do her best to get along, maintain the status quo. The last thing she needed right now was a trip to family court to discuss their custodial schedule.

Davy stood with both hands on the front hood of his car, chin on his chest, for several seconds. Then he threw open the door and got in. The car lurched from the curb and sped down the block. She watched it until it entered the shadow of a big oak on the corner. Its midnight blue blinked to colorless gray in the deep shade.

Her breath caught. With the color muted, she noticed its shape for the first time. The lone car that lay in wait for her in the Fishbowl's parking lot three weeks ago and Davy's sedan could have rolled off the same assembly line.

2.4.6

THE LAST CLASS of the day was canceled, so Olivia closed up the Fishbowl at eight instead of nine, called Sage and got the okay to come by for a refill of Brian's tincture. As she made the right at the end of Los Rios, she noticed the statue of St. Francis she'd seen on her first trip to Sage's house. He wasn't as welcoming tonight. A single bulb beamed up from the dirt at his base wreathing his face in eerie shadows. He made her think of a child about to tell a ghost story with a flashlight held under his chin.

Olivia parked on the gravel drive in front of Sage's and turned off the car. The world was submerged in that deep, midnight blue of moonless nights that eats up all other colors. When she opened the car door a cloying floral scent wrapped around her, and she wondered what it was.

She walked up the path toward the stand of oaks that sheltered Sage's home. As she entered their gloom, she heard a sound—the scratch of tin on tin. It came from the direction of the neighboring house. Olivia stepped deeper under the dark canopy where she could see without being seen. A figure clothed in a shirt so white it glowed in the light of a distant streetlamp stood at a mailbox at the edge of the drive-way. Nothing threatening, just a woman getting her mail.

"Abby." A tired male voice called from behind a screen door.

"Yes." The woman's voice was soft and sweet.

"Check for the paper, would you? I never got it this morning."

The woman walked, bent, retrieved a gray object from the grass, then disappeared into the house with a slap of a door.

Tension she hadn't known she'd been carrying dropped from Olivia's shoulders. She climbed the peeling stairs to the porch and opened the screen door. A voice came from a dark corner of the porch. "Olivia."

Olivia started.

"Sorry." Sage sounded amused. "I didn't mean to scare you. I've been sitting here since the sun set. I like to watch the lights come on and listen to the crickets and the frogs wake up. Have a seat." She gestured to a rattan chair covered in deep cushions.

"It's peaceful out here," Olivia said.

"Isn't it? Better than a Pilates class, but don't tell Fiona I said so."

"I won't." Olivia sat. "What's that scent? I smelled it as soon as I got out of the car."

"Angel's trumpet," Sage said. "I have a big bush in the yard. The blooms don't release their perfume until after the sun sets."

"Do you use it in creams or lotions? It's very strong, but nice."

"No, all parts of the plant are poisonous. I only keep it around because the scent brings back memories."

They sat and listened to the night songs for several moments, until the sound of a train in the distance disrupted the melody. "Well, that's that." Sage stood. "The seven o'clock from Irvine has arrived." The noise grew steadily louder until it sounded like the train was bearing down on the house itself, but it thundered past and screeched to a stop somewhere up the track.

"I didn't realize how close you were to the tracks," Olivia said.

"Living near a train station was a real bonus when the city sprang up. Kind of like living on a seaport before airplanes and tractor trailers took over the delivery business. Now it's mostly commuters going between LA and San Diego, but it used to be the city's connection to the world."

Olivia followed Sage into the house. The kitchen was bathed in cheerful yellow light and a kettle simmered on the stove. "Herb tea, or black?" Sage said.

"What are you having?" Olivia sat on a metal chair covered with a red plastic cushion and pulled up to an old Formica table. The dinette set, although free of rust or wear, looked like something out of the fifties.

"Herbal, I think. I make a special blend that helps me relax. You look like you could use a cup."

"Sounds good. I'm a bit stressed tonight."

Sage selected one of the canisters on her counter, filled two metal teaspoon diffusers with some of its contents, and placed them into ceramic mugs. "Why are you stressed? Tell me to mind my own business, if I'm nosy."

"No, you're not nosy. I'm the one who mentioned it. It's just life. Lots of little things."

"I hope it has nothing to do with that son of mine. He can be...," she sat across from Olivia and placed the cups in front of them, "... bossy. He means well, but he's a teacher. I guess they get used to telling people what to do all day long and forget to stop when the workday is over."

Olivia inhaled the fragrant steam rising from her cup and took a tentative sip. It tasted of flowers and garden loam and honey. "Tom isn't the problem. On the contrary, he's a big help. He took Brian to an away game this afternoon."

"Tomas loves spending time with kids."

What do you really know about the guy? Davy's words echoed through her mind. This was a golden opportunity to find out more—drinking tea with his mother. She worded her next question carefully, not wanting it to seem like she was pumping Sage for information. "Did Tom always know he wanted to be a teacher? Or did he find out by happy accident?"

"He had no idea what he wanted to do. I think the main reason he ended up in Idaho was to get out of Southern California for a while."

"How did he figure it out then?"

"Tomas had to work his way through school. I didn't have the funds to pay for it. His first year he tried all the typical college jobs; waiting tables, house painting, furniture moving. But they all have their drawbacks." Sage took a sip of her tea. Olivia waited for her to continue.

"Then one day in his sophomore year, he saw an ad on the school bulletin board. A tutoring start-up was looking for math tutors. Tomas had always been good at math. He applied. They took him, and he found his calling. He declared his major the next year."

"I'm envious of people who find their calling." Olivia leaned her elbows on the table, cradling her warm mug with both hands. "I love my work, but I'm not sure it's a calling."

"You're fortunate to have a lucrative business you enjoy. Some of us have callings that don't pay the bills," Sage said.

"You mean your garden? The things you make from it?"

"Yes. I've done a bit of work at the local nursery, but it's not the same. I like planting things and watching them grow. I like to walk around a garden, point to a tree, or shrub, or flower bed and tell you its history. Nurseries are exactly what the name implies; baby plants in incubators waiting for adoption."

"I've never thought about it like that," Olivia said. How did Sage survive if she didn't work or sell her lotions and potions? She must have some source of income. Olivia couldn't ask, but she was curious.

Sage supplied the answer. "I inherited my home, so I have no mortgage payments. Because of that, I've been able to make it on my husband's life insurance and the odd job here and there."

Olivia looked at Sage with questioning eyes.

"Tomas never told you about his father?" Sage didn't seem surprised.

"No. Honestly, I wondered. He talks about you all the time, but he never mentioned a father."

"Doug, my husband, was in a car accident. Drunk driver hit him. Like Brian, he had brain damage, but unlike Brian, he never recovered."

A shadow seemed to pass over the kitchen, muting its bright colors for a moment. "I'm so sorry," Olivia said.

"It was a long time ago. Can't mourn forever, can we?"

"Did he die from the injuries?"

"I guess you could say that." Sage rose from her seat and crossed the kitchen to the kettle on the stove. "More?"

"No, I'd better get going. Brian will be home soon."

Sage opened a pantry door, walked in and came out again with a jar of amber liquid. "Your tincture."

"Here's the empty," Olivia said taking the glass jar from her purse.

"I used to make this for Doug. That's why Tomas wanted Brian to have it."

"Did it help?"

"I think it was beginning to, but Doug died, so I'll never know." She gave Olivia a sad smile.

"Your calling may not pay the bills, but it's important." Olivia touched Sage's hand as she took the jar from it.

"I hope so."

"It is to me," Olivia said. "Can I give you something for it?"

"I hope you didn't think I was hinting around about payment." Sage looked horrified.

"Of course not. I just want to show my appreciation."

"Knowing it's helping Brian is all the payment I need."

"Well, you've got free classes at the studio for the month. I've already put them into your account."

"You didn't have to do that."

"I wanted to. It makes me feel important, like a real business owner."

"How does Fiona feel about it?"

"No problem. If you brought her a jar of your magic face cream, she'd give you free classes for life. She wants your complexion when she grows up."

Sage laughed. "I was going to mix up a batch for myself next week. I'll make it a double."

They hugged goodbye. Olivia headed toward her car but was stopped by a thought. Sage still stood in the doorway, a halo of light around her silhouetted form. "How long did Tom stay in Idaho?" Olivia asked.

"About seven years, I think. Why?"

"Just wondering where he was between college and moving home again."

"His first teaching job was in Boise, but he didn't like the winters. Then he transferred to a school in Arizona, but Phoenix was too hot. So, like Goldilocks, he came back to California where it was just right."

Olivia could hear the smile in Sage's voice. She said goodnight again and continued on to her car.

Idaho and Arizona. The same states the boys in the articles had lived in. It didn't mean anything though. They were big states. A lot of people lived in them. But it was a strange coincidence.

2.4.7

OLIVIA CHECKED herself in the mirror on her closet door and adjusted her skirt for the fifth time. She didn't look like herself. She wasn't sure if she'd ever worn a skirt this short or heels this high, but she did know she'd never worn any this expensive.

Davy's blow up the other day had backfired on him. If she was going to be accused of dating Tom, she figured she might as well do it. She'd asked Mike if his offer to keep Brian overnight was good for that Friday, firmed up plans with Tom, and cajoled Fiona into going shopping with her.

They went to the Irvine Spectrum, an overwhelming mini-city of boutiques, chains, and eateries. Fiona was an expert. She knew where to park. She knew the right stores, and she knew the wrong ones—which turned out to be the ones Olivia always shopped in. Fiona talked her into saying yes to the dress, then the shoes, the purse, and finally some costume jewelry.

Olivia pivoted on her heels and checked her profile. The dress fit like a glove—a very tight, very red glove. What had she been thinking? She couldn't wear this. Panic grabbed her. She hurried to her closet and pushed through the hanging garments like a hunter charging through a jungle. She found the long, pilled cotton skirt and black t-shirt—her old go-out-in-the-evening wear—laid them on the bed and kicked off her new heels. She grabbed the hem of the red dress to pull it over her head but was stopped by the doorbell.

Seven already? She closed her eyes in defeat, breathed deeply, and stepped into the shoes.

Tom stood on the stoop with a large bouquet of flowers in one hand. His eyes grew wide when he saw her. "Wow. You look... Wow." Olivia's cheeks flushed.

He took her to Chad's in Laguna Beach, one of those new restaurants with a five-star menu and blue-jean ambiance filled with old bricks and Napa wines. Afterward, they walked off dinner in the art galleries on Forest Avenue.

Laguna, like so many Orange County towns, had a personality all its own. It had once been a small beach community populated by artists and hippies. Now it was an international vacation destination with untouchable home prices. But Olivia could still taste the bohemian spice in the cosmopolitan stew, and she loved it.

She breathed in the damp, salt air, glad she'd worn the red dress after all. She didn't feel like herself tonight, and that was okay. She was someone prettier, someone more sophisticated. Tonight, she felt brilliant, and poised, and a touch wild. "You know what I want?" She leaned onto Tom's shoulder.

"No. What?" He smiled at her.

"I want wine. Lots of it. And I want to drink it on the beach."

"Your wish is my command."

They bought an expensive blend called Red Ravish, because she liked the name, glasses and a wine key in a market on Ocean Avenue. When they walked out into the balmy night, Tom turned toward Main Beach, but Olivia stopped him. "I have an idea."

"Another one?"

"Let's go to Diver's Cove. The house Fiona sold is on Cliff Drive. It overlooks that beach. I want to try to find it."

Five minutes later, Tom parked his Honda on Cliff Drive near the beach entrance. "Do you know which house it is?"

"I've heard a lot about it. I think I'll recognize it when I see it." They walked along a shrub-lined path dotted with short flights of stairs. Eucalyptus and jasmine perfumed the air. The path opened onto a moonlit cove. Soon it would be busy with scuba divers going for dawn dives, but now it was deserted. They trudged south, dodging the incoming tide, shoes dangling from their hands.

"There. Look." Olivia pointed to a moss-covered house crouching on the cliffs above them. Glowing French doors peered like eyes from a weathered face.

"It's kind of creepy looking, isn't it?" Tom said.

"It is. There was a murder there when Gwen Bishop had it listed."

"And you find this romantic?"

Olivia sat on a large rock, leaving room for Tom to sit next to her. He opened the wine, handed her a glass and poured one for himself. She pondered the moon's silvery path across the water, and the stars freckling the stretches of sky visible between purple-gray clouds before answering. It was a romantic setting, but Main Beach had all the same elements. She'd wanted to come here and sit with her back to Fiona's old house. She wasn't sure why. "Romantic isn't the word," she finally said.

"I'm relieved. I was beginning to wonder about you."

"Join the club." Olivia stared into her glass. The deep red liquid looked black on the darkened beach. "When I was a kid, my mom and I lived in Vermont on a farm for a while. There was an abandoned house up the road. It was broken down, the roof partially caved in, hidden by wild roses, blackberry vines, and overgrown lilac bushes. It was like a fairy tale. I'd go there to pick berries. On nice afternoons I half-expected Peter Rabbit, or the seven dwarves to show up. But at night, at night the place turned into something out of Grimm's."

Olivia took a sip of wine and let it roll around on her tongue. It was delicious. "Anyway, five of us, all under twelve, would go there after dark now and again just to scare the bejeezus out of ourselves. I never understood what the attraction was, why I wanted to go. I just did."

"When I was a kid, we used to play chicken on the train tracks." Tom's voice took on a sleepy quality, like he was telling her about a dream he'd had. "On full moons, a group of us would go there and see who could stand there the longest while the train was coming."

"That sounds dangerous." Olivia felt a tingle of fear imagining it.

"Wouldn't have proved how macho we were if it wasn't. The train would come roaring up the tracks like a giant bull, and I was the matador. It was a rush. I'd lay there in the dirt only feet away while it screamed past me feeling like I'd cheated death."

They sat and listened to the sound of the waves breaking on the shore for several long moments. Tom broke the silence. "Kind of like Brian."

"What's kind of like Brian?" Olivia said.

"Cheating death. Most people who get hit by a car don't make it."

Olivia didn't want to think about Brian's accident, not now, not here. She didn't respond.

Tom's voice grew lighter. "So why are we sitting here anyway? To scare the bejeezus out of ourselves?"

Olivia laughed. "I guess I'm making a statement, turning my back on the scary stuff. The past has haunted me far too long."

Since she was ten, as a matter of fact. Since that winter a battered Buick station wagon crunched up the long, ice-covered driveway at the commune in Vermont. The day before there'd been a big snow fall, then the temperature dropped. The world was blanketed in the uncanny silence that comes when all the moisture in the air has frozen.

Olivia stood at the window of the big, white house with Mark, one of Teach's kids, and watched the Buick park. It was hard to see the face of the man who exited the car. He was covered in shoulder length, tangled, brown hair, a bushy beard and mustache. He dressed like all the other men on the farm, dirty jeans, construction worker boots, flannel shirt, and a bulky, green, Army-issue jacket.

She watched him walk toward the house with nothing more than mild curiosity. Her feelings changed as soon as she heard his voice. It was too bright, too smooth, too smiling.

Olivia had a sixth sense about people when she was a kid. It was a survival mechanism. Her mother loved her, but she was the least protective person Olivia had ever known. Sarah Richards was a trusting soul who believed the best about everyone, even those who didn't deserve it. Olivia knew as soon as she heard Proctor say "hello," he was dangerous, but her mother was sleeping with him within a week.

Tom reached up and stroked Olivia's hair. "Anything I can do?"

"No. It's being handled." She hoped that was true. She and Sarah had met with Mike earlier in the week and told him about the blackmail attempt. He'd agreed to investigate. The waiting was hard though. Small ripples of anxiety rolled through her whenever her phone rang. "I saw your mother on Tuesday night. We talked about you." She moved on to an easier topic.

Tom dropped his hand, tipped his head and looked at the night sky. "Uh oh."

"No, no, it was all good things," Olivia said. "She told me how you'd found your calling in college, and how you worked in Idaho and Arizona before you got the job at St. Barnabas."

"All true."

"So why did you leave California in the first place?"

"I got accepted to Boise State. It seemed like a good excuse to see another part of the country." Tom leaned on one arm. "But the novelty of Idaho's snowy winters wore off in a couple of years. After a little traveling around the Southwest, I'm home."

"I'm glad you are." Olivia put her hand on top of his. His expression was unreadable in the dark, his eyes dark hollows, his cheeks shadowed stone. Only his lips glinted wetly in the moonlight. She leaned forward and kissed him.

"I wish we could go away together," he said when they broke apart.

His statement, so impetuous, so sudden, startled Olivia. "Where?"

"I don't care. Mexico. San Francisco. The wine country. I'd just like to get out of here. Go somewhere."

"How about Rome? Or I've always wanted to see the Parthenon. Oh, or Egypt. Egypt would be wonderful. So much history." Olivia waved her wine glass at the sky. "Or, why not the moon?" She refused to take him seriously. There was a hook in this conversation that threatened to snag her and drag her into the responsible, rational world. She wasn't ready.

He pulled away from her. She grabbed his arm and drew him close again, but the damage was done. She felt the magical braid of night and beach and wine unraveling. They finished their drinks, then in unspoken agreement began to pack up their things.

"I feel like all I do is apologize to you," he said as they trudged through the sand.

"Are you apologizing now?"

"Yeah. I shouldn't have talked about taking off together. I wasn't serious. I mean, of course, I'd love to go away with you, but this is only our third date. It was inappropriate."

"Fourth, if you count Turk's, but you don't need to apologize. It's just my life is... complicated. I can't take off whenever I want. I have a new business. I have Brian.'

"You have Fiona, and you have Davy."

"I could leave the Fishbowl for a week, but I can't leave Brian."

"I thought he was doing better?"

"He is. So much better. I don't want to upset the balance."

"Would you go away if he wasn't doing well?"

"Of course not." She bristled.

"So, whether he's well or sick, it doesn't make any difference. You wouldn't go away." There was an edge in Tom's voice that made her uncomfortable.

"I'm saying it's timing. Now is not good timing. Speaking of which, we'd better hurry." The tide was coming in quickly.

They darted up the beach, coordinating their runs around rocks and over tide pools with the waves. When they reached the first set of stairs, they collapsed with laughter. They were soaked with salt water, speckled with wet sand, and cleansed of tension.

Tom was looking for a serious relationship. He'd made that clear. She liked him—liked him a lot—but she wasn't ready. Not yet. There were too many loose threads in her life that needed tying up: the Safety Plan, Davy, Proctor. Especially Proctor.

He'd been a boogie man under her bed since she was a child. His invisible, but constant presence had infected her life with its poison. Her marriage, her relationship with her mother, and even her parenting had been tainted by it.

But that was about to change. At this moment Mike was shining his big police flashlight into dark closets and under furniture. He'd find Proctor's dirt. When he did, the omnipotent monster of her childhood would be defeated once and for all, and she'd be free.

MOLLY: So, Proctor is in town. That was a bombshell. He's in town, and he's blackmailing Olivia's mother. I'm pretty sure Olivia would like to pin all her problems on the guy, and maybe she'd be right to do it.

We also learned a little more about Tom today. Sage seems proud of him. Says he knew his calling at an early age. But she also said he can be a little controlling. "Bossy" was the word she used.

Is it just because he's a teacher and used to being in authority, as Sage said? Or is it something from his childhood? It's said that children who come from out-of-control homes often try to control their environments when they're adults. Maybe we'll find another clue in this week's entry from Sage's diary.

Saturday, June 27th, 1992

I heard frantic barking and raised voices from the garden. I threw down my trowel and ran toward the sound. "I'm going to kill your stupid mutt." That was Doug.

"Dad." That was Tomas.

"Get off my property." That was Paul Travers, our next-door neighbor.

I flew around the side of the house, across the driveway and into the yard next door. Spotlighted by a patch of sunlight like two actors on a stage, Doug and Paul stood a foot apart, faces red, hands fisted. The Travers's dog, Pepe, a small thing I always thought looked more like a dirty mop-head than a canine, hid behind his owner, nose to the sky, raising an alarm. Tomas, so small and skinny next to the two large men, shuffled from foot to foot and picked at his father's t-shirt.

"Doug. Come inside," I said, my words coming in a breathless rush.

"I'm going to break that yapper's neck if it doesn't stop."

"It's a dog. Dogs bark. Get over it." Paul's voice was laden with disdain.

"Paul, I'm sorry. He's not well." I reached for my husband, anxious to lead him to the house, away from the discord.

"There's nothing wrong with me." Doug flung out his arm. The blow landed between my breasts driving the air from my lungs. I fell to the dirt, stunned. He'd been unpredictable in the week since he'd been home from the hospital, but he hadn't been violent.

"Stay away from Mama," Tomas screamed at his father and dropped to his knees next to me. He wrapped his little arms around me.

Paul shoved Doug out of the way and kneeled beside me too. "You okay?" His forehead wrinkled with concern. "This is too much for you, Sage. Too much. I'm calling the cops."

"Please, no," was all I could gasp out.

"You come home with me. Mary can take care of you until the police get here."

"No police. I can handle it. We're okay."

"So, you two are having a thing behind my back? That's what's going on here?" Doug's gaunt face twisted into a rictus, a parody of his old smile.

"Doug. How could you say that?" I understood this was the brain damage talking, not my husband, but the statement hit me like a slap.

"You're sick." Paul shook his head and stuck out a hand to help me to my feet.

"Don't touch her." Doug charged like a bull. The two men hit the ground with a thud, dust billowing up around them. I rolled to my knees and crawled toward the skirmish, but Tomas tightened his grip on me. "Tomas. Let me go." I snapped at him.

"No, Mama." He sobbed the words.

The fight lasted less than a minute. Doug, although several inches taller than Paul, was still weak from the accident. Paul now sat on his chest, pinning Doug's arms with his knees. I stifled a laugh. This was the way most of Tomas and Lily's wrestling matches ended. The men looked like children, silly, teasing children. It struck me funny, hysteri-cally funny.

"The police are on their way." Mary stood nearby, cradling and shushing Pepe like a baby, her five-year-old, Abby, clinging to her leg. I hadn't noticed them come out of the house. "Come inside with me, Sage. I'll make you some coffee."

I looked toward their door. Scottie Travers, Tomas's best friend, stood at the screen, his eyes wide. I shook my head. I'd stay here with Doug. I'd explain to the police.

I didn't blame Mary for calling them. She was trying to protect the kids and me. Doug was loud. He sounded menacing. But I knew I could control him. At least I thought I could.

I saw the plume of dust behind the oak trees before I saw the black and white. The car crunched up the gravel and rolled to a stop between the houses. Two uniformed men, one short and Hispanic, the other a big Norwegian looking man, emerged.

"Hello there, folks." The Hispanic officer's tone was easy. "I'm Officer Rodriguez."

"Swanson," the blond man said, and extended a hand to Paul, who took it and rose to his feet.

"Is anybody hurt here?" Rodriguez said.

"My mother," Tomas said, but I shushed him.

"No, baby. Mama's fine. It's all a silly misunderstanding, Officer. Doug was mad about Pepe, their dog. He barks a lot. He didn't mean to knock me over."

"That man has seduced my wife." Doug jerked his chin toward Paul Travers. "What would you do if some jerk seduced your wife?" He sat up and leaned back on his arms.

"Tomas, go to Scottie's house." I pushed him gently toward the Travers's home.

"No, I—" he began.

"It's okay, son. Your mom will be okay." Officer Rodriguez gave Tomas a comforting smile. Tomas wiped his nose with his arm leaving a long brown smear across his upper lip and walked into Mary's waiting arms. Officer Swanson and Paul Travers followed. The screen door closed behind them.

"He's confused." I tipped my head toward Doug with a gesture I hoped communicated the problem.

Rodriguez thinned his lips. "Let's go into the house, sit down, and you can tell me your side of the story. Okay?"

Rodriguez helped me to my feet while Doug struggled to his. Before we made it to the porch, the screen door slapped closed next door, and Swanson walked across the patchy grass toward them. He directed a pointed look at Rodriguez, then one at the squad car.

"On second thought, we're going to go for a little drive. You can tell me all about it on the way," Officer Rodriguez said.

"I'm not going anywhere with you," Doug said.

"I'm afraid you are, sir." The policeman's hand went to his belt.

Swanson moved beside him. "Let's do this the easy way. Okay?"

Doug swung his fist in the direction of the big man's face. It made a jagged arc and fell short. A moment later, his wrists were handcuffed behind him. The officers moved so quickly, I never saw it happen.

Doug bellowed. "What do you think you're doing?"

"Where are you taking him?" I had to shout to be heard over my husband's rage.

"Usually, we take them to South Coast Hospital," Swanson said. Paul and Mary must have filled the officer in on Doug's condition.

"I have friends. Friends who can get you canned." Doug's face had turned a dangerous purple, veins throbbed on the sides of his forehead.

"Can you take him to Mission Hospital? I'll call his doctor and see if he can meet us there," I said.

"Sure," Rodriguez said. Swanson protected Doug's head while they lowered him into the squad car.

"Why don't you take that jerk next door in? Seducing somebody else's wife is illegal, isn't it?" The door closed with a thud and muffled his ranting.

"I have to find someone to watch the kids, and I'll be right there," I said.

"Take your time." Officer Rodriguez patted my shoulder. "He's not going anywhere."

I watched until the car was out of sight, then turned to my house.

Tomas stood at the Travers's door, nose pressed to the screen, face too stoic for a little boy. It almost broke my heart

MOLLY: Poor little Tomas. It must have been really traumatizing to see a parent fall apart like that. It makes you wonder if this was why he went into education—to make other kids' lives better than his own had been.

But back to our villain, Proctor. I couldn't find out anything about his childhood, and you know what? I don't care. There are no excuses for a creep like him.

What do you think? Is he the one leaving the messages for Olivia? And, if so, what's his motivation? Pop into the Facebook group and let's get the conversation going.

(cue music)

VO: This episode is brought to you by Fawkes Press, a small press with big ideas. *Murders Under the Sun* is edited by Jim Wilbourne, theme music by Eclectic Blends, and I'm your host, Molly Shure.

part six

MURDERS UNDER THE SUN
SEASON TWO; EPISODE FIVE

MOLLY: Welcome back to *Murders Under the Sun*. I'm Molly Shure, your host.

I can't believe we're in Episode Five already. By the end of today, we'll be halfway through the season. Generally, at the halfway point of a movie or a novel, the hero has an ah-ha kind of moment. They learn something about themselves that changes the rest of the story.

Sometimes reality is no different. Today, you'll hear Olivia find her voice. She faces down the demons of her past and rises victorious. It's pretty inspiring.

Regarding her past, it was interesting reading all your comments about Proctor. You had a healthy debate about whether he's the message culprit or if it's someone else. Those who believe it was him were sure he'd be coming after Olivia with a blackmail threat next. That the messages were an attempt to shake her up, make her more vulnerable. Those who believe it's someone else said he didn't have a sufficient motive for leaving the messages.

As to the question Rachel James asked regarding my old roommate: Did anyone ever look into Melissa's boyfriends when she disappeared? The answer is a resounding yes. That's always the first place the police go. Melissa wasn't dating anyone at the time, but she had left a few broken hearts in her wake. None of them became suspects. There simply wasn't enough evidence. And, no, there was no Proctor in her past. She had a happy childhood. The police ran into a dead end.

Similarly, the thing repeated most often in the Facebook page, is that you don't feel you have enough information to make an informed guess about who is stalking Olivia. There are always things the victim knows that others don't. In the case of Melissa, she can't tell us because we don't know where she is. Thankfully, Olivia can. Today you'll find out what Proctor did when she was a child.

So, without further ado, let's get into the story.

2.5.2

ON MONDAY NIGHT, Olivia, Mike, and Sarah sat in Sarah's gray-blue dining room with mugs of coffee in front of them while Brian watched television in the living room.

"This isn't Proctor's first rodeo," Mike said. "I called the people whose names you gave me, the judge..." He shuffled through some papers.

"Drew Reynolds." Sarah supplied the name.

"Right, and the Anderson woman. Once they heard I was working privately, not in any official capacity, they admitted he'd sold them photos. They didn't say what was in the pictures, but my guess is they're the same as the ones he's blackmailing you with."

Sarah's cheeks flushed. "Did he leave them alone after they gave him money?"

"Yes." The word came out long and stringy like he'd had to pull it out of himself. "But, Sarah, I think he's only on round one. Reynolds told me Proctor left a message on his phone a couple of days earlier saying he'd be back in town after he finished up some business in SoCal. Said he was hoping to get together for dinner."

Sarah digested the news. "What do you suggest we do?"

"Well, it took me a few days to find him, but I also called Greg Forsythe." Greg Forsythe was the man Olivia had known as Teach.

"Greg never made any money to speak of. Why would Proctor blackmail him?" Sarah said.

"He didn't. I went on an information gathering tour. Decided to contact as many people from that commune as I could find, which wasn't easy. Some were dead, some off the grid. But I did talk to Forsythe, and he told me something we might be able to use. Turns out he was browsing an art website looking for prints for his home and saw a picture that looked a heck of a lot like his son Mark when Mark was a kid. The artist's name was Jeff Proctor."

Jeff? Olivia had never heard his first name. She'd only known him as Proctor. It seemed wrong. Jeff was too benign, too ordinary.

"So what?" Sarah shrugged. "He was an artist. He was forever snapping photos and then sketching from them. He probably drew everybody at the farm at one time or another."

"The thing is the boy in the picture was naked. When Greg Forsythe asked his son about it, Mark was shocked. He'd never given Proctor permission to photograph him, sketch him, nada, nothing. In any case, he was too young to consent."

That didn't surprise Olivia. She had a vivid memory of sitting by the fire in the great room at the farm reading *The Hobbit* for the second time and feeling her skin prickle. There was no reason for it. She was in a pleasant part of the book, no orcs or Black Riders in the chapter, nothing to make goose bumps rise on her arms.

She glanced around the room. No one was there, not seated on any of the other furniture, not by the bookshelves, not in the doorway. She was about to return to her book when she saw him. Proctor stood outside the large paned window near her chair, not moving, arms by his side, his face only feet from hers.

Panic leaped into her throat, but she turned her eyes to her book and pretended to read. The words might as well have been hieroglyphs. She stared at the pages until she heard the sound of boots on gravel. It was the first time she'd caught him watching her.

After that it seemed he was everywhere. His predatory stare found and fixed on her wherever she was and whatever she was doing. No place was safe. When she played outside with the other kids, she'd see glimpses of him behind trees and outbuildings. When others weren't looking, he'd catch her eye across the table at meals. She lost so much weight that year, her jeans wouldn't stay up without a belt.

Once, when she was leaving the bathroom after a shower, he blocked her way in the upstairs hall. She stepped right to walk around him, but he mirrored her movements. She dodged left. He slid the same way. The strange, silent dance went on for several minutes before another adult climbed the stairs. She'd felt naked and ashamed despite her long terrycloth robe.

She tried to tell her mother about him, about his eyes. But her mom laughed and said, "What do you expect? You're a beautiful child. Proctor is an artist." The adults at the commune were so impressed with his talent for charcoal and pastels, they were blind to everything else.

"So how does that help us?" Sarah said.

"It's illegal." Mike swirled the coffee in his mug like it was wine. "You can't take pictures of a naked child without his parents' permission."

"But it's art." Sarah's voice rose.

"Contrary to popular opinion, being an artist doesn't give you immunity from the law."

Olivia spoke for the first time, her voice sounding rusty from lack of use. "Isn't there a statute of limitations?"

"Well, now, that's the interesting part. We could make a case that this was sexual exploitation of a minor. In Vermont, the statute of limitations on that is forty years, and it's only been twenty-something."

"But would Teach be willing—"

Mike interrupted Olivia. "It doesn't matter. I don't plan to take this to court. It would be a hard case to prove. The painting isn't an exact representation. A lawyer would argue it's art, not exploitation.

"But Proctor doesn't have to know any of that. Our message to him is: you may have something on Sarah, but we have something on you. We'll make it clear that if we did win that court case, the least of his worries would be public humiliation."

Sarah's face brightened. "Do you think it'll work?"

"I wouldn't take the chance if I was him. Would you?"

A flicker of anger ignited in Olivia's gut. It was all about Sarah Richards once again. What about the children he'd hurt years before? Proctor had exploited Mark, and her, and who knows how many others.

She'd had to take matters into her own hands when she was a child because there was no one else to turn to. Her mother had been so focused on her rocky romantic relationship with the man, she was deaf to Olivia's pleas for help.

Olivia had launched what, at the time, she thought was a brilliant intimidation campaign. She'd decided to give Proctor a taste of his own medicine, show him she wasn't afraid. Whenever she caught him watching her, she would lock eyes with him in a defiant gesture. It seemed to be working. More often than not, he was the first to look away.

Later Olivia realized he broke their staring matches whenever someone else came into the room, but at the time she thought she'd gained the upper hand. She was too young and too stupid to realize it wasn't a war she could win.

"So, we let him get away with what he did to Mark?" Olivia said.

Sarah and Mike both stared at her, surprise registering on their faces for several long moments. "Livvie—" her mother started to say.

Olivia pushed away from the table in a violent gesture and stood. "No one protected us from Proctor when we were children, and no one is standing up for us now."

"Did he hurt you?" Mike's voice was low, like a growl.

"She was fine. She is fine," Sarah said.

She and Olivia stared at each other mutely. "I've got to go." Olivia broke the spell.

"What do you want from me?" Sarah said.

"I don't know, Mom."

"I made a mistake. I tried to rectify it." Sarah looked at her hands.

"He may not win this battle, he may not get any money off you, but he gets to walk away. That bothers me."

"The painting isn't our fight," Mike said. "It's up to Mark Forsythe if he wants to open that can of worms. They're thinking things over, but they've agreed to let us use the information and not to do anything with it until Sarah is in the clear. If you have charges you want to bring against the guy, that's a whole different story. I'll help you if that's what you want to do."

Was that what she wanted to do? Olivia thought about walking into a court room, sitting on the stand, and reliving the events from her past. "No," she said. "Just get rid of him."

What she wanted was to put the past behind her. Bad memories and bitter feelings tunneled beneath her life like gophers in a garden, uprooting and destroying. If Proctor was no longer a threat, if he was gone for good, maybe she'd finally be able to build a future.

2.5.3

"**WHERE IS IT?**" Olivia said under her breath. It was Wednesday evening, and she and Fiona had stayed past closing to wait for a UPS shipment. In the meanwhile, she'd been doing a bit of online research and had discovered that clove oil could substitute for pine in a flu season mix she'd been playing around with. The original scent was too medicinal for her customers. She wanted to tweak it but couldn't find the recipe card.

Then she remembered she'd taken it home one night last week. She closed the cabinet drawer and fished out her tote from under the counter. She used the bag to cart around all the stuff that wouldn't fit in her purse and rarely cleaned it out. If she was searching for something—paperwork, overdue library books, last week's uneaten lunch—that was where she found it.

She rummaged around and pulled out the journal she used to log all the things she didn't want to forget. She leafed through a month's worth of notes and smiled. The recipe card was there, tucked into the book's spine.

"Hello, hello." Their UPS delivery woman struggled through the doorway with an overloaded dolly.

"Those aren't all for me, are they?" Olivia tossed the journal into her bag and hurried over to help.

"No. Only the top three."

Olivia signed for the packages, took them off the cart, and held the door while the delivery driver backed out. Then she turned to the boxes and got busy trying to find places to put things as she unpacked them. She fit the yoga pants and tops on shelves with others they sold. The aromatherapy candles snugged in next to the diffusers. But the big box of deflated exercise balls stymied her.

"Looks like Christmas in here," Fiona said as she walked in.

"Want to be elf to my Santa? I need help figuring out how to display this stuff." The packages of brightly colored balls were spread out on the counter.

Fiona bent and picked something up off the floor as she walked over. "What's this?" Olivia's heart skipped a beat. Fiona held the articles about the dead boys in her hand. They must have fallen out of the notebook when she threw it into her tote. She reached for them.

Fiona stepped back, her eyes on the papers. "Why do you have these?" She looked up, forehead creased.

Olivia's mind went blank. She didn't say anything, just reached for the pages again.

"Olivia. What's this about?" Fiona asked.

"Nothing. They're... nothing. Just some old stories someone gave me."

"Why would someone give you something like this?"

"I don't know."

"What do you mean you don't know."

Olivia sank into a swivel chair at the desk. "Someone left them on my windshield. I don't know who. I don't know why."

"What?" Fiona's voice raised. "When?"

"About three weeks ago." Olivia stared at her hands folded in her lap. She was a child again, being reprimanded by a teacher.

"You go out to your car one day and these articles are just sitting there?"

"Yes, and no."

"Would you stop being so cryptic and tell me what on earth happened?" Fiona's voice lowered in irritation.

Once the door opened, the story spilled out. Olivia told Fiona everything, about the flit of white at the Mission, the feeling of being followed and watched, the car in the lot, the graffiti, and finally the articles on her windshield.

"Have you called the police?" Fiona said when Olivia finished.

"No." Olivia's head snapped up. "What could they do about it, other than tell CPS? If CPS thinks Brian isn't safe with me..." her voice trailed off.

"But you *and* Brian could be in danger. Someone is obviously stalking you, trying to scare you."

"I think I know who's doing it, and it's being handled."

"Who? Who would do a thing like this?"

"A man from the past. He's bothering my mother. Mike's taking care of it."

"What do these articles have to do with your mother?"

That was a good question. What did the articles have to do with Sarah? Nothing as far as Olivia could see, but they had to have something to do with Proctor. In Olivia's experience whenever he showed up, bad things happened.

"This is crazy. I don't understand why you didn't go to the police when you found these." Fiona tossed the articles next to the computer.

"I didn't want to give Davy any ammunition. He was talking about joint custody. If he heard about this, he might go for full."

Fiona perched on the edge of the desk and looked out the window at the sea for several moments. Then she turned toward Olivia and said, "Could it be him?"

"Who? Davy?"

"Yeah. Maybe he's, I don't know, trying to scare you into getting back together with him?"

"The thought crossed my mind," Olivia said. "His new car, it looks like the one that was in the parking lot that night, and the one that trailed me when I met Tom at Turks. But there are a hundred cars on the road that look like that."

"Yeah, but not a hundred cars driven by your ex-husband. An ex-husband who has a reputation for pulling elaborate pranks."

"I thought about all that, but it doesn't fit." Olivia gestured to the articles. "How does sending me articles about little boys who died in other states help his cause?"

Fiona chewed on a thumbnail for several seconds, then said, "Okay, let's look at this logically. What do these articles have in common? What connections to you or Brian could there be?"

"I've already done this," Olivia said.

Fiona opened the computer printer drawer, took out several sheets of paper, and grabbed a pen. "Humor me. What do both boys have in common with Brian?"

"They're close in age. One was ten. The other eleven. Brian's eleven."

"Good." Fiona wrote that down.

Olivia reviewed the facts she remembered from her Internet search, and they came up with a list of commonalities. Both boys had single mothers, some kind of behavioral issue, and died in accidents after they wandered off.

"Now the differences." Fiona sat with a pen poised over the paper.

"Location, of course. The first boy, Peter Compton, lived in Boise. The other one lived in Phoenix." As soon as she said the names of the cities in sequence, Sage's words from the other night came back to her. *His first teaching job was in Boise, but he didn't like the winters. He transferred to a school in Arizona for several years, but Phoenix was too hot.* She paled.

"What? What's wrong?"

"It's nothing. A coincidence."

Fiona waited for her to go on.

"Tom lived in Boise and in Phoenix before he came home to Southern California." Olivia's voice sounded stilted even to her own ears.

"That's a heck of a coincidence," Fiona said.

Outside the large picture window, a cloud blew across the sun darkening the room. Olivia hugged her sweater around herself. "Those are big cities. We don't know if Tom even knew those kids."

"No. But we need to find out."

"Even if he did, the boys' deaths were accidents."

Fiona's mouth tightened into a stubborn line.

"How could we even find out?" Olivia said.

"You could ask him."

"I couldn't do that. How would he feel? Besides, if he had something to do with those boys, if he was guilty of something, he'd lie about it."

"How about Mike? Maybe he could give you some advice."

"Mike's pretty busy with my mom right now. And if I talk to him, he'd tell Davy. Davy would want to take Brian away until we figure this out. Maybe even use it to get custody."

Fiona stood and paced across the lobby. Olivia slumped in her chair. After several moments Fiona stopped mid-stride. "I have an idea." Olivia wondered if that was a good thing. "Tom is a teacher, right?"

"Yes. He teaches math," Olivia said.

"What if we call the schools these boys went to and pretend we're from the HR department at St. Barnabas? We don't ask a bunch of questions, nothing to get anyone suspicious. We just verify employment. Did Tom so-and-so—"

"Hartman," Olivia said.

"Hartman." Fiona repeated the name. "Did Tom Hartman work there in two thousand whatever? Then we'd find out if he could have known the boys."

"Don't they call back to make sure you're who you say you are?"

"No. Not if all you're doing is confirming employment. I call other studios all the time when I'm hiring new exercise instructors. Nobody ever checks."

"I think this whole thing is going to go away when my mother's problem goes away."

"Maybe, and maybe someone knows something about Tom we don't."

Olivia stood. "It seems so sneaky. What if Tom found out?"

"He won't." Fiona picked up two of the packages of exercise balls. "I'll do it next week. Now, where should we display these?"

2.5.4

"YOU SHOULD HAVE SEEN IT; Crackers found Brian in like two minutes." Olivia shouted to be heard over the music. Tom had finally made good on his threat to take her to the Swallows Inn. She'd already said yes to the date before Fiona found the clippings, but she wouldn't have said no anyway. Olivia couldn't believe the articles had anything to do with Tom.

A local rockabilly band filled the dance floor with boot-scooting boogiers and Texas two-steppers. Cowboys and bikers cozied up to the bar together in unlikely camaraderie. Bras and other undergarments hung from the ceiling like party banners. Olivia sat with Tom at a table in the corner enjoying the show.

Tom leaned toward her. "How long did it take?"

"I told you, about two minutes."

"No," Tom yelled. "To train the dog."

"Oh. I don't know. The prior owner had him in a program. I didn't want a dog, but I have to admit Crackers has been good for Brian. He's almost like his old, pre-accident self."

"President self?" Tom looked confused.

Olivia laughed. "Pre-accident. Pre-accident self." She enunciated the words carefully.

"Oh. Hard to hear."

She nodded and sipped her beer. They listened to the music without talking for two more songs, and the band announced they were taking a short break. The noise level dropped several decibels.

"They're good, but not good for conversation," Tom said.

"No," Olivia agreed.

"So back to Brian. He's doing well?"

"Great, really."

"Not con ...con ..."

"Confabulating. No. Only once in the past month."

"Wandering?"

"Nope. I think Davy was right to choose a dog with search and rescue training. It seems to be having an impact, hearing all the stories about dogs finding people lost in the wilderness. It's like he finally understands the danger of wandering off."

"How's school going?" Tom said.

"So much better. I got an update from Mrs. Margolis. All his grades are up, except math. He's still pulling a C minus, but math has always been hardest for him."

"Maybe I could help. That's my subject." Tom picked up his beer and took a slug.

Olivia thought before responding. She didn't know how Davy would feel about that. Correction. She did know how Davy would feel about it. He wouldn't like it. Wouldn't like it at all. On the other hand, it would give Brian and Tom a chance to bond. Brian never said anything negative about Tom anymore, but he was still reserved around him.

She and Tom had been dating for a month now, and it was a strange dance. He, always moving closer. She, always backing away. She didn't know how much longer she could keep it up before they fell off the dance floor altogether, and she didn't want that to happen. She liked him. Once or twice she'd even slipped into a fantasy about a future that included a three-bedroom house with a garden for him and a cat for her.

"That would be great," she said.

Tom beamed at her. "Why don't we start after the week after next, after Thanksgiving break?" The PA system in the corner of the bar came to life with a screech. He grimaced. "The band is back."

"I think we have to dance." Olivia pushed out her chair. "Can't talk, that's for sure."

"Yeah, well, I can't dance either."

"I don't believe it. You've been coming here for years. You must have picked something up."

"Who told you about her?" Tom feigned shock.

Olivia slapped his arm. "Just for that, you're dancing with me."

An hour and a half later, Tom pulled up to the curb in front of Olivia's dark condo. He turned off the ignition and wrapped his arms around her. His kiss was hard. Demanding. "Are you going to invite me in?" He spoke into her hair.

Olivia froze. She couldn't. This wasn't just her home. It was Brian's too. He would see Tom spending the night as an invasion. "I don't think Brian would—"

"Isn't it Davy's weekend?"

"It is."

Tom pulled away from her. "Then what's the problem?"

"He wouldn't be comfortable..." her words trailed off.

"He's not here." Frustration punctuated Tom's words.

"I know, but this is his home. Home has to be a safe place."

Tom pulled as far away from her as he could get in the front seat of his car. "What are you saying? Do you think I pose a threat to your son?"

"No. No, of course not. It's just he may see you that way."

Tom's jaw tightened. "I'm starting to feel like Brian's an excuse."

"Excuse for what?" Olivia's voice rose.

"For not getting close. He's like a shield you hold up to keep me away from you."

"That's not true."

Tom sat and stared out the window without speaking, but waves of tension flowed from him.

"Listen." Olivia pivoted in her seat so she could face him. "When I was a child my mother dated around a lot. It didn't work out well for me. I promised myself if I ever became a mother my children wouldn't have to deal with my boyfriends." What she'd really promised herself was that her children would be raised with a father. Their father. But Davy had screwed that up.

"So how does this end?" Tom said. Olivia didn't answer. "If Brian never has to deal with his mom's boyfriends, how can I ever become more than that?"

A mix of emotions flooded through Olivia: warmth, hope, excitement, despair, and fear. She knew Tom wanted more than a casual relationship, but it was the first time he'd said it. The thought of having a solid, reliable presence in her home was something she'd longed for her whole life. She'd never had a father to protect her.

When she'd married Davy, and inherited Mike as a father-in-law, she'd thought that dream had been realized. She had not one, but two strong men in her life. But it hadn't lasted long. She'd barely begun to settle into the whole family thing when financial trials came, and Davy failed the test. He'd hidden in a bottle when things got tough.

Tom wouldn't do that. She knew it. Strength emanated from him. "Let's take it slow," she said.

"I thought that's what we were doing."

"You've been wooing me. It's time to woo Brian."

"I've been trying, Olivia. He's not interested. He has a father. The most I'll ever be to him is the man who's in love with his mother."

In love with his mother. That was anything but slow. She said, "Nobody will ever replace Davy in Brian's heart. I know that. But there are other kinds of relationships. You two could become friends."

"It's not easy to make friends with an eleven-year-old when you're thirty-seven. Especially if the eleven-year-old isn't interested."

"Tutoring is a great idea. If he sees you want to help him, I think it could make a difference."

Tom shrugged. A small, resigned gesture. "Right. Well, we'll give it a go."

She got out of the car and watched him drive away. Even though it had been her decision for him to leave, her throat constricted. Brian came first. He was her priority. But tonight, she felt as empty as her house behind her.

2.5.5

THE STUDIO WAS quiet on Monday. Thursday was Thanksgiving, and most of their students were taking the week off. Fiona and Karen had been the only instructors that morning, and they'd left after lunch. Olivia was wrapping up some paperwork, then planned to head home. Brian had a short week at school, and she had things to do so she'd be free to enjoy their time together.

It was a vacation week, and the Idaho and Arizona schools Fiona called were short staffed and unhelpful. Her plan to check up on Tom was a wash. She'd had to postpone it until after the holiday. Olivia wasn't worried about it. By tonight, the situation would most likely be resolved. Mike and her mother were meeting with Proctor today. Sarah said she'd call as soon as it was over.

Sunlight streamed through the large picture window by the desk, wrapping Olivia in its warmth. She yawned and pivoted her laptop out of its rays so she could read the screen. Her eyes were tired. She'd been at the computer for over an hour.

Her cell phone vibrated across the desktop. Fatigue fled. Her nerves jangled as she read her mother's name on the screen.

"He's gone," her mother said as soon as Olivia picked up.

"What happened?"

"Mike told him about Mark, about the picture. He denied it. He said it was an image from his imagination, that it wasn't Mark or anybody else. But Mike said, 'I guess we can see if a jury would buy that.' And he backed right off."

"Did you get the pictures he had of you?"

"Yes, but I don't think that means much. I'm sure he's got copies."

"Well, it's over anyway."

"For now."

"What do you mean for now?"

"It kind of depends on Mark. If he somehow intimates he won't prosecute, all bets are off. It's the only thing I have over Proctor."

There was a long silence on the phone. An uncomfortable idea struck Olivia. "You're not saying you want me to—"

"Maybe it's time," Sarah said.

Rage bubbled in a stagnant place in Olivia's heart. "All these years, you've kept silent about what happened and now, when it suits your purposes, you want me to dig up the bones?"

"I kept silent for your sake."

"For my sake?" Olivia was incredulous. "How did keeping silent help me?"

"What if I'd have gone to the police?" Sarah's voice raised in anger. "How do you think those conservative New England cops felt about the farm? We were leftovers from the hippie days. They were sure we were all perverts and drug addicts. They'd have taken you away from me so fast it would have made your head spin. No. I wasn't taking that chance."

Olivia was silent. She couldn't see past her own anger to her mother's point of view.

"I took you three thousand miles away," her mother continued. "I took you to the safest place I knew, my parents' house. And I changed our lives. I've been trying to make it up to you ever since."

"I know, Mom." Olivia had heard this all before.

"Just think about it, Livvie. Not just for me. For us. The past has caught up with us. Maybe we have to deal with it."

"I'll think about it." Olivia hung up, leaned back in her chair, into the sunlight and closed her eyes. Could she go there? Could she take the stand and relive that time in her life? That time she'd tried so hard to forget?

Proctor had lain in wait for her all that winter, playing the part of Sarah's attentive boyfriend. He'd lulled Olivia into letting down her guard by making her think she was winning the battle of the stare-downs. He waited until the weather grew warm and struck in the spring.

Lambing season had begun, and Olivia had gone into the barn to see the newborns. Adorable twin cotton bundles wobbled on pencil-thin legs beside their mother. Olivia was so entranced; she didn't hear him enter. She didn't notice him until he stood beside her.

"Cute, huh?" he said.

She couldn't answer. Her heart took up too much room in her throat for words to edge past it.

"Asked you a question, didn't I?" He chewed on a bit of straw.

An incoherent sound eked from her lips, and she moved toward the big barn doors. He grabbed her arm. "Where're you off to?"

"Mom." She meant to tell him her mother knew she was in the barn, that she was waiting for her, that she'd be there any minute if Olivia didn't show up at the house. But the only thing that came out was *Mom.*

"Your mother left for town. I saw her get into the car with Rainy." He spat the straw from his mouth and yanked her close. His flannel shirt smelled of pastel chalk and old sweat.

"I'm supposed to go with her." Olivia couldn't move. Fear had turned her to stone. "I need to leave." She stared with more defiance than she felt, but he didn't look away this time. Her heart knocked hard against her rib cage.

Proctor moved closer. Panic and bile bubbled into her throat. She didn't fully understand what he wanted, but she knew it wasn't something she wanted to give him.

Mom. Where are you? Unspoken words screamed through her brain. An image of her mother's face flickered to life behind her eyes. Olivia willed her to come to the barn.

Proctor put a hand on her shoulder, drew his chin back and examined her. A smile crawled across the stubble on his face. She was confused, but like the restless sheep nearby she smelled danger.

The ewe bleated again. The sound jarred Olivia into action. She bolted for the barn door. but before she reached the sunlight, she slammed into a blue t-shirt. Her fists came up and battered the obstacle.

Gentle hands held her wrists. "Olivia. What's wrong, honey?" A soft voice swam upstream against her terror. "Shh. Shh. It's okay. I'm here."

Teach. Here. Help. Realization came in stutters.

She threw herself into Teach's comforting arms and breathed in the clean cotton smell of him. "Explain yourself." His comforting tone was gone. It was angry and held a threat, but he wasn't addressing Olivia.

"Don't know what's her problem. She was watching the lambs one minute, screaming like a banshee the next. Musta' startled her," Proctor said.

"Is that what happened, Livvie?"

She shook her head, burying it deeper into his wide chest.

"I think you'd better leave," Teach said.

"I was just about to, but I wanted to make sure the girl was okay first."

"I mean *leave*. Leave the farm. Leave before I call the cops."

Proctor didn't say any more, but she felt his scent move past her and heard his footfalls fade away on the gravel drive outside.

The memory was so strong, she smelled his smell again, faint but defined—sweat and chalk and tobacco. "Well, look at you." She heard his voice.

Olivia's eyes snapped open. Adrenaline surged. Heart thudded.

Proctor stood in the doorway of the Fishbowl; washed-out denim eyes focused on her.

"ALL GROWN UP." He took three steps toward Olivia before she leaped to her feet. "Grown up real pretty, just like your mama."

Olivia opened her mouth to speak, but nothing came. She was like a fish on a dock, gasping for oxygen.

"So happy to see me you're speechless?" He came into the sunlit space, walking with a slight limp. The light revealed a frayed and faded version of the man of her memories, a ghost of the past. Revulsion, more than fear, coursed through Olivia. She backed up until her hands rested on the windowsill.

"I understand you're one of the proud owners of this establishment. Congratulations, darlin'." She wondered how he knew that but didn't ask. He went on. "You're probably wondering why I'm stopping by, after all these years. Other than the fact that I wished to see your lovely face again and satisfy my curiosity as to the kind of adult you've become, I'm also here to deliver a message. Do you mind if I sit?"

He didn't wait for her to answer but pulled a stool out from the sales counter and perched on it. He was so close, every sag and wrinkle stood out in clear relief. He looked old, older than his sixty-odd years, and he wore the road map of his life on his face. The lines etched there told a story. Proctor had leered instead of smiled, lusted instead of loved, taken instead of given.

"You're probably aware I've just come from your mama's home, where I met with her and your ex-father-in-law. Mike, I believe, is his name. Oh, on a side note, I'm sorry you've had to live through a divorce. I hear it's painful. It's one reason I never married. Although I did think about marrying your mama at one time. But I'm still available if you're interested."

He smirked. For a moment he looked like the Proctor of her childhood, and she shuddered.

"No? Well, I'll say my piece then. I couldn't get in a word edgewise with that father-in-law of yours beating on his chest like some kind of senior citizen King Kong. I think he's got a thing for your mama." He winked a reptilian eye.

"Livvie, darlin', if you love that woman, you need to help her understand that generosity is in her best interest. I'm leaving town now, but I'll be back. I don't give up easy, especially not when I'm angry. And that Mike makes me angry."

"I'm not your errand girl." Olivia found her voice.

"She speaks." He threw up his hands as if amazed. "If you won't help me for your mama's sake, think of your son. Scandal won't help your case with Child Protective Services, and I have the means to start a scandal."

A muscle in Olivia's eyelid twitched. Scandal. His life was a scandal. He didn't have a record. That was the first thing Mike had checked. Apparently, Proctor had lived below the radar, using his reputation in the art world to cover his perverted behavior. Over the past five to ten years, his work had lost popularity, however. Whether it was because he'd angered one too many people, or tastes and opinions had changed, Olivia didn't know. What she did know was, he'd started digging up old dirt to start a new career—as a blackmailer.

He knew about CPS. Which proved her assumption correct. He'd dug around, found out everything he could about her. The idea of him following her, following Brian, leaving her messages, made her skin crawl.

He stepped off the stool, winced as he straightened his back, and walked toward the door with arthritic bravado.

"Wait." Olivia couldn't let him leave without being sure. He stopped and turned. "What do those boys have to do with me?"

Proctor raised his eyebrows in question.

"The boys in the articles," she said. "Did you hurt them? Did you want me to know what you were capable of?"

He stared at her with pale eyes that didn't deny the accusation. A sudden anger surged through her. "You need to stop it. Stop your threats and innuendos. You don't scare me. Not anymore."

As she said the words, she realized they were true. "You're a pathetic old man who preys on children because he's afraid of adults. You couldn't stand up to Mike and my mother, so you came here thinking I'm the same frightened girl I once was. I'm not."

Olivia stepped away from the window toward him. "And I have a message for you, Proctor." She almost growled his name. "If you know what's good for you, you'll stay away from my family and me. I could put you away for a long time."

"My, my. She's a little spitfire." He attempted a leer, but it died on his face. He turned and limped from the studio.

MOLLY: Go Olivia! I was so proud of her when she told me the way she reacted to that man. He's vermin, and she crushed him.

I'd love to leave you on that high note, but we still have a diary entry to read. Sage has an ah-ha moment here, as well. But, unlike Olivia, it's not something she can walk away from or throw out of her Pilates studio. Her revelation is about the depth of the damage that's been done to Doug's brain.

Let's hear from Sage.

Saturday, July 11th, 1992

I hummed to myself as I washed up the breakfast dishes. It was a sunny Saturday morning, and Doug had woken up in such a good mood and seemed so much like his old self, I'd made pancakes to celebrate. I even let him take the kids to the petting zoo across from the train station without me.

His doctor had adjusted his medications after his fight with Paul two weeks ago. I'd increased the strength of the tea I'd been making him. He was doing better, and I was encouraged.

The tea was an old recipe of Abuela Maria's. She'd used it to treat depression, senility, nerves, what today would be called ADHD, and any other malady of the brain or mood. Every few days, I would send Tomas up the ginkgo biloba tree in the garden to bring me the brightest green leaves he could find. I washed them well, placed a handful with sprigs of rosemary into a bowl, covered them with three cups of boiling water and let them steep for at least ten minutes. After I strained the mixture, I would add in ten to twelve drops of the St. John's Wort tincture Lily and I made whenever the small yellow flowers were in bloom.

My children had grown up knowing the ways of the garden. Although many of the plants were used to flavor food or had medicinal properties, some were deadly. To my way of thinking, having a garden was like having a swimming pool. It was a pleasure and a blessing, as long as one taught children to respect it.

Just as I placed the last dish into the dishwasher, there was a knock on the front door. I dried my hands on a towel and headed there. Paul Travers stood on the front porch.

As soon as I saw his face, tight and drawn, I knew something bad had happened. My thoughts ran ahead to the petting zoo, to Doug and the children. Had I trusted him too soon?

Paul spoke in a formal tone, not at all like our usual friendly way with one another. "Is your husband home?"

Relief cooled some of my worry. If he was asking for Doug, he wasn't bringing news of my family. Yet. I could see something was wrong. "No. He's taken the kids to the petting zoo. I'm sure they'll be home soon. Can I help?" I said.

"Little late for that."

I didn't respond.

Paul continued in a weary, emotionless voice. "It's Pepe. He's been poisoned. The vet says he'll make it, but it'll cost a small fortune. Just wanted to let Doug know, although I'm sure he already does."

"Oh, Paul. I'm so sorry. But you can't believe Doug would have..." Paul gave me a hard smile, a smile that said that's exactly what he believed. "Did the vet know what kind of poison? Maybe Pepe got into someone's rat traps. I know the city was talking about putting something down to get rid of the rabbits in the parks."

"He thought it might be sago palm. The symptoms fit, and he found seeds in Pepe's vomit along with half-digested beef. We don't have sago palm in our yard, and we don't feed our dog steak." He and I locked eyes. I had sago in mine. "Sage, I'm going to have to file a report. I know it's not Doug's fault, but he's dangerous. If he'd do this—"

"But he didn't do this." My words shot out high and sharp. "How can you think that? He's been better, Paul. So much better."

"I'm sorry. I can't have that kind of threat near my family. What if he goes after Mary or the kids next time?"

"Paul, please. I'm sure Doug wouldn't have hurt the dog. He—"

"He said he wanted to kill him, then Pepe gets into some poison. Odd coincidence, don't you think?"

"People say things like that all the time. They don't mean it."

"People who don't have brain damage say things like that and don't mean it. Obviously, Doug did."

I heard Lily's piping soprano, and Tomas's laugh before I saw my family trudging up the driveway. Why did they have to come home now? If Paul accused Doug, and if Doug threw another punch, it wouldn't go as easily as it did before. The police had warned me. They said if Doug presented a danger to others, he'd have to be institutionalized.

"I'll find out what happened, Paul. You go home now." I wanted him to leave.

But Paul turned and followed my gaze. He stepped off the porch and met Doug at the edge of the grass, his shoulders set and determined. "You'll be sad to know, Pepe is going to make it," he said.

A small smile crept across Doug's features. "What are you talking about?"

"Like you don't know."

"I don't know."

"I'm filing a report with the police." Paul shoved past Doug, heading toward his house.

"What are you going to say in that report, Paul?" Doug called to his retreating form. "How're you going to prove I had anything to do with anything?" Paul didn't answer, just kept walking. "Because I didn't, you know. I didn't poison your dog."

Paul froze for several moments, then pivoted to face him. "What did you say?"

"I said, I didn't do anything to your dog."

"No. That's not what you said. You said: 'I didn't poison your dog.' How did you know Pepe was poisoned?"

It was Doug's turn to freeze. The smile he'd been wearing slid off his face. "I don't know. I figured, if he'd been hit by a car, we'd have heard about it."

"Right," Paul said. A moment later, I heard the slam of his screen door.

Lily stared at me. Tomas stared at the ground. I opened my arms, but only Lily ran into them. Tomas didn't move, his face hard. Doug mounted the stairs to the porch, gaze straight ahead, avoiding my eyes. "Doug, what did you do?" I said. He walked into the house without answering.

MOLLY: All I can say is thank God Pepe was okay. If Doug really did poison that dog, and it seems he did, he was worse than Sage thought. My heart goes out to her at this point. She lost the man that she loved and instead found his evil doppelgänger.

The question I am posing for you this week is: Do you think Doug's brain damage had an impact on the way Tom related to Brian? Remember, in the first few episodes, Brian didn't like Tom. He thought he was mean. Was Tom mean? Did he have a knee-jerk reaction to Brian because of his father? Or was it just as he'd said? He didn't know about the accident and thought Brian was being rebellious?

Tom did seem to care. He asked his mother to make a tincture to help Brian, and he said he wanted to befriend the kid. But was it sincere? Or was he just trying to make points with Olivia? Let's hash it out on Facebook.

(cue music)

VO: If you enjoyed this episode, please leave us a five-star review on your favorite podcast service—it really helps. *Murders Under the Sun* is edited by Jim Wilbourne, theme music is by Eclectic Blends, and I'm your host, Molly Shure.

part seven

MURDERS UNDER THE SUN
SEASON TWO; EPISODE SIX

MOLLY: Welcome back to Season Two of *Murders Under the Sun*. This is Molly Shure, your host.

There was a lot of rage on in the online group this week, and for good reason. Nobody likes to see an innocent animal get hurt, but to console those who are worried, I have it on good authority that Pepe lived an exceptionally long and happy canine life after his NDE—Near Death Experience.

In fact, you were so incensed over poor Pepe; I didn't get many answers to my questions about Tom. A few of you felt sorry for him because he had such a horrible father, and a few of you thought Olivia should steer clear. You thought the early childhood trauma must have left a mark, and she already had her hands full with Brian. Fair enough.

This episode will show us just how full her hands actually were. You're in for a roller coaster ride, people. The vine is twisting.

Let's get into it.

2.6.2

OLIVIA AND BRIAN passed a quiet and grateful Thanksgiving at her mother's home with some of Sarah's single friends in attendance. They'd discussed inviting Mike, but he was planning to eat with Davy. Asking them both felt awkward, and Davy had Brian beginning Friday morning for a long weekend anyway.

Olivia and Tom drove to San Diego on Saturday. They visited the Old Point Loma Lighthouse, now a museum, walked on the beach and ate terrible, overpriced Mexican food in the Gaslamp District. It had been a wonderful day. The showdown with Proctor had started the destruction of an invisible wall in Olivia's heart, one that had been there since childhood. Behind it, she saw glimpses of courage, confidence and a new sense of freedom.

On Tuesday afternoon, Olivia pulled into the St. Barnabas parking lot. Brian had stayed after school to spend time in the library. The good thing about it being so late was there was no pick-up line. The bad thing was, she had to hurry. It was a packed evening. She had her last parenting class, and she had to drop Brian at Davy's on the way.

Thank goodness, Brian was sitting on a grassy hill waiting for her. He waved as she drove up. She didn't bother parking, just stopped in the drive.

He stood, gathered his things, and jogged toward her. As he opened the door to stow his stuff in the backseat, a car horn sounded. Olivia hadn't noticed there was a driver in the minivan she'd pulled in front of.

"Hurry," she said to Brian, but he didn't. He zipped and unzipped his bags, rearranging who knew what. The woman tapped her horn again. Brian opened the passenger side door to get inside but dropped his water bottle. It rolled under the Explorer.

"Wait, honey. Let me move the car," Olivia said, but it was too late. Brian was on his knees reaching for his water. She couldn't pull forward without running him over.

"Excuse me." An angry voice shot through her open window. The minivan mom was yelling at her. "Would you move your car? You're blocking me."

"One minute." Olivia sent her an apologetic smile. A long moment later Brian popped up with a bottle in his now filthy hand. "Get in. Quickly," Olivia said.

But before he'd closed the door behind him, Minivan Mom appeared in front of Olivia's car, hands on her hips. "What is your problem?" Dark hair tumbled into her narrowed eyes.

"I'm sorry." Olivia leaned from her window. "He dropped his water bottle."

"If you pulled into a parking space like everyone else, he could drop his stuff all day long without bothering anybody."

"I'll get out of your way now." Impatience rippled up Olivia's spine.

The woman didn't budge. "Oh, do you want to leave?" Her eyes opened wide in mock surprise.

Olivia stared at her. The woman shifted her weight onto one leg, lifted a hand and inspected her fingernails.

"What's she doing, Mom?" Brian asked.

"I don't know, honey."

"Teaching your inconsiderate, self-absorbed mother a lesson. Honey." Minivan Mom's voice dripped with artificial sweetener.

Olivia felt an unfamiliar heat burning in her chest. She didn't have time for this, but she wasn't going to put up with the woman's attitude, especially not in front of Brian. She put a hand on the door handle.

"Nicole." A man's voice. Olivia stopped.

"Coach Tom." Minivan Mom came to attention.

"What's going on here?" Tom walked out between two large vehicles.

"Nothing. We were just having a conversation." She pushed her bangs off her forehead.

Tom glanced at Olivia and raised an eyebrow. Olivia shook her head.

Brian stuck his face out of the passenger side window. "She said she wanted to teach my inconsiderate, self-something mother a lesson."

"Oh?" Tom gave Nicole a quizzical look.

"She blocked my car." Her voice was subdued.

"Looks like she's ready to move now."

The woman walked to her minivan without a word. Olivia pulled into a space but left the motor running.

"You causing trouble again?" Tom leaned into her car window and brought his face eye-level.

"Good lord. She just missed getting an earful."

"Sometimes it's best to give people the opportunity to be embarrassed." His green eyes lit with amusement. All the worries she'd had about dating him, that he and Brian would never bond, that they might be moving too fast, spun away like smoke through the open car window. He was kind, stable, feet-on-the-ground Tom. Things would work out, one way or another. He was a good man.

"I had a great time Saturday," he said.

"Me too."

"What are you doing Friday night?"

"Actually..." A slow smile spread across her face. "As it so happens, I'm free. Brian's grandfather is taking him to Knott's Berry Farm for law enforcement and military night and then over to his place."

"Hey, I'm jealous." Tom looked past her to Brian.

Brian grinned. "Grandpa Mike only has two tickets. Even Dad doesn't get to go."

Tom turned his gaze onto Olivia. "I'll call, and we can make plans."

Olivia turned out of the parking lot toward home. Confronting her old fears, confronting Proctor, had created new space in her life. She'd be wrapping up parenting classes tonight, another thing to check off the list of heavy concerns. She and Davy had been co-parenting amicably of late. And if everything continued in the positive direction it was headed, she'd be free of CPS in about two months.

It was as if she was cleaning out a large closet stuffed with the detritus of the past. Soon it would be empty. She was excited about the prospect of filling it with shiny, new things.

She flipped on the radio. A classic rock station Brian loved came on. He began belting out his off-key appreciation for California girls along with The Beach Boys. Olivia laughed and joined in.

A half mile from home, Olivia's phone lit up and played a Tinker-bell tune from where it sat in the middle console. She lowered the volume on the radio. "Brian, you want to answer that? It's Fiona."

Brian did. "Hi," he said. "No, she's driving. Just say what? Okay. Yeah. See you soon." He hung up. "Rolling Stones, Mom. Turn up the radio."

"What did she say?" Olivia's hand paused on the button.

"She said to tell you Boise said he worked there. Who's Boise?"

Olivia felt nothing but confusion for several heartbeats, then she remembered. Fiona was calling the out-of-state schools to investigate Tom. Olivia had never told her about Proctor's visit to the Fishbowl, or that he had all but confessed to leaving the articles to intimidate her.

"Mom, who's Boise?"

"It's a place, not a person."

"But how can a place talk? She said, 'Boise said...'"

"It's just an expression. Not literal." What did it matter? So what if Tom had taught school in Boise?

"Who worked in Boise anyway?" Brian fiddled with the phone, tossing it from hand to hand.

"Put that down," Olivia snapped. He looked at her, hurt in his eyes. The only sound in the car for the next few blocks was Mick Jagger's lament about satisfaction, or the lack thereof. When she pulled up to the curb, she put her hand on Brian's leg. "Sorry."

"Are you mad about Boise?"

"No. Don't worry about it. It's nothing. Okay?"

He brightened. "Okay. I need to be at Dad's by six-thirty. We're going to take Crackers to training."

"Get your homework done as soon as we get home."

Olivia waited until Brian was in his room with the door shut before she called Fiona back. "I have to tell you something," she said as soon as Fiona answered.

"The Boise school said he worked there." Fiona sounded distracted.

"You don't need to make any more calls. I know who—"

"See you next Wednesday at three." Fiona's voice was muffled, and Olivia could hear another woman in the background.

"Fiona." Olivia itched with impatience.

"Great job today."

"Fiona, talk to me."

"Okay, I'm here." The sound of papers shuffling came through the phone. "He worked there from 2001 to 2008. That fits, doesn't it?"

"Yes. Peter Compton died in 2008, but it has nothing to do with Tom."

Neither woman said anything for a moment, then both spoke at once. Olivia said, "I know who—"

Fiona said, "I don't know why you'd—"

Olivia waited for a beat and Fiona said, "I don't know why you'd say that. It seems significant to me."

"Listen, it's a long story but I know who left the articles."

"Who?"

"A man who was involved with my mother a long time ago."

"Why does he care if you're dating Tom?"

"He doesn't." Olivia heard the exasperation in her tone and adjusted it. "The man wanted to scare me. He was trying to extort money from my mother. I was his backup plan, in case plan A didn't pan out."

"He said that?"

"He didn't deny it."

There was a moment of silence, then Fiona said, "I still don't get how he knew you were dating Tom."

"He didn't. Tom doesn't—" Olivia heard a beep.

"I've got another call. I'll call you back." Fiona rang off.

Olivia walked into the kitchen. She would explain the whole thing to Fiona tomorrow and tell her she didn't need to keep looking into Tom's past.

She opened the refrigerator and peered in looking for something fast to make for dinner. She pulled a couple of zucchinis from the vegetable bin and tossed them into the sink. Then she took a spiralizer from the cupboard.

She'd finally found a way to get vegetables into Brian. The device turned zucchini, sweet potatoes, carrots, all kinds of things, into long, noodle-like strips. She then mixed them with regular pasta, put spaghetti sauce over all, and Brian ate them happily.

By the time she'd turned two squash into a hill of noodles, the phone rang again. She rinsed and dried her hands, then rushed to the counter to pick it up before it went to voice mail. "Hi." Her voice sounded breathless.

"Okay. This is confusing," Fiona said. Olivia waited. "Tom didn't work at the school in Phoenix."

Relief washed over Olivia, and she berated herself. She had nothing to be relieved about. "Good. That's good."

"I guess."

"What do you mean you guess? Of course, it's good. It confirms what I told you. Tom didn't have anything to do with those boys, the articles, any of that."

"Probably." Fiona enunciated every syllable.

"Oh, come on. Phoenix is a big city. If he didn't work at Trevor Johnson's school, how would he know him? It's not like grown men hang around with other people's kids when they're not getting paid to do it."

"Maybe you should think about getting a private detective." Fiona's words dropped with a thud.

"Why would I spend money to run down a blind alley?"

"Done." Brian slid into the room in his socks. "Can we go to Dad's now?"

Olivia muffled the phone against her chest. "We have to eat first." She returned it to her ear. "Fiona, I've got to go but thank you. Thank you for looking into this. I'm sorry I didn't tell you sooner it had been resolved, sorry you wasted your time."

"But—"

Olivia cut her off. "I've got to go. I'll see you tomorrow, okay?"

2.6.3

"LOOK, I don't want to delve into the past, not here, not now. Just believe me when I say children aren't safe around the man," Olivia said. Fiona pursed her lips and gave a small nod.

Fiona had taken Wednesday off, and Thursday morning had been so busy at the Fishbowl, Olivia had little time to fill her in. She'd told Fiona about Proctor showing up in town, blackmailing her mother, stopping by the Fishbowl after Mike scared him away in disconnected bits and pieces between classes and customers. Fiona listened but didn't say much.

When the final client cleared the door, Fiona turned to Olivia. "I think it was Davy."

"Davy?"

"Who left the articles."

"But I just told you—"

Fiona held up a hand. "Hear me."

Olivia closed her mouth hard.

"Tom worked in Boise when the first boy was killed. We know he was living in Phoenix when the second boy died. This is too big of a coincidence to be a coincidence."

"So, you think Tom is a danger to young boys?"

"No. I think someone is trying to make you suspicious of him. And

I don't think it's this Proctor guy. Why would he care who you were dating?"

"How would Davy know anything about Tom's past?"

"He could have paid one of those Internet search companies. They figure out where people have lived based on public records, like real estate transactions, court appearances, parking tickets. Then checked for tragedies involving boys Brian's age in those towns in those time frames. He could have left you the articles and hoping you'd come to your own conclusions. That's probably why he got one school right, but not the other. He didn't actually know where Tom worked."

"That's a lot of work," Olivia said.

Fiona shrugged one shoulder. "He's got a motive, and you said he's pulled some pretty elaborate pranks in the past."

"But why would Davy assume I'd put two and two together? I'd have to know Tom's history, where he worked and when he worked there."

"That's a pretty safe assumption. You're dating the guy."

"I don't know."

"Besides, there might be another layer to the plan. Maybe there are more messages coming. He might be doling out the clues."

"If you want to talk about coincidences," Olivia's voice rose, "I think it's a heck of a coincidence that Proctor, a known child predator, shows up in town after twenty-two years, and I start receiving messages about children in danger at the same time. That's the real coincidence."

"Maybe you're right." Fiona chewed her lip. "But watch Davy. He doesn't like Tom. He's threatened by the man. This could be his way of trying to warn you off, make himself the only safe option."

"I've got to go," Olivia said. "I've got to pick up Brian from tutoring."

Olivia simmered on the way to St. Barnabas. The mystery had been solved. It had all been taken care of. It was Proctor. He'd admitted it. Well, he hadn't denied it, which was pretty much the same thing. She wished Fiona would leave it.

She parked in the almost empty lot, walked up the school's stone steps, and opened the heavy glass doors. She was greeted by the scents of rubber erasers, crayons, and cafeteria food. School. She'd loved it as much as Davy had hated it.

When Olivia and her mother left Vermont, they'd moved to California and Olivia enrolled in public school. Her favorite day of the year was the day they shopped for school supplies. She'd thrilled at the reams of clean, white notebook paper, freshly sharpened pencils, and textbooks with un-cracked spines.

Davy told her when he was a kid, he'd always said he liked the last day of school best. Summer trips to the beach, sleeping in, and running around his neighborhood with the gang who lived on his block, that was his idea of heaven. Shopping for notebooks and backpacks had sent him into depression. She and Davy were so different. But no matter how different they were, she didn't believe he would do what Fiona accused him of.

She climbed the empty staircase to the third floor and turned right.

As she approached Tom's classroom, she could hear the rumble of voices. One low. The other higher. She peered through the window in the door.

Tom sat across from Brian at a child's desk, his long legs straddling its base. Brian bowed over a textbook, a can of soda at his elbow. Olivia smiled at the scene—teacher and student in deep concentration. Brian raised his head to look at Tom, and her smile faded. His eyes were unfocused. Guardedness covered his face like a caul. His expression echoed the one he'd worn in the early days after the coma.

A draft blew through the long, empty hallway, and she shivered. She hesitated, watching for a moment more, then turned the knob. The blankness on Brian's face lifted as soon as he saw her. "Mom." Warm relief drove away the cold that had seeped into her limbs while she stood in the window.

"Hey, sweetheart. You done?" It was obvious he was. Brian had jumped up and begun stuffing papers into his backpack the moment she'd entered. "How'd it go?"

"Great," Tom said a broad grin on his face. "He did well. I think we'll have long division mastered by the end of the month."

Olivia turned to place a congratulatory arm around Brian's shoulders, but he was already at the door. "Ready? It's Dad's night. We're going to a movie. I gotta finish the rest of my homework."

"How about saying thank you to Coach Hartman?"

"Soccer season's almost over. As long as the other kids aren't around, you can call me plain old Tom."

"Thanks, Mr. Hartman," Brian said.

"Brian, honey, he said you could call him Tom."

The bland expression slid over Brian's face for a heartbeat. "I'd better not. I forget sometimes, and I might call him Tom in front of the other kids or something."

Tom looked at the floor and nodded. Olivia smiled an apology she wasn't sure he saw.

As soon as the classroom door closed behind them, Brian started talking. "Dad said he'd take me to see the new *Wolf Rider* movie. We saw the coming attractions when we went to see *Mothvader*. It looked so good. I've been waiting to see it for, like, months."

Olivia tuned him out as he gave her a blow-by-blow recitation of the *Wolf Rider* trailer. She was relieved to see him animated and excited, but she worried about the vacant look she'd seen through the window. Was his brain shutting down for seconds here and there? Or was it boredom?

Brian had never liked math, but she'd never seen him disconnect like that before the accident. She'd have to ask his teacher, talk to Davy and her mother about it. If others had seen it, they'd have to make a doctor's appointment.

By the time they reached the car, he was quoting, in character, the lines he found funniest. How could he remember such minute details about a film, but not where he'd left his shoes?

She slid behind the wheel and was about to put the car into reverse when she saw something stuck under her windshield wiper. Her first thought was that it was a flier. Probably a discount for a new gym, or spa. But her heart skipped a beat anyway. When she stepped out of her car to retrieve it, she noticed the newsprint.

Dread gripped her. She forced her hand forward, pulled the paper free, balled it up, and threw it into her tote bag.

"What is it?" Brian asked.

"Nothing. An advertisement." Her throat tightened around the words. "Tell me about *Mothvader*. I don't think you ever did."

She didn't have to ask twice. Brian dove into a detailed plot summary that took the entire car ride. When they got home, Olivia watched him run to his room. After his door shut behind him, she walked into the kitchen. With trembling hands, she took the paper from her bag and spread it out on the counter smoothing the wrinkles. It was an obituary.

2.6.4

THE COPY in the obituary wasn't as clear as the copy in the other two articles. The newsprint was smudged in some places, and the picture of the smiling boy at the top of the page was almost sepia in color.

The boy's name was Scott Travers. He was survived by his parents and a sister. The paper didn't mention how he'd died, only that his death was sudden.

There were several significant differences between this story and the other two Olivia had read. It seemed his parents were still married. He wasn't being raised by a single mother. And nothing was said that gave her any indication he had any brain issues. Of course, this was only a short obituary, not a newspaper story like the others had been.

She stared at it without understanding, a hollow, aching place opening in her chest. Proctor was gone. She'd thought the nightmare was over. She was about to throw the paper into her tote, when the family's hometown caught her eye—San Juan Capistrano.

Another town Tom had lived in. Someone wanted her to connect the children's deaths with him, that was for certain. A deep sadness flowed over her. It had to be Davy. Fiona was right. He was the only one who had a reason to want her and Tom to break up.

She walked to the living room window and gazed with unseeing eyes out to the street for several moments, then returned to the article on the counter. She read it again as if it might yield a secret she'd missed the first five times she'd read it. But no. Scott Travers was beloved by his surviving family, Mary and Paul Travers and his younger sister Abigail Travers. The closed casket memorial service was held at the San Juan Capistrano Mission Church on August 9th, 1992.

The date. 1992. Tom was... what? She did the math in her head—twelve, thirteen? He couldn't have anything to do with this. He was only a child at the time, only a few years older than Brian.

Davy hadn't done his research very well. This was sloppy, desperate. Tom had no connection to the school in Phoenix, and now Davy was trying to create suspicion over something that happened when Tom was only a kid.

She picked up the obituary, tore it in half and threw it into the trash. This was it. She wasn't going to play this game anymore. She had to confront Davy, let him know his plan wasn't going to work. Confrontation seemed to be an everyday occurrence these days.

She yanked her tote bag off the chair and onto the table and began riffling through it to find the other two articles. They were going in the trash too, where they belonged. Before they came to hand, the doorbell rang.

It was Davy. "You're early," she said.

"I know. I—"

"Dad." Brian slid into the room and launched himself at his father. "I'm ready. Let's go."

"You couldn't have done all your homework that quickly," Olivia said. They'd only been home for about fifteen minutes.

"I'm almost done. I'll get up at six and finish in the morning."

Olivia opened her mouth to protest, but Davy said, "Hey, champ, I got here early so I could talk to your mom. Go finish up. We're not leaving yet."

Brian screwed up his mouth like he'd bit an especially sour lemon, then relaxed it into a smile. "All right. But don't talk too long. I'm almost done." He marched to his room.

"What's up?" Olivia's voice was as heavy as her heart.

"You're in a good mood," Davy said. "How about some coffee?"

Olivia spun on her heel and walked into the kitchen. Davy sat at the counter in his usual spot.

"I have to talk to you about the tutoring." His tone was calm and even. It was the tone he always used when he had to bring up a sensitive subject. Her jaw clenched.

She kept her back to him. "What about the tutoring?"

"It's nice of your friend, John—"

"Tom."

"Right, Tom, to offer to tutor Brian in math, but I don't think it's a good fit."

"Not a good fit?"

"Right. I don't think Brian's comfortable with him."

"Not comfortable with him."

"Why are you repeating everything I say? I'm trying to have an adult conversation with you about our son. I feel like I'm in junior high." The humor in his voice sent waves of anxiety through her. Why was he doing this? Didn't he understand the careful balance of power between them? Did he want to force her into battle?

Olivia flipped around and braced herself on the counter. "How do you know Tom is tutoring Brian?"

"Brian told me, over the weekend."

"What did he say?"

"He said your friend was going to tutor him two days a week after school starting today. He also said the man makes him feel stupid. Brian doesn't like the guy, Olivia." Davy's face wore the sincere expression she'd come to associate with manipulation.

"And you have nothing to do with his attitude."

"Of course not." He sat up straighter. "Listen, I may not be happy about you and Ron—"

"Tom."

"Tom. I won't pretend I am, but I wouldn't try to influence Brian. I appreciate the guy is trying to do a nice thing for our son, but I don't think it's a good idea. That's all I'm saying."

Olivia folded her arms across her chest and looked at the white linoleum floor. Her next words had to be uttered with extreme caution. She modulated her voice, kept it light, like what she was saying held little importance. "I know Tom didn't have anything to do with those accidents."

Silence dropped like a stone into her small kitchen.

The wall clock ticked nine times.

Davy said, "What are you talking about?"

Olivia looked up. His face was a mask of confusion.

"I know you've been following me. I recognized your car. I know it's you who's been leaving the newspaper clippings. I had a hard time believing you'd sneak into a women's bathroom after me to graffiti that message, but I guess I have to. I understand why you've done what you've done, but it's time to stop now." Her speech was absorbed into the unnatural quiet between them.

Seven ticks of the clock, then Davy said, "Someone has been following you and leaving messages?"

"It won't fly. The innocent act won't fly."

Davy looked down, then up again. "I swear to you, Olivia, whatever is going on, it isn't me."

A tiny pebble of doubt entered her mind, but she tossed it out. They had to resolve this for Brian's sake. "I'm sorry you feel threatened by Tom, but you had to know someone would come into my life sooner or later."

"Please." Davy held his palms up in supplication.

"We have to be honest with each other if this co-parenting thing is going to work. Believe me when I tell you I don't want to take Brian away from you, replace you with another man. Your son loves you and needs you. You've been doing a great job with him. You can stop this... this..." She didn't know what to call it.

"I am being honest with you. I know in the past I've—"

"Done." Brian skated into the room, shoes in hand, jacket on. "Let's go, Dad." He looked from parent to parent, the brightness on his face fading. "What's wrong, Mom?" Olivia couldn't answer. Emotion choked off her words.

"Nothing, buddy," Davy said. "Let's go." He rose from the counter and ushered Brian in front of him toward the front door. When Brian stepped outside, he turned. "I'll talk to you when I bring him home. I'm worried about you, Olivia." He left before she could respond.

2.6.5

AN HOUR and a half after Davy and Brian left, the phone rang. Olivia leaped at it, hoping it might be Davy, ready to talk, but knowing it wouldn't be. It wasn't. It was Tom. "The math part was fine, but I don't think tutoring is going to help with the friendship thing," he said after they'd said hello.

"Give it time. You've only had one session." Olivia made her tone comforting, but she wasn't paying attention to her words. Confronting Davy had left her agitated and unfocused. She paced from the kitchen, through the dining area, circled the living room, through the dining area, and into the kitchen, reverse, and repeat. She was on her fifth lap.

"By the way, I hope you don't mind me giving Brian a soda today. I know you're trying to keep him away from sugar, but I thought it might make staying after school less painful. A spoonful of sugar and all."

When she saw the soda, it had annoyed her, but it no longer seemed important. "It's okay."

"Don't take this the wrong way, but I wonder if the medications he's on are doing the job."

Olivia stopped walking and stiffened. "What do you mean?"

"He has this way of going blank on me. Have you seen it? His face. It goes slack, like he's not taking anything in."

"He doesn't do that at home." She heard the defensiveness in her voice and tried to soften it. "I did see it through the window of your classroom today though. It worried me."

"Did you call the doctor?"

"No." She felt herself bristle again. "I just saw it this afternoon for the first time. I thought I'd talk to Mrs. Margolis, my mom and... and Davy first. See if anyone else has noticed it."

"Or, if it's just me."

"No. That's not what I said." She didn't have the emotional reserves to spar with Tom tonight. "It could be it's math. He's never liked it and maybe thinking so analytically bothers him. The brain is complicated. He recited almost every word from the movie trailer for *Wolf Rider* today, but he can't remember what he ate for lunch."

Tom didn't say anything for a moment, and she could hear the rustling of paper in the background. "Okay, so I have an idea," he said.

"I'm listening."

"*Calavia* is opening in Irvine tomorrow. I want to take him."

"Is that the horse show with the acrobats?"

"Yeah, it's supposed to be amazing. I know how much he likes animals."

"I saw a TV commercial for it. I'd love to go. I'm sure—"

"No. I didn't mean with you. Don't be hurt, but I want to do something with him. Alone. Something fun that has nothing to do with soccer, or school, or math."

"That's so sweet of you." Olivia didn't know what to say. She appreciated the gesture, but she didn't think either Davy or Brian would like the idea.

Tom must have heard the hesitation in her voice. "What's wrong? Is it Davy's weekend?"

"Yes, but he's not taking Brian until Saturday morning."

"Then?"

"No, it's a great idea. I'm sure Brian would love it." She wanted Tom and Brian to bond, and she had to show Davy she wasn't going to be manipulated by his ridiculous behavior.

"Then it's settled. I'll pick him up in the late afternoon, and we'll get dinner after."

"I'll let him know." Olivia tried to match Tom's excitement.

"On the medicine note, I'll talk to Mom. Maybe she can mix up something a little stronger for him."

"That'd be great," Olivia said absentmindedly. Her thoughts had returned to the conversation she was going to have with Davy when he brought Brian home. She resumed pacing.

It was the small things Davy did that bothered Olivia the most. He threw himself on the green couch like he was throwing down a gauntlet. She had to sit in an armchair she never sat in. He knew she always sat on the couch.

She took three deep breaths through her nose and focused on the sweet scent of the essential oils she'd filled her diffuser with. Lavender, rose, and bergamot wrapped their calming fragrances around her head. She rallied. "Is he asleep?"

"Yeah. I turned off the light," Davy said.

They'd waited until Brian was asleep to talk. Olivia didn't want him overhearing their conversation. As insane as this campaign Davy had been waging was, she knew it was motivated by love and insecurity. She'd thought about it a lot while they were at the movies. She would forgive Davy, take the high road. She wouldn't tell anyone. If he'd only come clean.

"Now." Davy laid an arm over the back of the sofa and crossed a foot over a knee. "Tell me what's been going on."

Olivia looked at the ceiling and inhaled again. *Stay calm. Be sensitive. Be compassionate.* She repeated the mantra under her breath. "Stop. I understand why you did it, but we can't move on until we're honest with each other."

"I know you think I know what you're talking about. I know you think I'm behind whatever has been happening to you, but I don't and I'm not. How can I convince you?"

The doubt that had crept into her mind earlier, came galloping back. He looked genuinely concerned. But Davy always looked genuinely concerned. It was one of his secret weapons.

Whenever there were stormy seas, he became a lighthouse. He drew his brows together, furrowed his forehead and sent his blinding blue gaze into the darkness. People flocked to the light. But Olivia had been shipwrecked on that shore in the past.

"Why do we have to do this?" she said.

Davy's eyes darkened. He rose from the couch and walked across the room. "I deserve this. I do. The past four or five years, I've been an idiot, an absolute idiot. But I swear to you, I've turned a corner. I've changed." He put up one hand like a traffic cop. "Not perfect. I still screw things up, but you have to believe I wouldn't stalk you, terrorize you." His hand moved to his head, and he ran it through his hair. "Never. Not you. Not Brian."

Olivia knew the shadows and shades of Davy. The way his left eyelid twitched when he was irritated. The way his eyes opened a little too wide when he wasn't being completely truthful. And the way he tugged at his hair when he was distraught. He was distraught now.

She stood, walked to her tote bag and brought it over. She dumped it on the coffee table and pawed through the contents until she found her journal and the newspaper stories inside it. She handed them to Davy.

As confusion transformed his face, her suspicions began to deflate. When he finished, he laid the clippings in his lap and looked at her. "What does this mean?"

"I was hoping you could tell me. Someone left them on my windshield."

"You said someone was following you."

"I think so, yes."

"I'm in the dark here. You better start at the beginning. Tell me everything that's happened."

Olivia told him about the nights she was followed, the graffiti on the bathroom stall, and the latest newspaper clipping she'd found. His dawning expression of horror finally convinced her he wasn't guilty of the events she'd described.

"Where's the last one?" he asked.

"In the trash. I'll get it." Olivia went into the kitchen and returned with the torn page. "There's something else I didn't tell you." She gestured at the papers. "Tom lived in each of those places at the times the accidents occurred. He lived in Boise and worked at the school the first boy went to." Davy leaned forward and opened his mouth to speak, but Olivia raised a hand to quiet him. "Before you jump to conclusions, he did live in Phoenix when the second boy died, but he had no connection to him."

"How do you know?"

"He worked at a different school, a school across town."

"That doesn't mean he didn't know the boy," Davy said.

"It doesn't mean he did."

"You'd think if someone was trying to build a case against him, they'd provide the connection. The lack of detail almost makes it more believable to me."

"Or more random," Olivia said.

"But they gave you a third story. San Juan Capistrano is a small town. I'll bet Tom knew this boy." Davy rapped the article with his knuckles.

"But he was only a kid at the time—twelve or thirteen." Davy shrugged. Olivia grew more insistent. "I think someone is trying to make me afraid of Tom, so I'll stop seeing him."

"And I'm the only one with a motive." Davy said in a resigned tone.

"As far as I—"

"But I didn't do any of this."

"I don't know why, but I believe you. Which means I'm at square one." Olivia slumped into her chair, despair and anger vying for top emotion. "I was convinced it was Proctor. But he wasn't in town when this one was delivered."

"Are you sure about that?"

Olivia looked into Davy's eyes. "No. No, I guess I'm not sure. I just assumed..."

"Let me take these to my dad. He can call in a favor and find out where Proctor was. He can also find out things that never made it into the papers about these accidents. Things that might shed some light on this."

"Maybe." Olivia felt the tension in her shoulders that she'd been carrying all day release a little. "Fiona was sure the articles were about

Tom because of the locations of the accidents, but I don't want him dragged into this."

"It's possible they are about Tom. Maybe he's guilty of something. Maybe he's an innocent victim. Maybe somebody has a crazy vendetta against him. At this point, you have no idea what's happening here."

Innocent victim, the words rang with sudden clarity. Olivia sat up straighter. "I've been so focused on Brian, on us, I didn't stop to think it could be someone from Tom's past. It could be an old girlfriend, a woman scorned."

One side of Davy's mouth went up in a doubtful smile. "Anything is possible."

"No, think about it. It makes sense. Someone doesn't want Tom and me together. I assumed it was you, for obvious reasons, but it could just as easily be someone Tom knows."

"Or it could be someone trying to warn you about Tom because they're concerned for Brian's sake."

"Then why not ask me out for coffee and talk to me? Why all the subterfuge?"

"Maybe the person is afraid of him, doesn't want him to find out he or she is involved."

Olivia dismissed that notion with a wave of her hand. "Tom is a gentle person." But as the words left her lips, she realized she had to work with Davy on this. If he felt she wasn't taking every possible action to keep their son safe, he'd be within his rights to try to take him from her.

"Okay," she said. "Talk to Mike, but please, ask him to keep it on the QT. I don't want it to get back to Tom. I don't want him to feel like I'm investigating him."

"Can I take these?" Davy held up the articles. She agreed. "Promise me you'll stay away from the guy until we figure all this out, okay?"

Olivia smiled, but she didn't promise.

2.6.6

"YOU'LL HAVE FUN." Olivia poured a large spoonful of Sage's tincture into a glass of orange juice and put it in front of her son.

"I'd rather go to Dad's." Brian's mouth tightened into a thin line.

"Your dad has to work tonight. He's picking you up tomorrow morning." Olivia ran hot water into the kitchen sink.

Brian took a half-hearted bite out of his peanut butter toast and tossed it onto the plate. "Why can't you come too?" He spoke around the food in his cheek, words sounding thick.

"Don't talk with your mouth full." Olivia scrubbed the remains of their breakfast from a frying pan. How could she explain it to Brian, so he'd understand? "Tom wants to spend time with you. He wants to get to know you better."

Brian washed his food down with a sip of juice. "He knows me."

"All you guys ever do together is school stuff. He wants to do something fun with you." She opened the dishwasher and began loading it.

"I'd have more fun if you were there." Brian put an elbow on the table and dropped his head onto his hand like it was too heavy to hold up without help.

His reluctance to go to the horse show with Tom weighed on Olivia. She didn't know how to change his attitude. She didn't tell him until that morning, the day of the event, so he hadn't had much time to adjust to the idea. She hadn't wanted to bring it up in front of Davy the night before, and by the time he left, Brian was sound asleep. It was better if Davy didn't know about it until after the fact. It was always easier to ask for forgiveness than permission.

She dried her hands on a dishtowel, crossed to the counter where Brian sat and rested her cheek on the top of his head. His hair smelled like fruit shampoo and peanuts. Maternal love gripped her heart. He was her joy, her pain, her reason for going on when she wanted to give up. She hated making him unhappy, but sometimes it was necessary.

Olivia wasn't sure Tom was the right man for her. Not yet. But she did know growing up without a father had made her vulnerable. She wanted a father's protective presence for her son. Yes, Brian had Davy, but Davy wasn't around all the time. He didn't drop Brian off at school in the morning or pick him up in the afternoons. He didn't have dinner with him every night, or sleep in the same house. He wasn't there to comfort Brian when he was awakened by a nightmare at three in the morning. Tom wanted to be there. She ought to give him a chance.

"I think you'll like *Calavia*," Olivia said.

"What do they do there?"

"Well, there's acrobats and horses."

Brian lifted his head and looked at her. "Any dogs?"

"I don't think so. There are people who balance on horses while they're galloping around the ring, though. And there's music and lights and I think the horses dance."

Brian gave her a disbelieving smile. "Horses can't dance."

"They don't do ballet or anything, but they can do some pretty fancy steps."

"You're not making that up?"

"Would I do that?" Olivia widened her eyes.

He wiped a hand under his nose. "Okay."

"Okay, what?"

"Okay, I'll go."

"Good. Now finish your toast. You don't want to be late for school."

"Hello," Olivia answered her cell.

"Where are you?" It was Davy. His words were rushed.

"At work. Why?" His tone made the skin on her arms tingle with anxiety. Not that it took much to stress her out today. She'd been so restless after Tom and Brian left for *Calavia*, she'd decided to go into the Fishbowl and lose herself in work.

"Stay there. I'm coming to talk to you."

"But—" she said into a dead phone.

By the time he arrived the sun was beginning to set, turning the light in the Fishbowl a lovely rose color she wasn't able to appreciate. As soon as she heard his footsteps on the outside landing, she shut off her computer and picked up her purse. "I thought you were working late?"

"I didn't think this news should wait until tomorrow," Davy said. "Where's Brian?"

"At *Calavia*." She told as much of the truth as she was comfortable telling.

"*Calavia?*" Surprise registered on his face. "Those are pretty expensive tickets. Who did he go with?" Olivia hesitated, and before she answered, he said, "It doesn't matter. I need to talk to you."

"News from your dad?" She swung her purse over her shoulder.

Davy nodded. "Let's go get coffee."

He followed her out and paced the landing while she locked the front door and set the alarm code. They exited the building in the opposite direction than she usually took. Here the stairs dropped into an alley which opened onto a side street that led to Dana Point Harbor. It wasn't far, but Olivia was glad for even a short walk. She needed to move.

"What did he say?" she said.

"First, let me tell you what I found out. I did some research of my own. The boy who died in 1992 in San Juan was hit by a train."

"God." Olivia's hand flew to her chest. "How awful." She'd thought it strange that the Travers boy had a closed casket service in a Catholic church. In her experience, Catholics had viewings before the actual funeral mass and kept the body on display until it was time for the burial. A train would explain the departure from tradition. She wondered if it was a game of chicken gone wrong and shuddered. She was afraid to ask the next question. "How did it happen?"

"Sounds like he had a bike accident and somehow ended up unconscious on the tracks."

"Tom couldn't have had anything to do with that," she said with relief.

Davy shrugged. "Now for Dad's news. The bad first. I guess it's bad. According to his airline reservation and credit card, Proctor was in Massachusetts when that last paper showed up on your windshield."

Olivia didn't react. The hope Proctor was behind the messages had been such a small flame, she hardly noticed when it was snuffed out.

"Then Dad contacted a friend who moved to Boise when he retired from the Orange County Sheriff's Department. It took some time, but that guy was able to find out who handled the paperwork on Peter Compton. They never had an official investigation. The coroner ruled it accidental, so it fell off their radar pretty quickly."

Olivia and Davy caught up to a young couple they'd been trailing at the corner of Coast Highway. They stopped talking while they waited for the traffic light to change. When it turned green, the couple bounced off the sidewalk ahead of them, and Davy picked up his story.

"This guy says there were no suspects, because nothing about the accident seemed suspicious. He did say the mother, Anne Compton, was dating a man named John, or Don, or Tom. He couldn't remember which."

"The Boise cop also talked to the school. They confirmed that Tom had worked there during the time Peter attended, but they didn't know if Peter was in any of Tom's classes. The records didn't go back that far."

They crossed Harbor Drive without waiting for a signal and headed for the coffee shop near the docks. "So, nothing we didn't already know," Olivia said.

"Except that Peter's mother may have been dating Tom."

"Or John, or Don."

Olivia was surprised to see there was a line at the coffee shop after the sun set. Happy hour was the happening thing to do on a Friday night. After they got their coffee, they settled at a table on a patio illuminated by twinkling lights.

"The news from Phoenix was more interesting," Davy said.

Olivia's pulse quickened. She wished she had a glass of wine instead of coffee, but she wasn't about to tempt Davy. "Yeah?"

"Dad knows a couple of guys on the force there—transfers. You know Trevor Johnson's mother filed a lawsuit against that father-son backpacking club?" Olivia nodded. "Dad was able to pull the transcripts, and you'll never guess who testified."

"Not Tom." Her hand shook. Hot coffee slopped over the side of her cup. She set it down and dried her hand with a napkin, the pain from the burn barely registering.

"Yes, Tom. Apparently, he was one of the adult chaperones on the camping trip."

"I thought it was a father-son thing."

"It was." Davy's eyes locked on hers. "He was standing in as Trevor's dad. He'd been dating the boy's mother."

The metallic clank of rigging against masts, the slap of sails, and the keening of gulls were all Olivia heard for several long moments. A cold wind whipped up, and she shivered. Davy's warm hand covered hers. "I know. This is upsetting. You like Tom; I get it. But there's something weird going on here. You need to stay away from him until we figure it out. Keep Brian away."

"Oh, God." She dropped her head in her hands.

"It's a good thing we found out before you got more involved with him." Davy's voice was soothing. "Nothing is conclusive, but it's pretty suspicious. Dad is going to keep looking into Tom's history. We won't take anything to Art until we have solid facts."

"Art?" She didn't understand. Her brain was still reeling from the new information.

"Art Bishop, the principal at St. Barnabas."

"I know who Art is." She closed her eyes in frustration. Why were they talking about Art when Brian could be in danger?

"I know you don't like it, but we will need to inform the school. We'll do it discreetly. It'll be okay." Davy smiled at her over the rim of his coffee cup.

He thought her pride was bruised. He thought she was embarrassed she'd been taken in by Tom. "No. You don't understand." She almost shouted the words. "Brian is with Tom. Now. He's the one who took him to see *Calavia*."

"What?" Davy pushed away his chair like he'd been shoved.

"Tom said he wanted to do something fun with Brian, something that wasn't math." The look of horror on Davy's face hit her like a punch. "I trusted him. I'm sorry. I'm so sorry."

"I asked you... How could you..."

"Davy, please. I'm sorry." Her voice broke.

He stared at the table for a moment, his body rigid. "When are they supposed to be back?"

"Not until eight-ish. They're going out to eat after the show."

Davy looked at his watch. "Let's call."

Olivia had already pulled out her phone and hit Brian's number on her speed dial. It rang five times and went to his mailbox. She forced a cheerful note into her voice. "Hi, honey, call me when you get a chance. I want to hear all about the show."

"Tom. Call Tom," Davy said as soon as she put her phone down.

"What do I say?"

"Tell him you forgot I was supposed to take Brian out for dinner. He has to get back."

"I can't say that. I already told him you were working."

"Tell him I canceled. Tell him it's a special occasion. Tell him it's my birthday."

"He knows your birthday is in June."

Davy slammed a hand on the tabletop. "Tell him it's my dad's birthday, or Crackers's birthday. I don't care what you tell him. Get my son away from him, now." A couple at the next table stood, cleared their coffee things, and left, looking at Davy over their shoulders.

Olivia punched in Tom's number with nervous fingers. His phone rang six times and went to voice mail. She shook her head at Davy.

He leaped from his seat and strode toward the water, both hands clutching his hair. Olivia hurried after him. "Listen, it'll be okay. I know it'll be okay." She was comforting herself as much as she was him.

"Forgive me if I don't have a lot of confidence in your judgment right now." He shot the words at her without breaking stride.

"I know but hear me out. Even if Tom wanted to hurt Brian—

which I can't believe is true—everybody knows where Brian is and who he's with. The other boys, their accidents all happened when they were alone, out in nature with no one around. Tom and Brian are in a public place. He wouldn't hurt him now."

Davy's pace slowed. "Why aren't they answering their phones?"

"Brian never answers his. You know that. It makes me crazy. And Tom is probably driving. The show was over about twenty minutes ago."

Davy stopped and turned; hope etched on his face. "Do you know where they're going to dinner?" Her look must have told him she didn't. He pivoted and continued his race to the car.

"Let's go to my place and wait for them there," she said between breaths when she caught up to him.

"There's nothing else we can do."

2.6.7

SEVEN-THIRTY HAD COME AND GONE, and still there was no word from Tom or Brian. Davy had drunk half a pot of coffee and worn a path in living room rug. "I'm going to call my dad," he said for the fifth time.

Olivia wouldn't argue anymore. If he wanted to call Mike, she wasn't going to stop him even though she didn't think it would do any good. Brian was out for the evening with a well-respected teacher from his school. A teacher who tutored him, coached him, had taken him to away games and returned him safely. And she'd given the outing her blessing. The cops weren't going to start scouring the hundreds of possible restaurants in Orange County where they could be having dinner. Not under the circumstances.

"I'm sure they'll be home any minute." She kept her voice calm. She and Davy had switched roles. Usually, she was the one panicking when Brian was out of sight, and he was the one comforting her. But she knew Tom; Davy didn't. Whatever happened in his past, she couldn't believe Tom would harm her child.

"Call him again," Davy said.

Olivia walked toward the kitchen counter where she'd dropped her purse. Before she reached it, she heard her cell ring. She lunged the rest of the way and fished it out of her bag as it stopped. "Hello. Hello." No one answered. The call had been from Tom. She hit return, but it rang half a dozen times then went to voice mail. She hung up. "Damn it. I missed him."

"Why wouldn't he answer? He's got his phone right there. He just called you." Davy's voice rose in exasperation.

"Maybe the calls crossed. I'll try again." She hit call.

Tom answered on the second ring. "Hey there." He sounded cheerful. She could hear Brian in the background saying, "Is that Mom?" A tsunami of relief broke over her. She leaned against the wall and slid to the floor. "Just checking on you guys." Her voice came in a hoarse whisper.

"You okay? You sound like you're getting sick," Tom said.

"No, I'm just ...I'm just tired. Long day. I was wondering when you two would be home."

"We were going to grab a frozen yogurt, then head over. Just had burgers at Ruby's. That's why I didn't hear your call, by the way. The noise level in that place is off the charts."

"When are they coming home?" Davy mouthed the words. Olivia waved him off.

"We can skip yogurt if you want us home sooner for some reason," Tom said.

"We're not getting yogurt?" Brian sounded disappointed.

"No. That's okay. Go ahead and get dessert," she said.

Davy slashed the air and mouthed. "No. I want him home."

Olivia shook her head at him and continued, "Just have him home before eight-thirty if you can."

"No problem. See you soon." The phone was quiet for a brief second, then she heard, "Love you," and Tom disconnected.

"What were you thinking?" Davy's voice was tight with anger. "Why would you let him keep Brian out any longer than he already has?"

"Brian is fine. I heard him."

"So why not get him home while he's still fine?"

"And what was I supposed to say? It's a Friday night. No school tomorrow. Why shouldn't they get frozen yogurt to top off a fun day?"

"I don't know." Davy resumed his pacing. "You could have thought of something."

"No, I couldn't." When she heard Brian's voice through the phone, the tension she'd been under all evening had drained away, leaving her limp and exhausted. She didn't have the energy to argue with Davy, or Tom, or anyone else. "Nothing that wouldn't sound incredibly suspicious and, frankly, ungrateful. This man has spent all kinds of time and money to make our son happy. And Brian sounded happy."

"I don't care if he's happy. I want him safe."

"If Tom is the monster you think he is, the last thing we want to do is make him angry. Not while Brian is alone with him."

Davy clamped his jaw shut. Her point must have hit home. He walked into the kitchen, and she heard him pour himself another cup of coffee. He returned to the living room, set his mug on the coffee table, offered her a hand, and pulled her to her feet. As soon as she was standing, he put his arms around her and drew her close.

The familiar planes of his chest, the smell of him, the rough texture of his sweater against her cheek combined to create a symphony of emotions. Nostalgia, yearning, anger, and loss overwhelmed her. She pushed him away with a gentle shove.

"So how do we handle it when they get here?" He stepped away from her and wiped his eyes with his sleeve.

"Maybe you should go."

"No, I want—"

"It'll look strange. You being here."

He glanced around the room as if he was seeing it for the first time. "Maybe you're right."

"I am right."

"I'm going to wait down the street."

"Why?"

"I want to make sure you're safe. If Tom isn't outside within fifteen minutes or less from the time he gets here, I'm coming in."

"Davy, I—"

"Don't bother." He held up a hand. "Nothing you can say is going to change my mind."

The set of his jaw told her he was speaking the truth. "Don't let him see you."

Davy nodded. "I'll park under the trees and turn off the car. He'll never notice me."

Olivia remembered how his car almost disappeared in the shade of those trees in daylight. "Okay."

Davy walked out the door and halfway up the path to the street, stopped, then turned to look at her. "I know I didn't take care of you as I should have. I failed you when you needed me. I'm not going to do it again. No matter what happens between us, Olivia, I'm here for you and for Brian. I'm going to keep you safe."

He walked the rest of the way to the car, started it and pulled it into the darkness at the end of the block, invisible but present. Something comforting and warm wrapped around her like a flannel robe, and she relaxed for the first time that day.

MOLLY: Sorry to leave you on such a cliffhanger, but we're almost out of time. Those were quite the revelations about Tom. Based on the new info, I'd dump him. After he brought my kid home safe and sound, though.

It definitely seems that neither Proctor nor Davy left the messages for Olivia. So, who did? Tom? But wouldn't that be counterproductive to him?

Oh, and what did Scottie Travers' death have to do with the boys in the other articles? Was it accidental, as the papers reported? This episode created more questions than it answered.

Let's hear from Sage. Maybe her diary will give us some clues.

Sunday, July 19th, 1992

Lily, Tomas, Doug, and I all lined up in the pew my family had called their own for as long as I could remember. Father Junipero Serra, founder of the San Juan Capistrano Mission, was the first to celebrate mass in this chapel in 1783, and the tradition had been continued through the centuries. Abuela Maria claimed to be descended on her mother's side from the Juaneño Native Americans who built the very walls surrounding me now. The familiar scent of incense, the intonations of priest and congregants, the rhythms of the mass echoing from the ancient stones were as comforting to me as my grandmother's arms.

Today was the first Sunday Doug had attended mass since the accident. When he'd first come home, he wasn't strong enough to make the walk, or even to sit up on the wood bench if I'd driven him. Later, he wasn't interested. Whether he was angry at God, or no longer believed He existed, he never said, and I was afraid to ask.

This morning, he came out of the bedroom dressed in chinos, a shirt and tie, face shaved, and hair combed. He didn't explain, and I didn't question him. I made a decision right then and there to enjoy the morning. Walking in the sunshine, husband at my side, children skipping on ahead—just the way it had been before. It was a break in the windstorm of my present life, and it was as welcome as rain after a drought.

That little bit of joy disappeared as soon as I saw my neighbors. We'd been avoiding each other in the week since Pepe's poisoning. Now we'd have to pass by them to leave the building.

If we dawdled, maybe they'd exit first, but we'd surely run into them outside. After mass, adults congregated in small circles to catch up on neighborhood gossip, plan bake sales, and argue about who would win whatever game was on TV that day. Children ran off the steam they'd built during mass. My only hope was to hurry my family past as quickly as I could.

After the benediction, I rose, pushed Lily and Tomas ahead of me and joined the stream moving toward the doors. When I got outside, I reached for my children. I took Lily's hand first, but before I could grab Tomas, he took off at a run. "Tomas," I called after him.

"Let him go," Doug said.

"I have a roast to put in the oven."

"It'll keep. I'm not going to be run out of my own church." Doug's voice was harsh. We'd never talked about Pepe's poisoning. The day after Paul came over, I'd found bloody butcher paper under a bag in the outside trash. I knew the truth. I didn't need to talk about it. Pepe had recovered. Paul never called the police. The event was behind us, at least that's what I'd thought.

Doug walked over to a group of men he used to do an early morning Bible study with and left Lily and me where we stood. Lily looked up at me, a question in her eyes. "Go play," I said. She skipped off in the direction her brother had gone.

I shielded my eyes with a hand and looked over all the cliques, trying to decide which to join. There was a time I'd have made a beeline to Mary, but our friendship had been strained to the breaking point.

Three ladies from the church decorating committee stood together at the end of the path. I was in charge of the floral arrangements for an upcoming service. I'd wanted to run my idea of including lavender in with the traditional yellow roses by them. It was a good excuse to avoid the group gathered around Mary.

Before I'd gone even five steps in their direction, a shout stopped me. A second later the sound of children's voices, excited and distressed, were raised. Adults began to break away from their groups, first one, then another, then in twos and threes. All hurried toward the noise.

I didn't follow. My feet felt fixed to the sidewalk. There'd been so much pain in my life lately, surely this disturbance, whatever it was, belonged to somebody else. But then I heard Lily scream. I broke free from the concrete and ran.

By the time I reached the crowd on the Mission courtyard, Tomas and Scottie had been pulled apart. Paul's arms were wrapped around his son. Father O'Brien held Tomas by the collar.

Both were filthy. Streaks of dirty tears and snot striped their faces. Blood poured from Scottie's nose. A purple bruise was already forming around Tomas's right eye. Lily hugged herself with thin arms and wept. Doug stood by, still as one of the icons in the sanctuary. He neither reprimanded his son nor comforted his daughter.

"What's going on here?" I heard my voice as if from a distance.

"Now, now. It's just boys being boys." Father O'Brien, wise as he was in many ways, wasn't a modern parent. Men were hardly allowed to be men anymore; boys certainly couldn't plead testosterone as a defense. "There's nothing to see here." The priest waved away his parishioners.

Parents collected children and moved slowly toward the chapel, glancing over their shoulders at our two families left on the grass.

"Now what's all the kerfuffle?" Father O'Brien addressed the boys with a humorous lilt, trying to lift the mood with his voice. But the boys stared at each other silently. "It can't be that bad. Why don't we shake and be done with it?" No one said a word.

The priest looked from Doug to Paul and back again. "Best you try to get to the bottom of things at home then." Paul nodded, and Father O'Brien walked into his church.

Paul, arm around his shaking son, led his family across the grass toward home. I wanted to give them a head start. We were all going the same way. I couldn't imagine anything more awkward than walking side by side up Los Rios Street. But Doug clamped a strong hand at the nape of Tomas's neck and steered him in the same direction.

Lily and I hung back. When Doug realized we weren't behind him, he spun around and glared. The look on his face sent fear trickling like ice water through my veins. I followed. Our two families trudged through the streets—a tragic parade for the neighborhood.

After the trek up the long gravel drive, the Travers family veered right to their home. Doug pushed Tomas up onto the porch and through the front door. He started yelling as soon as the screen slapped closed behind them.

I sat on the steps and pulled Lily into my lap. At that moment I thought this might be the worst day of my life. I was wrong.

MOLLY: It appears that Doug did more than poison a dog. He poisoned two families. There were so many relationships ruined. Tomas and Scottie's,

Mary and Sage's, even Abby and Lily's, were irrevocably damaged by that one act.

It still doesn't answer our questions about Scottie's death, however. We'll have to wait for a future episode for more information.

Our question for the week is: Do you think Davy was being self-serving or paranoid for wanting Olivia to keep Brian away from Tom? Or were his suspicions legitimate? I know what I think, but I know the end of the story.

(cue music)

VO: This episode is sponsored by Nightshade Gallery in Laguna Beach, for collectors of avant-garde fine art. *Murders Under the Sun* is edited by Jim Wilbourne, theme music is by Eclectic Blends, and I'm your host, Molly Shure.

part eight

MURDERS UNDER THE SUN
SEASON TWO; EPISODE SEVEN

MOLLY: Welcome back to Season Two of *Murders Under the Sun*. This is episode seven, and I'm Molly Shure, your host.

Things are going to get gritty today, people. Just want to warn you up front, you're not going to need a latte to get through the afternoon after listening to this one. Your adrenaline will be pumping.

Brian did come home safe and sound, as many of you guessed in the group chat. And it seems Olivia also agreed with the bulk of you regarding what she should do about Tom. We discover almost immediately that she decided to avoid him. Maybe she felt a little guilty about it, but she knew it was best for Brian. Whew.

Except we don't get to exhale for long.

I don't want to give anything away, though, so I'd better stop talking. Here's Olivia.

2.7.2

OLIVIA HADN'T SEEN Tom in over a week, not since the night he took Brian to the horse show. Avoiding him hadn't been difficult. Brian had come down with a cold the next day. He couldn't go to school or his tutoring sessions all week. By Wednesday, Olivia was running a fever and coughing along with her son.

The forced vacation from her usual nonstop schedule had given her a chance to think. She'd come to the conclusion she had to end things with Tom. Not because she believed he'd done some terrible thing, but because she didn't believe he hadn't. She couldn't be with a man she didn't fully trust. Not again.

Her suspicions made her feel guilty. She couldn't shake the idea the newspaper articles were from a scorned lover from Tom's past who wanted to punish him for something or keep him for herself. But it didn't matter. She had to get back to the business of rebuilding her own life and her son's. She didn't have the time, or energy for the drama. Nor could she risk CPS getting wind of anything even remotely threatening to her son's safety.

Davy had brought offerings when he heard she was sick too: chicken soup, ice cream, and pizza. He'd stayed to play video games and watch movies, and generally hovered. It surprised her how nice it had been to have him around, how comfortable. She'd allowed herself to feel hopeful about him for the first time since they'd broken up. Not that they'd get back together, never that. But maybe they could be friends again. Davy had been a friend before he was a husband.

He was in her Statistics class. She'd watched him flirt with the girls and yuck it up with the guys and dismissed him as a shallow frat boy. Until the first quiz. She sat at her desk after class was dismissed, paper in hand, and tears in her eyes, staring at the large "66" at the top of her page.

"Ouch." Davy sat in the chair in front of her.

"I'm hopeless at this stuff. It doesn't make sense, no matter how hard I study."

"Maybe I can help. Statistics is one of the few subjects I'm good at." His smile was self-deprecating.

She hadn't thought about their tutoring sessions in years, and the memory brought a smile to her face. They'd met in a quiet corner of the library, which was their first mistake. After two weeks, they'd found it impossible to keep their minds on their books and their hands off each other. Olivia had almost flunked Statistics.

It was Sunday night, and Davy had brought Brian home early. The boys were at her place now playing *Iron Kingdom*, while she picked up Chinese food. They hadn't had a real meal together, all three of them, in over a year.

She passed her ATM card to a teenage boy behind the counter, grabbed a couple of extra chopsticks and the fragrant, white bag. He ran the card and returned it. She pushed open the restaurant door with one hip as she fiddled with all the items in her hands. She shifted the bag of food under her arm. She needed both hands to stuff her card into her overstuffed wallet. She dropped the wallet into her purse and began searching through it for her car keys. Halfway across the parking lot, she found them. That was the first time she looked up. When she did, she stopped short. Her heart jumped a hurdle.

Tom leaned on the front fender of her SUV, ankles and arms crossed, watching her. What was he doing here? She plastered an uneasy smile on her face and walked toward him with measured steps. She didn't want to see him. Not now. Her plan had been to talk to him when they went out this week, to tell him face to face she was breaking things off. For an awkward second, she worried he'd read her mind and had come to confront her.

"What's up?" she asked when she got close.

"Waiting for you." A flash of bright teeth.

"Nice surprise." It wasn't.

"I thought maybe you were avoiding me." He put his hands on her shoulders and leaned in for a kiss. Olivia turned her head, and it landed on her cheek.

"Wouldn't kiss me." She kept her voice light. "I might still be contagious."

He backed away with his hands up. "You look so good, I forgot."

The sun was setting behind him, leaving his face in dark silhouette, making it hard to read his expression. "How did you know I'd be here?" she said.

"I didn't. I stopped by the grocery store." He pointed to the big market that anchored the shopping center. "And saw your car. You haven't been very communicative this week. I figured if Mohamed wouldn't come to the mountain, and all that."

"So, you saw the mountain and decided to park in front of it?" Olivia's nerves were singing.

"Pretty much."

The lights in the parking lot popped on all at once. She jumped.

"I missed you." His voice quieted. Shadows deepened the furrows in his forehead.

"Tuesday..." She changed the subject.

"Right, are we still on?"

"Sure." She could feel the Chinese food cooling in her hands. It was getting late, and she wanted to go home.

"Great. Pick you up at six-thirty," he said.

"Why don't I meet you at Korba's? I'll be coming straight from work." Korba's was a family-owned Greek restaurant she often went to. It was a quiet spot, good for a somber conversation. She didn't want Tom to come to her condo. She didn't want to go to his home either. A public place, neutral territory, seemed best.

"That's the place on Crown Valley, right?"

Olivia nodded.

"Sounds great." He moved toward her, but she retreated.

"Cold. Remember?"

"Oh, right." He waved a hand instead, then walked past her into the next row of cars. He raised his electronic key and a nearby vehicle chirped to life. She watched him pull out of the lot. A feeling of emptiness washed over her. It had been nice having a man in her life again.

2.7.3

KORBA'S WAS busy and boisterous. Olivia had forgotten about the *balalaika* player who sometimes performed on Tuesdays. They followed Phil, the owner, through the maze of tables to a spot in the corner close to the kitchen door. It was far enough away from the music to carry on a conversation without shouting, so she didn't complain about the constant inhale and exhale of warm air and the parade of platters streaming past.

After they were seated and ordered a carafe of Greek wine, Tom straightened in his chair. He looked like he was bracing himself. "You've been mysterious lately."

"I haven't meant to be. Just home. With Brian."

"I wish you'd have let me come by. I could've brought Mom's famous herbal cold remedy."

"No sense in you getting sick." She wasn't sure how much longer she could keep up the small talk, or how much longer she should. She didn't want to order dinner, give him the bad news during appetizers, then talk about the weather while they ate their main meal. On the other hand, dumping him after he paid the bill seemed like bad form.

She didn't have much experience with break-ups. Only Davy, and she'd ended their marriage by throwing his things onto the front lawn and changing the locks. That hardly seemed appropriate here.

"So, what have you been doing for the past week and a half?" Tom asked.

"Oh, let's see, I watched three Disney movies, two superhero films, passed the first level of *Iron Kingdom* with a lot of help from Brian and ate. A ton. This week I have to catch up on all the work I didn't do last week."

"Cold didn't bother your appetite?"

"Oh, no."

"So where were you when I called Tuesday? Or Wednesday, or Friday for that matter. I figured you'd be bouncing off the walls with boredom."

Olivia didn't know how to answer. She'd seen the calls but let them go to voice mail. She hadn't been ready to talk to him, but she couldn't say that. "I don't know, sleeping or taking care of Brian."

"You could've returned the calls."

He'd just pushed right past the small talk phase of the date, so that answered her first question. The second question was more complicated. How did one do this kind of thing? "Listen—"

But she was saved from having to stammer out what she'd come to say by their server. He set the carafe and two glasses on the table, pulled a pad from his apron, and stood at the ready.

"Do you want to share the falafel?" Tom asked her. "Then we could get some appetizers."

She nodded. She didn't care what they ordered. She wouldn't be able to eat anyway. Her stomach was in tangles.

As soon as the server walked away, the *balalaika* player struck up a rowdy tune. Two children, maybe four and six years of age, brother and sister by the look of them, leaped up from their seats and began to dance with abandon between the tables. Several customers clapped to the song's rhythm and cheered them on while their parents watched with fond faces.

This wasn't the time or place for the serious conversation Olivia had planned. She couldn't imagine delivering her news over the heads of the jigging youngsters. *I like you, Tom, but...*

When the song ended, the children sat, but the atmosphere in the restaurant remained festive. It stayed festive throughout the hummus and pita bread, the salad, and the main course. Olivia wracked her brain for safe topics, redirected their dialog when it strayed too close to the cliffs, and glued interested smiles onto her face. By the time the *loukoumades* arrived, her cheeks hurt. She drained the dregs of wine from her glass, and nibbled on a donut, exhausted.

"Full?" Tom asked as he signed the check.

She nodded, the weight of what she was about to do piled atop the heavy dinner in her gut. It made her queasy. She marched the length of the restaurant like a condemned prisoner on the way to a painful, but just, punishment. When they stepped out into the evening chill, Tom wrapped an arm around her shoulders and pulled her close. "Where to now?"

Olivia pondered her answer. It was too cold to talk to him here, on the street—both literally and figuratively. Resistance rose up strong and solid at the idea of having him in her home. "How about your place?"

As soon as the words left her lips, she doubted the wisdom of them. She fretted all the way along Coast Highway, and inland toward San Juan Capistrano. He probably thought she was finally acquiescing about spending the night. He'd mentioned it two or three times.

She'd never slept with him, and she knew it bothered him, made him feel she didn't take their relationship seriously. Now she had to tell him she never would.

The truth was Davy was the only man she'd ever been with. Not that she was a prude. Her abstinence came more from anxiety than morality. She'd gotten close with Craig Caldwell—high school math class nerd—once. But as soon as she saw the excitement in his eyes, she'd shut down. It had reminded her too much of Proctor.

She pulled up to the curb in front of Tom's place and turned off the ignition. She would make this short, sweet, and to the point. No nightcap. No long-winded explanations. She'd deliver the blow, and leave.

Tom hurried inside, turning on lights as he went. She followed behind him, struck again by the austere perfection of his home. How had she ever believed they'd be good together? Her house was comfortable, like a favorite worn and faded sweatshirt. His was an Armani suit. It soothed her conscience to think it would never have worked.

Even if she hadn't known about the boy from the Boise school, or the other child and his mother from Phoenix, she knew she and Tom didn't mix. He was cold-pressed extra virgin olive oil. She was plain old tap water.

"Come over by the fire and get warm," Tom said, shaking out the match he'd used to light the gas logs. "I'll open a bottle of wine."

"No wine for me. I have to drive."

"You only had one glass at dinner." His eyebrows raised in surprise.

"We need to talk." There she'd said it, the trite phrase that started every breakup. The gauntlet was thrown.

"Oh." His eyes narrowed.

"I'm so sorry—"

He held up a hand, stopping her. "Why don't you tell me the issues."

"It's me. It's my life. It's—"

"Don't jack me around, Olivia."

"But it is my life. It's Brian. It's the new business. I don't... I can't be someone's girlfriend right now. I don't have time to do it right."

Tom sat in a chair near the fire and stared at her with blank eyes. "Brian doesn't want me around."

"He hasn't said that."

"But he doesn't have to, does he?"

The room was cold, but Olivia didn't want to move closer to the fire, closer to him. She hugged herself instead. "What do you mean?"

Tom's eyes flashed green in the firelight. "I've tried, Olivia. I reached out during soccer season. I've tutored him. I took him to the horse show."

"I know you have. I appreciate it."

"He's not going to accept anybody but Davy. You do know that, right? He'll sabotage every relationship you have until he's old enough to move out."

"It's not about Brian."

"But you said it was." The frost in his voice startled her.

"I mean, it's not that Brian doesn't like you, doesn't approve. He had a great time at *Calavia*. He talked about it for a week."

"Good, because regardless of what happens here, between us, it doesn't impact my offer to tutor him."

She'd let Brian finish out the year. He only had a few more sessions.

Not continuing after the Christmas break would be less awkward than pulling him now, and Brian had to see Tom at school. She didn't want to create anymore strain on their relationship than there already was.

"What is the problem, Olivia?" he said.

She searched her mind for an explanation. "It's this." She gestured to the room around her. "Your home, it's like you. So put together. You have such a tight rein on your life. I'm not like that." She realized the truth of her words as she said them.

"So, what, I'm wound too tight for you?"

"Maybe. That's part of it. It's also that you're so decided about things." The more she spoke the more confident she felt. She'd had qualms about Tom from the beginning, but she hadn't wanted to examine them. She'd wanted it to work. The vague doubts now grew distinct and sharp-edged as she voiced them. "You know what you want. You know where you're going. I need space to figure those things out for myself."

"Is it Davy?"

"No." She spoke too quickly. His abrupt change in topic threw her. And, of course, it was Davy. Not in the way Tom meant, but she had promised Davy she'd do what she had to do to keep Brian's and Tom's relationship purely professional. If information surfaced about Tom's past that resulted in his firing, Davy didn't want Brian hurt or confused.

"Davy and I have a reluctant friendship, which is good for Brian. Davy is making an effort. I'm beginning to forgive, let go of the anger. But it's not romantic."

"There's something you're not telling me." Tom's voice was emotionless, like he was puzzling over a math problem.

"I don't know what you want me to say. Nobody gave me a script. I just know this isn't right for either one of us."

"Speak for yourself." His words were cold and blunt.

She felt as if she'd been slapped. She suppressed the anger that was beginning to simmer in her belly. He was hurt. What was that her mother used to say, *hurt people hurt people*? "Okay. Speaking for myself then, it isn't right. For me." She pivoted and began to walk out of the room. She'd better leave before she said something she'd regret later.

"I'll give you time," he said to her retreating form.

She turned to look at him so he could see her resolve. "I don't need time."

A small, condescending smile crept across his face. "I think you do."

2.7.4

FIONA WINCED as she rearranged herself in the chair next to the lobby desk and stretched her spine. "I'm so glad I paid extra for ergonomically designed office furniture." Olivia smiled at the sarcasm in her voice, remembering how uncomfortable even the first months of pregnancy could be. "So, you broke up with him on Tuesday night?" Fiona continued the conversation they'd been having before her condition interrupted them.

"I did, but I'm not sure he believes it." Olivia checked the last two boxes on the order form she'd been working on, hit send and closed her laptop.

"How can that be?"

"I told him we weren't right for each other, and he said, 'I'll give you some time.'"

"Time for what?"

"To change my mind, I guess."

"But you're not going to." It was a statement, not a question. Fiona had sided with Davy as soon as she learned that Tom had dated the Phoenix boy's mother.

"No. Especially not now. I may have had some qualms about it at first, but I knew I'd done the right thing as soon as I told him."

"It's too bad." Fiona ran a lazy finger in circles around her belly like she was playing with a lock of her child's hair. "He seemed like such a nice guy in the beginning. So perfect for you."

"Yeah, well, looks can be deceiving. Even his mother admitted he's controlling."

"I wonder if Sage knows you broke up. She was in this morning, but she didn't say anything. Not to me, anyway. Did she say anything to you?"

"No, but it's only been two days."

"I'm sure she'll take it in stride."

"I hope so. The tincture has helped Brian so much. I don't know where else to get it."

Fiona anchored her hands, one on the desk, the other on the chair, and heaved herself up. "I'm looking forward to carrying this child in my arms."

Olivia smiled. If Fiona was this uncomfortable at five months, she couldn't imagine what she'd be like at the end of her pregnancy. "Just wait. My last trimester Davy had to cut my toenails for me. I couldn't reach them."

"Devon gave me a pedicure last week." She pointed a sandaled foot, nails painted metallic blue, in Olivia's direction. "He's practicing. I want my feet to look good in the stirrups."

"That's important." Olivia slid the pile of work she'd been assembling all day into her tote bag and checked her watch. She had to pick up Brian from school right on time. He had math tutoring until 4:30, and she'd asked him to meet her out front, so she didn't have to see Tom.

"You're not too sad?" Fiona said, pulling on a long sweater.

"Off and on," Olivia said. "But nothing like when Davy and I broke up. That was like an amputation." Olivia's cell phone chirped from somewhere. She followed the sound and found it under a pile of exercise tops she'd been folding earlier.

"Is Ms. Richards there," the voice on the other end said.

"This is she."

"I'm calling from the infirmary at St. Barnabas. Your son, Brian— don't worry, he's fine—but he's had an incident."

"What kind of incident?" A band of tension slid around the top of Olivia's head.

"He's disoriented, confused. One of the staff found him wandering off campus. I thought maybe he'd hit his head on the playground, but I can't find any sign of injury."

"Confused how?" Olivia grabbed her bags and moved toward the door.

"What's wrong?" Fiona's face was filled with concern.

"I don't know," Olivia mouthed to her.

"He wasn't sure where he was for a while, but he's coming around. Aren't you, Brian?" Olivia heard her son's voice in the distance. "I'm at school." He sounded distant and disinterested.

"I'll be there in ten minutes," Olivia said and raced to her car.

2.7.5

THE NEXT WEEK and a half were a roller coaster ride. As soon as Olivia had brought Brian home from school, she'd called Dr. Gallagher's office. His nurse suggested she keep an incident diary like the one she'd kept right after the accident, then make an appointment in a couple of weeks.

The doctor wanted to see if this was an anomaly, or if there was a pattern. The diary would be important to present to CPS as well. Olivia needed Fred to see she was on top of the problem. She looked at the pages now as she sat in the waiting room of the Children's Hospital of Orange County center in Mission Hospital.

Thursday, December 14th - Brian became confused and disoriented. Tried to leave school. When a teacher stopped him, he wasn't sure where he was.

Friday, December 15th - Brian told Mrs. Margolis, his teacher, that Crackers, his dog, had given birth to a litter of puppies the night before. When Mrs. Margolis said she'd thought Crackers was male, Brian became visibly disturbed. He approached her several times during the remainder of the day, asking if he could leave the room to call his father. He wanted to tell him they were wrong about the sex of the dog.

Saturday, December 16th - Brian went to his father's during the day and returned home at night. No incidents.

Sunday, December 17th - Brian spent the day with his dad again and returned home at night. Neither his father, nor I noticed any unusual behavior.

Monday, December 18th - There were no incidents.

Tuesday, December 19th - Brian wandered into the wrong classroom in the late afternoon, sat in an empty chair, and watched the instructor marking papers for several minutes before he was noticed. The teacher brought him to the school nurse, who called me.

Wednesday, December 20th - A male teacher ran into the boy's restroom when he heard a scream. Brian stood against a wall and directed the teacher's attention to one of the stalls. He claimed there was a dead kitten in the toilet. The toilet was empty.

There had been another incident after she'd entered Wednesday's record. Olivia brought Brian home, called the doctor and made an appointment for Friday morning. He went to bed early, complaining of fatigue. At about 11:45 that night, she was awakened by his screams.

She ran into his room and found him kneeling in his bed, eyes wide open, and gibbering about an armored man with an ax. She held him while he slapped at imaginary monsters and waited for Davy to come. It seemed she'd done nothing but wait since.

They'd waited in the ER until three in the morning for Brian to be seen. A four-car pileup had come in an hour before she, Davy, and Brian had gotten there. Bleeding patients get top priority. By the time anyone could see Brian he was sound asleep with his head on Davy's shoulder. The young attending doctor had to wake him to examine him. After hearing the saga of the past weeks and talking to Dr. Gallagher on the phone, he had Brian admitted.

Returning to the CHOC center was a homecoming of sorts. The staff welcomed Olivia like a long-lost cousin. She'd lived a lifetime in its rooms once.

It was now 2:15 in the afternoon. She'd been waiting in the appropriately named waiting room to hear the results of the battery of tests performed on her son. Her life had taken on the familiar unreality of an isolation tank. She was suspended in the ebb and flow of medical staff, other children's waiting family members, and cups of tepid coffee. The Fishbowl, Tom, Sage, Proctor everything that had happened the past two and a half months seemed like a dream.

Her only lifeline to the world outside the hospital walls was Davy. He gave her hope the passage of time hadn't been an illusion. Brian had been better. She had been optimistic about their future. She held onto the knowledge that the last time she'd been here, she'd been alone. Davy had been drowning in his own alcohol-soaked despair and unable to help her. Now he was here.

Dr. Gallagher entered the room. Davy stood, but Olivia's knees were too weak to hold her. The doctor shook his gray head, and she braced herself for bad news.

"I can't find anything wrong with him," he said. She wasn't sure she'd heard him right. "Passed all the tests with flying colors."

"Then why the hallucinations, the memory lapses?" Davy asked.

Dr. Gallagher answered, but Olivia couldn't hear him. She was still trying to process his words; *I can't find anything wrong with him. Nothing wrong with him.* A tentative joy bubbled up inside her. *Nothing wrong.*

Was that good news, or bad? Nothing wrong certainly sounded good. Every mother wants to hear test results are negative and their child has a clean bill of health. But if nothing was wrong, why was he losing his grip on reality again?

"I don't think they were hallucinations in the strictest sense. I believe Brian is confabulating again—filling in some memory lapses with segments from his dreams. Now that's a guess, but it makes sense. We know he's struggled with TGAs—incidents of temporary global amnesia—since the accident, but he's never hallucinated.

"However, there's a lot about the brain we don't understand. Sometimes healing is three steps forward and two steps back. I'd like to prescribe an antidepressant, anti-anxiety drug. Very short term. Just to see if we can get him to focus, sleep soundly at night. Maybe we can reverse this thing. Let's keep a close watch. Keep the diary going. Barring a big change, I'll see him in a couple of weeks."

The joy in Olivia's chest burst into full flower. Davy enveloped her in a bear hug and lifted her off the floor. "Let's go get him and take him home."

2.7.6

OLIVIA LEANED over the passenger side of her car for a better view of the St. Barnabas students grouped on the sidewalk waiting to be picked up. She'd kept Brian home on Thursday, but today was the last day of school before Christmas break, and his class was having a party. He'd wanted to go.

She didn't see Brian, but the assembly of kids were a blur of blue and white uniforms from where she sat. There was a long line of minivans and SUVs in front of her. She wished she'd arrived earlier, before the crush of parents arrived.

Brian hadn't had an episode since he'd been released from the hospital but worry still dogged her. She didn't like the subdued behavior the prescription had brought on. He'd slept a lot the past two days, ate little, and talked even less.

Seven cars later, Olivia pulled up to the curb in front of the school and scanned the children's faces. Brian's wasn't among them. A ripple of concern passed over her. She rolled down her window, leaned out and addressed the traffic monitor—a pretty mom volunteer with dark eyes whose slender frame swam in the orange uniform vest. "Has Mrs. Margolis's class been dismissed? I don't see my son."

"I don't know the fourth-grade students," the monitor said, an apology in her voice. "My daughter is in kindergarten."

Olivia didn't recognize any of the children still grouped on the sidewalk. Most of them looked older than Brian. A horn honked behind her. "Why don't you make a left up ahead and park in the teacher's lot? Just tell the monitor there Chihiro said to move the cones for you." Two more horns sounded behind Olivia as she pulled away from the curb.

She parked at the end of the teachers' lot and headed toward the building, keeping an eye out for Brian as she walked. Even though the scream in the bathroom and the nightmare were more dramatic than his attempt to leave campus two weeks ago, it was the wandering that upset her most. She'd worried ever since that he might try it again and succeed.

She climbed the stone steps of the school two at a time, weaving her way between the high school students pouring through the front doors. The high school and junior high dismissed a half hour after elementary school in the hopes of staggering pickup times and reducing the traffic jam. Brian should have been at the curb thirty minutes ago.

She reached the second floor and strode to his classroom. Mrs. Margolis looked up as Olivia entered. "Olivia. Hi." Her voice lilted upward in an unspoken question.

"I'm looking for Brian. He wasn't at pickup."

"He left," the teacher looked at her watch, "at least twenty minutes ago. I dismissed class a little late, but he had plenty of time to get to the curb."

"He wasn't there."

Adrienne Margolis's mouth tightened into a thin line. She was aware of Brian's problems and had agreed to help keep a close eye on him. She shouldn't have let him walk out alone. "Have you checked the principal's office? If anything happened between here and the exit, that's where he'd be taken. There or the infirmary."

Olivia jogged to the stairwell and up another flight. She shouldn't have trusted Adrienne Margolis. The woman's attention was always on the bright students, the easy students. The difficult ones weren't on her radar screen. Olivia's heart rate rose both from anger and the sudden exertion of the stairs. She was breathing hard by the time she opened the door to Art's office.

Millie Abraham, personal assistant to St. Barnabas principals for almost as long as the school had been in existence, sat behind an aged mahogany desk the same color as her skin. "Olivia." A smile flashed, then faded when she saw Olivia's expression. "What's the matter?"

"I can't find Brian." Olivia said, hoping her words didn't sound as desperate as she felt.

"You went to his class—"

"Yes." Olivia interrupted. "Mrs. Margolis thought he might be here."

"I'm sorry, dear." Millie shook her head, sympathy in her eyes. "I'll let Art know. We can alert the traffic team. They all have walkie-talkies. Did you try the nurse's office?"

Back to the stairwell, down three flights this time, and right toward the cafeteria. By the time Olivia reached the infirmary, she was in a rolling sweat. The school nurse wasn't at her desk. Olivia crossed the short hall behind it and pushed a partially opened door to reveal a small exam room.

Nurse Phillips, a plump middle-aged woman in scarlet scrubs, pressed a tissue to the nose of a boy lying on the table. Her head snapped around; indignation written on her face. "Can I help you?"

Olivia was past propriety. "I'm looking for my son."

With deliberate movements, the nurse placed the boy's hand on the tissue, patted it and said, "Hold onto that. It'll stop in a minute." She moved in slow motion into the hall and closed the door behind her. She turned toward Olivia, crossed her arms over her ample bosom and said, "Now, what can I do for you? Mrs. Richards, isn't it?"

It was Ms. Richards, but Olivia didn't bother correcting her. "I'm looking for my son, Brian. He was in here a couple of weeks ago."

"I remember. He was confused about where he was." She offered Olivia a small, sympathetic smile. "How is he doing?"

"Up and down," Olivia said, her words brisk. "I need to find him. He wasn't at the curb."

"Have you checked his class—"

"Yes." Olivia cut her short and bolted out the infirmary door. Why did everyone keep asking her if she'd gone to his classroom? Did they think she was an idiot? She ran halfway down the hall, then stopped. She had no idea where she was going. Think. Think. Where might Brian go?

He left his room with the rest of the class but never made it to the curb. Somewhere in the building? Or, he had gone to the curb, but didn't stop there? Had he decided to go home on his own? It was a long walk, a couple of miles, but they'd done it together once or twice when her car was in the shop. She stood, torn by indecision. Should she get into the car and take the route they'd walked? Or stay and search the school grounds?

"Olivia." A reluctant voice broke into her chaotic thoughts. Tom stood several yards away, a stack of files in his arms.

A wave of emotions washed over her--guilt, longing, regret, and, when she saw the look of concern on his face, relief. Even though they'd broken up, even though she knew he wasn't right for her, for her son, she was drawn to his strength. "Have you seen Brian?"

He hesitated, then came toward her. "No. I haven't."

"I can't find him anywhere." Olivia choked back a sob. Her hands flew to her face. She heard the files hit the floor with a slap and felt arms encircle her.

"Tell me. What's happening?" he said.

"He wasn't at pickup." She allowed herself to collapse into the solid wall of his chest for a short moment, pushed gently away and wiped her eyes with her hand. "And before you ask me, he wasn't in his classroom, Art's office, or the infirmary."

"I heard someone stopped him from wandering off a while ago. Do you know where they found him? Which way he was going?"

"No. Who would know that? That's a good idea. A place to start."

Olivia called Davy while Tom took charge of contacting all the members of the traffic team. No one remembered who stopped Brian the last time he'd tried to leave, or where he'd been exactly, but many dropped what they were doing to come help with the search. Volunteers were sent out to walk the campus perimeters and the neighborhoods that bordered the school.

Davy arrived within fifteen minutes of Olivia's call. She met him in the parking lot. "Any word?" he said. The agony on his face shocked her into reality. She'd gotten so involved in the logistics of finding Brian, the angst of losing him had been shoved into a dark inner corner.

She blinked, trying to clear her eyes of tears. "The police are patrolling the area. He couldn't have gotten far on foot."

"What about an AMBER Alert?" Davy ran a hand through his hair.

"They don't activate AMBER Alerts for kids who wander off, only for ones they suspect have been taken."

"They don't know if someone's taken him or not." His voice rose an octave. "Kids who wander off on their own make great targets for predators."

"Don't say that." She put both hands on her chest to stop the panic thudding through her.

"I'm sorry." Davy hugged her hard. "I didn't mean that. I'm just frantic. I don't know what I'm saying." He broke away and headed toward the school. Olivia had to jog to keep up with him.

"We've set up an emergency station in Art's office. Millie is organizing teachers, volunteers, even some high school students to look for Brian," she said between breaths.

Based on the somber look on Millie's face when they reached the office, there'd been no news. Several of the children from his class had been called, but none had noticed where Brian had gone after they'd been released. He hadn't made any close friends since the accident, and his old ones had fallen away. He didn't have a buddy to walk out of class with. Olivia vowed she'd change that when they found him.

She sat in a chair across from Millie's desk, stared at the phone and chewed her fingernails to stubs while Davy paced and pulled his hair into spikes. A walkie-talkie crackled to life. Millie answered it.

"Sun's setting in about an hour. I'm heading home," a female voice on the other end said. "I'm sorry, but I have to get my kids from the sitter."

"No problem, Kathy. Thanks for all your hard work."

"Keep me posted. I'm worried about the little guy."

"Will do." Millie gave Olivia a sad smile.

Every few minutes another call came through to let Millie know someone else was giving up the search for the night. Each contact was another stab of pain. Tom was the last to call. He asked to speak to Olivia. Davy looked at her, a troubled question in his eyes. She ignored him.

"I'm so sorry. I have a commitment I can't get out of, but I'll only be gone for a couple of hours," Tom said.

"No. That's okay. I appreciate all you've done."

"We'll find him, Olivia. It's only a matter of time."

"I know." She said the words but was no longer sure she believed them. A movie had been looping on instant replay in her mind for the past hour. It began with Brian's birth, the cord around his neck and the blue hue of his skin. The pediatrician saying, "It was a close call."

Scene two: Brian, four years old in the arms of a uniformed officer with a stern face. "Lady, you need to keep better tabs on your kid."

Pan to Brian, age seven, covered in mud, being led by another child's mother back to the birthday party in the park after an agonizing forty-five minutes. "He was by the stream."

And, the most painful scene, Brian, small at ten, lying in a hospital bed covered in bruises. The doctor saying, "We don't know the extent of the damage." It seemed no matter how desperately Olivia tried to hold onto him, Brian slipped through her hands like water.

The office door opened. She pivoted toward it hoping for one crazy minute to see her son walk through dragging his gym bag, crooked cowlick pointing to heaven, but it was only Art. The slump of his shoulders told her Brian hadn't been found.

"The police are out there looking now. I'm just in for a cup of coffee and a jacket. It's getting cold." A pang of regret crossed his features as soon as he said the words. Cold. It was getting cold. Brian didn't have a jacket. Typical Southern California winter, the days were warm, but the temperatures began to drop as soon as the sun went down. The thought clutched her heart and squeezed.

Davy spun toward her. "Crackers."

Olivia's mind leaped to the day Crackers trailed Brian into the bushes by Davy's community pool. "Can he..."

"I don't know. He's young. He hasn't had a lot of training, but we've been working him. It's better than standing here doing nothing."

"I'll walk you to the car." Anxiety made Olivia restless.

"I'll call your cell if there's—" Millie's words were cut off by the slam of the office door.

2.7.7

BY THE TIME Davy returned with Crackers it was dark, and the school was deserted except for Art and the night maintenance man, Alejandro. Art had asked Alejandro to hold off cleaning so he wouldn't wash away any trail that might still exist. The four of them assembled outside Brian's classroom on the second floor. The empty hallway yawned on either side, cold and silent.

"Do you have something of his?" Davy said.

"Yeah. His gym bag was in my car." Olivia pulled a soiled T-shirt out of her tote bag. Davy commanded Crackers to sit and offered him the shirt. The dog sniffed daintily at first, then with more excitement. His ears picked up. His tail thumped the linoleum floor. "He smells Brian. Don't you, boy?" Crackers whined in response. The sound seemed to increase in volume as it bounced off the cinderblock walls, then echoed through the corridors.

"How does this work?" Art shifted his weight from hip to hip as if loosening his joints, readying himself for action.

"Dogs are smelling machines. We have about six million olfactory receptors in our noses, they have 300 million." Davy launched into the lecture Olivia had heard from Brian more times than she could count. She knew Davy was calming himself with the familiar recitation. "A drug sniffing dog once found a sealed bag of marijuana submerged inside a can of gasoline. They're amazing. There are even dogs that can locate cancer cells in people doctors have pronounced well."

"About 400 stinky kids been walking all over this place today." Alejandro waved a hand down the corridor. "How's he going to know which smell belongs to your kid?"

"A huge section of a dog's brain is devoted to analyzing odors. They may not be as smart as we are, but they have about forty times more horsepower in that department." Davy scratched Crackers behind his ears. "He hasn't had much proper search and rescue training. He's only a pup. But he loves Brian, and we've been working on tracking. We figured it was worth a shot."

Brian was alone, maybe cold, probably afraid. Olivia had a sudden image of a stream of students pouring out through the school doors like blood from a wound, her boy trapped somewhere in the drained building. A draft, like a dying breath, blew past her. She wrapped her arms around herself. "If we're going to do it, let's do it."

"Right," Davy said. He held the shirt out to Crackers one more time. "Find."

Crackers, nose to the floor, circled three or four times then zeroed in on an invisible trail. He moved in the direction of the stairwell, tail and ears lifted. The group followed.

The lab stopped for a moment at the top of the stairs as if making a decision, then pulled them past into the left wing of St. Barnabas. Halfway along that corridor, they came to a wall of lockers. Crackers whistled high in his throat and lunged toward one of them. He sniffed the perimeter of the door, barked once, then sat and looked at Davy.

"Is that Brian's locker?" Olivia asked.

"It can't be," Art said. "Only high school students have lockers. Brian is in elementary school."

The glimmer of hope Olivia had been nursing went dark and floated away like a wisp of smoke. It was no good. The dog was too young. Too inexperienced. Or, worse, Brian had disappeared and left no trace of himself behind, like he'd never been.

"Good boy." Davy's voice held false cheer. He handed two small treats to the dog one after the other and patted his head. He pulled out the t-shirt he'd hung from his pocket, put it under Crackers's nose again and said, "Find."

The dog hesitated, confusion filled his luminous brown eyes, but he dutifully put his nose to the floor again. He wandered farther down the hall, slowly zigzagging its length.

He stopped.

He fixated on a spot. His nose locked in place, and he drew in small puffs of air for several seconds. He pivoted and trotted past the lockers toward the stairwell.

"He's got it again," Davy said.

The group jogged up another flight to the third floor. At the top, they made a left and wound deeper into the labyrinth of student odors. Crackers stopped in front of a classroom door, but after a quick whiff changed his mind and moved on. About three-quarters of the way down the corridor, he halted in front of another room. This time he stayed in place and snuffled with excitement at the door jamb.

"This is Tom's room." Olivia said, her chest constricting.

"How do we get in?" Davy appeared calm, but Olivia saw a muscle twitching near his jaw, and knew he felt the same anxiety she did.

"I got the master here." Alejandro detached a wide, metal ring from his belt loop and shuffled through keys. He inserted one into the lock and clicked the door open. Crackers pushed it ajar with his head and strained toward the rear of the room where a gray cabinet stood against the far wall. Davy dropped the leash. The dog ran to the cabinet and let loose three short, sharp volleys.

The metal cupboard had two narrow doors, each with a handle at its center. It was the kind that usually had shelves of supplies running its entire width leaving no room for a person. Still, the sight of it filled Olivia with dread.

She knew she should look inside but couldn't make herself move any closer. The others seemed transfixed as well. Even Crackers sat immobile before it.

It was Art who broke the spell. He strode across the room, pushed the dog aside and reached for one of the silver handles. A quick turn, and the left door swung open.

Olivia could see three shelves descending from the top and a large plastic tub jammed underneath them. This side of the cupboard was packed, but what about the other side? Only the top half was lined with shelves. Crackers whined. Art pushed open the second door.

Nothing.

An empty space gaped to the right of the tub; a space big enough to hold an eleven-year-old boy. Especially if the eleven-year-old was small for his age.

Nobody said anything for a long moment, then everyone spoke at once. "He must have crawled in there," Davy said.

"Why would he do that?" Alejandro threw up his hands.

Art shook his head. "No offense, but I think the dog needs more training."

They were in Tom's classroom. The coincidence sent a chill through Olivia. "Maybe Tom scared him, and he hid." She didn't want to believe Brian had been shoved inside.

Art shrugged. "Crackers didn't get the locker right. This has got to be a miss too."

Davy dragged a hand through his hair leaving it standing on end. "There's something we haven't told you." He opened his mouth to explain, but his phone rang. "Dad, hi. Any word?" Davy walked out of the room, the cell to his ear.

"What's he talking about?" Art looked at Olivia.

"It's a long, strange story. We were going to tell you about it when we had more facts. Mike, Davy's dad, has been looking into it."

"Into what?"

"Someone was in here." Alejandro, who'd kneeled by the cabinet, reached in, took something from the back corner, and handed it to Art.

It was a phone. Brian's phone.

Olivia covered her mouth with a hand to keep herself from crying out. Although she'd believed Crackers's nose hadn't lied, that Brian had been in the classroom, this was stark proof. The theory had become fact.

"Olivia, I need to know what's going on." Art crossed his arms over his chest.

Before she could organize her thoughts, Davy rushed into the room. "Dad has got a lead. A woman. She's the sister of the first boy who died. I told him we'd meet them at her home. He's there now." He stopped short when he saw Olivia's face. "What?"

"Brian's phone." She pointed to the object in Art's hand.

"The dog was right," Art said.

Davy closed his eyes for a second, then reopened them. "I'll call the police on our way."

"Where are we going?" Although she knew it was unreasonable, Olivia didn't want to leave this room. Brian had left his scent on its floor, burrowed into the cupboard against its wall, lost his phone in its corner. She felt the ghost of his presence here.

"Tom's place." The words echoed from the hallway Davy was already charging through. She shook off her resistance and followed, Art close on her heels.

"I'll wait for the police and show them where we found the phone," Alejandro called after them.

They climbed into Davy's sedan, Olivia in the front passenger seat and Art and Crackers in the back. Davy called the police while they drove and told the dispatcher about finding Brian's phone. "They're sending a squad car to the school now," Davy said when he hung up. "How do we get to Tom's?"

Olivia gave him directions. Art sat quiet and tense in the backseat. Olivia knew he was anxious for information, but he was patient. He understood better than anyone what they were going through. Eight months ago, someone he loved disappeared. He had experienced this same fear. A fear that roared through you, flattening everything that stood between you and what you've lost.

They'd reached Tom's neighborhood. Davy parked around the corner from the house. Art brought Crackers out of the rear seat and handed the leash to him. He gave the dog Brian's t-shirt to smell, and the group waited.

Crackers sniffed the blacktop with little interest. Davy began walking in the direction of Tom's place. Crackers trotted beside him, nose in the air, tail waving. It was apparent the dog wasn't picking up Brian's scent. "If he took Brian to his house, he wouldn't have parked a block away and walked. Crackers might get something when we reach the property," Davy said.

Olivia took a small measure of comfort from his words. They turned the corner onto Tom's street. His house was dark, and the driveway was empty. "Doesn't look like he's home," Art said.

"He parks in the garage." Olivia remembered how surprised she'd been by the organized, spotless condition of it. Most people she knew used their garages for storage or game rooms.

Davy moved ahead when they reached the house. "Wait here."

Olivia and Art stopped in the shadows outside the reach of the streetlights and watched as Davy and Crackers crossed the lawn. Davy edged along the stucco to one of the front windows, angled himself so he wouldn't be seen by anyone inside and peered through. He stayed in that position so long; it was all Olivia could do to keep from running up to see for herself.

Davy dodged past the other front window and onto the driveway. He gave Crackers another whiff of Brian's t-shirt and said, "Find." They walked the length of the roll-up door without any results. Davy and the dog then rounded some shrubbery and disappeared through a gate at the far side of the house.

Olivia's neck locked into a knot. She fisted her hands so tightly her fingernails dug into her palms. She embraced the discomfort. It helped her to keep from screaming.

An eternity later, Davy returned. He trudged toward them with shoulders slumped, all stealth gone from his gait. "No one's here." He spoke in normal tones, no longer bothering to keep his voice lowered. Disappointment, as miserable as a wave of nausea, washed over Olivia. "Let's go meet my dad," Davy said.

"Where are the police? Why aren't they here? Why aren't they searching his house?" Her voice was laced with hysteria.

"I'm sure they'll come." Art put a hand on her shoulder and squeezed.

They got into Davy's car and turned toward the Los Rios district.

No one spoke for several long minutes. Olivia broke the silence. "We need to find Brian. How is ancient history going to help us do that?"

"I don't know," Davy said. "But I know my dad. He was one of the best investigators the Sheriff's department ever had. If he thinks this is important, it's important."

A moan escaped her lips. She dropped her face into her hands. She was beyond words. She didn't care about Mike's record. She didn't care about anonymous women from Tom's past. She only cared about Brian.

Davy placed a hand on her knee. "Maybe this woman can help us find him. It's all we've got right now. I can't do *nothing*." Olivia lifted her face and looked at Davy's profile. She saw her pain and fear mirrored there. He was as desperate to find their son as she was. He was all she had right now.

"Can someone, please, fill me in while we drive?" Art said from the rear. Olivia started. She'd forgotten he was there for a moment.

Davy began at the beginning; from the first article she'd found on her windshield. As she listened to the saga of her failure, guilt draped over her like a dusty shroud. She was the one who'd put her son at risk. Her desire for the man she'd believed Tom to be had blinded her to the truth. The irony wasn't lost on her.

For years she'd nursed bitterness and anger at her mother for not shielding her from Proctor, for not being there when Olivia needed her. She'd accused her mother of selfishness, accused her of making a romantic relationship more important than the needs of her child. But Sarah had been deceived, Olivia realized, just as she had been.

Olivia was as culpable as her mother, worse really. Brian's life was at risk. Olivia's innocence, self-worth, maybe even sanity had been in jeopardy, but not her life.

MOLLY: This might be the worst possible place to leave you hanging, but, honestly, we're ten minutes from the top of the hour, and you still need to hear from Sage.

Let's just recap some of the things we learned. Brian was confabulating again, but worse than confabulating, he was hallucinating. He was so confused he tried to wander away from school. However, on the last day of this installment, thanks to Crackers, we know he didn't wander, but was in a supply closet in Tom's classroom.

A supply closet.

Why would he get into a supply closet, people?

Obviously, he wouldn't. He must have been put there and removed after the fact. But it didn't appear Tom had brought Brian to his home. So where was he? And what will Olivia and Davy learn when they meet with Mike? I'm chewing my finger-nails, and I know what's going to happen.

Before I say sign off, I need to read this diary entry. It's hard. It's gritty. But you need to hear it before you meet Mike's person of interest.

Here's Sage.

Wednesday, July 22nd, 1992

I saw the police car as soon as I turned onto the long gravel drive. My heart stopped for a cold second. No. *Dios mío*, please, please let it not be Doug. Or worse, something Doug did.

By the time I reached the end of the driveway, my hands were shaking so badly my fingers couldn't hold the key to turn off the ignition. I left the motor running, threw open the door, and ran up the wooden steps. Doug and Tomas stood at the far end of the porch watching Travers's house through the screen.

I sat on the edge of a chair before my knees gave out. "What? What's happened?"

"It's Scottie," Doug said.

"He fell off his bike." Tomas turned to look at me, his face expressionless.

"How bad?" I covered my heart with my hand.

"Bad, I think." Doug said. "All I know is Abby found him by the railroad tracks, came home and told her mother. An awful lot of emergency vehicles are there now. That police car brought Mary and Abby to the house about five minutes ago."

"What was Abby doing by the railroad tracks by herself?"

Doug shrugged.

A jolt of adrenaline flooded through me when I thought about the vulnerability of that little girl near the fast-moving trains. My anxiety shifted to my daughter. "Where's Lily?"

"Your sister came to get her. She took the girls to a movie."

That's right. I'd forgotten. Lily had spent so much time at Clarice's since Doug's accident, she and Clarice's girls had become more like sisters than cousins.

A sudden desire to go to Mary came over me. I stood and moved toward the door. We had been friends, close friends. Like sisters. Mary might need me.

"Where are you going?" Doug asked.

"To see Mary. To see if there's anything I can do."

"She won't want you."

I didn't bother answering. As I drew close to the Travers back door, I could hear the voices of the police, low and quick. Mary's replies sounded strangled. I hesitated. Maybe Doug was right. Maybe she wouldn't want me.

The door burst open. Mary stumbled out holding Abby by one hand. A uniformed officer walked next to her, an arm around her shoulders. She looked as if she'd fall without the support.

Our eyes met. "What can I do," I said. Mary shook her head. "Can I watch Abby?"

Mary's eyes grew large. "You want to do something for me?" Her voice was little more than a hiss. "Keep your husband away from my family."

I stepped back like I'd been slapped. Mary reached down, lifted Abby onto one hip and followed the police officer into the waiting squad car. I stared at the driveway long after the vehicle disappeared.

When I reached my front yard, Doug was leaning into the car. He'd switched off the engine. "You left the car running. That's a waste of gas."

A waste of gas? His words were meaningless.

"Don't you have groceries? We'd better get them inside before they spoil." He popped the trunk and lifted out several bags. "Can you manage the rest?"

I nodded. I carried in the remaining bags and placed them on the kitchen counter. I put the things into the fridge and the cupboards on autopilot, my mind full of questions. What had happened to Scottie? Mary implied Doug was involved in whatever it was. It couldn't be true. Could it? If you'd have asked me that before the accident I'd have laughed. Doug was one of the most gentle men on the planet.

Then.

But now, I didn't know. I didn't know my husband anymore.

Doug entered the kitchen and opened the refrigerator. "What's for lunch?"

I had to lean on the counter for support. "How can you be so unfeeling?" The words came from someplace deep in my gut. "Paul and Mary's child has had a terrible accident. He's injured, or dead for all we know, and you want lunch?"

Doug's face registered confusion. "I'm hungry."

"I can't do this anymore." I spun around. "I can't go on pretending that everything is fine, that you're fine. What did you do to Scottie?"

A spasm flickered across his features. "What did I do to Scottie? I didn't do anything to Scottie. Scottie fell off his bike."

"That's not what Mary thinks."

"What does Mary think?"

"She thinks you hurt her child." I lowered her voice. "Like you hurt her dog."

Doug strode toward the doorway, thought better of it and pivoted.

His voice was tight with rage. "A child isn't the same thing as a dog. What kind of monster do you think I am?"

"I don't know." I heard the hysterical edge in my voice, but now that the words were flowing, I couldn't stop them. "My husband wouldn't poison a poor little dog. I think that's monstrous. A man who does that might hurt a boy."

Doug took two swift steps toward me. He was a stranger—a red, squint-eyed, gape-mouthed stranger. His arm came up again. I raised my own for protection and cowered against the counter.

"Dad. No." A small brown head bobbed behind Doug. Thin arms wrapped around his waist. Doug wrenched away. The movement slammed Tomas against a wall of cupboards. He slid to the floor, cradling his head in his hands.

I darted between them, no longer afraid of Doug. "Don't come near him."

Doug left the kitchen. A moment later, I heard the front door slam.

I squatted next to Tomas and pulled him into my arms. He resisted for a moment, but relaxed and then allowed me to rock him. I held him that way until the sun's rays, now slanting through the windows diagonally, turned from white to gold.

Tomas lifted his head and wiped his cheeks with the sleeve of his shirt. I hadn't realized he'd been crying. "I hate him."

"Don't say that," I said. "He's your father." Tomas didn't speak. "Why did you and Scottie fight at church?" I broke the silence. Tomas shrugged. "Did Scottie accuse your dad of poisoning Pepe?"

He shrugged again.

"Mama." Lily's voice rang from the entryway.

I forced a cheerful note into mine. "In here."

"Auntie Clarice bought me a purse."

I took Tomas's face in my hands. "Don't tell your sister. She doesn't need to know any of this." Then I put on my brightest smile, and Tomas and I rose from the tile floor. "Bring it into the kitchen, *corazon*. I can't wait to see it."

MOLLY: Sad and chilling. Whether it was true or not, we learn that Mary, Scottie's mother, blamed Doug for her son's death. His obituary said it was an accident. She didn't think so. Tuck this info into a file in your brain. It'll be relevant in Season Three of the podcast.

But back to this season. Doug certainly didn't display any emotions when he heard what happened to Scottie. He was more worried about wasting gas and about what he was having for lunch than the death of his neighbor's child.

We also see Tom trying to defend his mother in this entry, which paints him in a better light than he was painted in Olivia's segment. When did he go wrong? Or did he? We still don't know where Brian is or if Tom had plans to harm him.

All this leads me to the final question of the season: Did Tom take Brian? If so, why? Solve the crime, people.

(cue music)

VO: If you enjoyed this episode, please leave us a five-star review on your favorite podcast service—it really helps. *Murders Under the Sun* is edited by Jim Wilbourne, theme music is by Eclectic Blends, and I'm your host, Molly Shure.

part nine

MURDERS UNDER THE SUN
SEASON TWO; EPISODE EIGHT

MOLLY: Welcome back to *Murders Under the Sun*. This is Season Two, *The Garden*, and I'm Molly Shure, your host.

I thought you were going to draw and quarter me this week in the Facebook group. I know you wanted to know where Brian was and if he was okay. But my producers only give me so much time per episode and there's still a lot of story to go.

I never thought when I started *Murders Under the Sun* we'd be talking about my murder. Just joking, people. I know you didn't mean half the things you said on social media. People never do. But the language did get pretty ripe.

Anyway, today we're going to answer all your questions. So, I should be back in your good graces. Right?

You're going to hear not one, but two diary entries. They'll help us tie up all the threads of this strange crime. I know you want to get right to it, so I'll stop talking and start reading. We'll begin the episode where we left off in Olivia's story.

2.8.2

OLIVIA SAW Saint Francis at the end of Los Rios as they rounded the corner. He was illuminated by a light at his base, like he'd been the previous time she was there. But tonight it wasn't his face that demanded her attention. It was his open arms and raised palms. He seemed at once to be offering hope and asking for it.

She released her rigid fingers. They'd been balled into fists since Davy and Crackers had circled Tom's house. The red slashes in her palms stung when the air hit them. She cradled her hands on her lap, palms heavenward like the statue, and breathed another prayer for her son.

Davy made a right onto the long driveway toward Sage's house. Why were they here? At Tom's mother's? But he drove past Sage's and pulled up to the house next door. Gravel crunched under the tires, the engine died, and the soft croaking of frogs filled Olivia's ears. "She lives next door? The woman we're going to see?"

"Next door to who?" Davy's eyes glittered in the streetlamp.

"Sage. Sage lives there." Olivia pointed to the squat yellow building that shared a side yard with the home they sat before.

"Who's Sage?"

"Tom's mother."

The news seemed to surprise him. He didn't say anything for a moment. "They must have been neighbors when it happened." It, she knew, referred to the 1992 death of the boy from San Juan Capistrano.

Olivia had never seen the front of this house, only the side with the screen door. It was smaller than Sage's and newer—a white, single-story bungalow, probably built in the late 1950s. The door was opened before they knocked. Mike stood in the light spilling from the doorway.

Olivia had always thought of Mike as ageless. He had a strong, wide face that looked the same when she'd met him as it had in pictures she'd seen of him as a young father. Tonight, he looked old. His white hair was tousled and greasy, his face lined with deep furrows. "Come on in." His voice sounded weak and tired. He ushered them through an entryway into a small living room.

The young woman Olivia had seen taking in the mail from the box outside huddled on a brown couch against the far wall. Her face was familiar. It couldn't be from that night. Olivia hadn't seen it clearly in the dark, but she couldn't place where she had. The woman was older than the impression Olivia had gotten from her voice—early thirties maybe. A man, who must have been her father, stood next to her. His hand rested on her shoulder protectively.

"Abby and Paul Travers, this is my son, Davy, and Olivia, Brian's mother, and this is—"

Art interrupted Mike. "Abby and I know each other. She works at St. Barnabas. In the school library." Abby nodded a greeting to Art. A flashback to the day two months ago when a young woman with interesting eyes had trailed Olivia from the St. Barnabas parking lot flickered through her mind. This was that girl. That was where she'd seen her.

"Abby, why don't you tell them what you told me?" Mike leaned against the wall and folded his arms across his chest.

The living room was small and sparse. What little furniture there was looked like it had been in place since the 1990s. Olivia sank into a floral print easy chair. Davy perched on the side of the couch closest to her.

"Brian is missing. If you have something that—" Davy said.

Mike held up a hand. "The police are out there. They're looking in all the obvious places, following up any leads we have. We need to look in the less obvious places. Hear her out, Davy."

"I'll tell you what I told your father, but I'm not sure how it will help now." Abby's voice was a rasp of air, soft and brittle. Olivia had to lean forward to hear her.

"I was only about five when my brother died." Abby launched into her story with the expressionless tone people use for well-rehearsed bits. "It was the worst day of my life. Scottie had made a jump for his BMX bike out of scrounged bits of plywood. He kept it in the side yard. The one we share with Sage. He and Tomas used to ride circles out there, flying off the jump. Mom hated it. She thought it was dangerous, and it was ruining the grass."

Abby glanced up at the gathering, a sad smile on her face. "Mom told Scottie to get rid of the jump, but he dragged it to the railroad tracks and hid it behind a utility shed. I knew about it, but he made me promise not to tell. One day, about a week later, he told me he was heading to the tracks to practice his jumps. I said he shouldn't go. I did say it." She crossed her arms over her belly, folded in on herself.

"It's okay, Abby," Mike said. "Just tell your story."

"I was only five," she said again. "Scottie took off. I wasn't allowed to leave the yard by myself, but I followed him. I worshipped my brother."

"We worship God, Abby." Paul Travers's voice was gentle but firm.

"It's just an expression, Daddy." She cleared her throat as if the story had lodged there. "I got to the tracks in time to see him go off the jump once and head around the circle. When he hit it the second time, it cracked in half." The placid mask of her face shattered into tragic fragments. She covered it with her hands for a moment. When she looked up again, it was repaired.

"The whole thing, it broke right in half. Scottie lost control of the bike. He went over the handlebars, and landed on the tracks." Her voice sank so low, Olivia had to strain to hear her. "He was so still. I thought he was dead. I tried to wake him, but I couldn't. There was blood everywhere. I... I ran home to tell Mama. I shouldn't have left him. By the time we got back..."

Silence rang in the small room. Olivia knew what had happened.

The train, the giant metal monster, had borne down on him like it had so many times in the past. But he hadn't jumped out of the way this time. She felt the walls closing in, and had a sudden urge to go outside, to feel the cold night air on her face.

"I'm sorry for your loss, but I don't see how..." Davy said.

"Let her finish." Mike's tone was impatient. "Go on, Abby."

She sat up straighter, her detached expression in place again. "A couple of years later, I saw Tomas sawing a branch off a tree in his front yard, and I remembered something I'd completely forgotten. The day Scottie died, in the morning, I'd seen him coming up from the direction of the tracks with that saw in his hand. I guess I'd been so traumatized by the accident it'd gone out of my head."

"I didn't want to upset Daddy, but I tried to tell Mama. She wouldn't listen. When Scottie died, she'd decided Doug, Tomas's father, killed him. She got strength from that, from her rage. She almost lost her mind when Doug died. There wasn't anybody to hate anymore, nobody to blame. Cancer took her about five years later."

"You think Tom vandalized the jump?" Olivia fidgeted with restless energy in her chair. She wanted Abby to get to the point, give them something that would help Brian now, today.

"I do. I've thought so ever since I had that memory. But what could I do about it? Tomas went away to college in Boise. I saw him every so often when he came home on vacation; then I heard he got a teaching job there. I thought, I hoped, he was gone for good."

"When he came home from Boise, I never talked to him if I could help it. I was scared. Tomas had a mean streak when we were kids. I didn't want him to know I'd remembered about the saw."

He's mean. Brian's words came back to Olivia. Why hadn't she listened to him? Regret, pointed and painful, gripped her.

"Sage told me things though. She told me he was looking for another job. That he'd left his school because a boy in his class had drowned. That didn't make sense. Why would he have to leave his job because a kid in his class died?" Abby's eyes widened, and she looked around the room. "But then he got a job in Phoenix, and he went away again. I put it out of my head."

"We know all this." Davy's voice filled with impatience. Abby's lips thinned, and she stared at her hands.

"What you don't know is that Abby is the one who left the messages for Olivia," Mike said.

Olivia's head snapped up. "What?"

"I was worried. Worried he might do something to Brian." Abby's eyes pleaded with Olivia to understand. "I heard about the other boy when Tomas got the job at St. Barnabas. The one in Phoenix who died when he was on a camping trip. I looked it up on the Internet and found out Tomas knew him. That he was dating his mother. That made three boys." She paused and let the words sink in.

"I started watching him. I wanted to see if he was spending extra time with any of the St. Barnabas boys. I couldn't sit by." She turned her head to look at Davy. "I like Brian."

Brian. His name brought a pain so deep Olivia almost doubled over. A phone rang. Mike pulled his cell from his pocket and walked out the front door, closing it behind him.

"Was it you then, following me?" Olivia said.

Abby nodded, eyes down. "When I found out he dated the mother of that Phoenix boy, I wanted to know if you and he were..."

Davy's voice grew hard. "If you suspected Tom Hartman was dangerous, why didn't you go to Art, or the police? Or talk to Olivia? Why leave messages on bathroom stalls and windshields?"

"Who would believe me? Sage, Tomas, they're respected here in town. I'm the daughter of the crazy woman who never got over her son's death. The woman who accused Doug Hartman of a murder everybody believed was an accident until the day she died. What I had, what I knew, it wasn't proof."

"But you wanted to warn me." Olivia softened her tone.

"I gave you everything I had. You could make up your own mind." Abby turned her palms up like the Saint Francis statue.

Mike returned to the house with a blast of chilly air, and all eyes turned toward him. Olivia's heart tapped extra beats. He gave a small shake of his head. "They haven't found Tom yet. They're trying to get a search warrant for his house."

Davy burst from his seat and moved toward the door. "What the hell are we doing here? We should be out there. Looking for Brian."

Mike strode forth and blocked his way. "Son, listen to me." He put his hands on Davy's shoulders. "Let's think this through. What do we know? What's the pattern?"

"He likes to hook up with the mothers of young boys." Davy spat the words.

"Right," Mike said softly. "Then the boys have accidents. Accidents related to an outdoor activity they routinely did or wanted to do." He released Davy and took his position against the wall again. "Scottie was always on that jump. The child in Boise drowned in the river he loved to play nearby. The boy on the camping trip had been begging to go rock climbing."

"Brian's not an outdoors kind of kid. I don't see how this helps us." Davy said.

Olivia said, "He wanders."

"That's not exactly a sport," Davy said.

"No, now, if our theory is correct, Tom staged each boy's death to look like an accident. Everybody knows Brian is a wanderer. Then he disappears from school two weeks after he tries to leave campus on his own. Most people would assume he was successful this time," Mike said.

"Right." Davy tugged at his hair, leaving it standing in tufts on his head. "But where could he go that would prove fatal? Wandering in and of itself isn't dangerous, not like bike jumps, rivers, and rock cliffs."

"He could wander out in front of traffic." Art spoke for the first time. His deep voice resonated through the room, and everyone turned to look at him. "Brian got hit by a pickup eight months ago. It could be a pattern."

"I thought about that," Mike said. "But a car accident is hard to stage unless you're the one doing the driving. If you're not, you've got an unknown factor and a possible witness."

"If he was going to stage a car accident, why not do it already? Do it near the school? That would be the most believable," Davy said.

"The other deaths occurred in solitary situations. The area around St. Barnabas is pretty busy." Mike said.

Olivia sobbed. "How can you talk like this? Like you're trying to solve an episode of *Murder, She Wrote*? This is my child." She hugged herself. Warm tears slid down her cheeks.

Davy kneeled next to her chair and pulled her into an embrace. "I'm sorry, baby. I'm so sorry."

"Maybe you should take her outside. Get some fresh air." Mike's voice was soft but firm. This wasn't a request. She rose, and Davy led her through the front door.

2.8.3

OLIVIA SHIVERED in the cold night air. Brian hadn't taken a jacket to school that morning. The sun had been shining, the temperatures in the seventies. She'd thought he would be home well before nightfall.

"Let's water Crackers." Davy walked toward his car and paused. When they'd arrived, Olivia hadn't noticed the other vehicle in the driveway. It was the same make and model as Davy's. In fact, she wasn't sure which was his. The only difference between them was the color—one was a slightly darker shade. No wonder she'd made the mistake of thinking Davy was the one following her. Abby's car was almost identical.

Davy opened the door of the lighter colored one, and the dog bounded from the car. He was so delighted to see Davy, his entire hind-end wagged. Davy stroked Crackers's head. The stoic lines of his face broke. His distress was only visible for an instant, before he rebuilt the expression he'd worn all evening. "How far could an eleven-year-old boy walk in—" he looked at the watch on his wrist, "a little more than two and a half hours?"

"I don't know. Why?"

"If I wanted to make it look like Brian wandered away and had an accident, I'd have to make the location a reasonable distance from where he was last seen. He was last seen at 4:00 in Dana Point. It's about 6:45 now."

Distress mounded over Olivia's ability to understand like dirt atop a freshly filled grave. "Explain."

"If Brian walked about three miles an hour, the farthest he could have gone is six or seven miles from school."

"But Tom has a car. They could be anywhere."

"Not if Tom sticks to his M.O. He wants everyone to think Brian wandered off, right? At least that's our assumption. Given that kids get distracted, stop and fool around, I think anywhere from three to five miles would be a believable distance."

Light inched into Olivia's darkened mind as the truth of his words dawned. "The police and the searchers created a grid around the school, but I don't think it was any larger than a mile." She pulled her phone out of her purse and plugged in the St. Barnabas address. A map app opened, and a red pin dropped to show the school's location. A blinking blue dot in the corner of the screen indicated where she and Davy stood. "We're about three miles from school here, but it's a big circle."

Davy took the phone from her hand and stared at the screen. "Three miles west would put them in the ocean. Every other direction lands them either in a suburban community, park, or..." His voice dropped, "Onto a freeway."

"The freeway would make the most sense if Mike's theory about a traffic accident was correct." Helplessness overwhelmed her as the words left her lips. A three-mile circumference around the school was a huge area. How would they ever find Brian? Davy dropped the phone to his side and stared at the night sky. He took her hand with his empty one.

They stood that way for a long time, silent, defeated, frogs and crickets the only sounds. The same sounds she'd thought so peaceful the night she'd sat on Sage's porch. It had only been a little over a month, but it seemed a lifetime ago. Tonight, the quiet felt empty and ominous.

A train whistled in the distance—the seven o'clock to Los Angeles. That's what Sage had told her. It came through every weeknight. A commuter train. Tom had played chicken with that train as a child. He'd told her about the adrenaline that flooded his bloodstream like a drug when he stood watching the sleek bullet barreling toward him.

How bold he felt when he leaped away at the last minute, like he'd cheated death.

Cheated death.

Brian had cheated death in Tom's mind. That's what he'd said that night at the beach. "The train." Panic welled up like bile in Olivia's throat. She gripped Davy's arm.

"No," he said, but his eyes widened with fear.

She ran toward the sound.

She cut across the yard, down the gravel drive, and onto the street that led toward the train tracks, Davy right behind her. The horn sounded again, closer this time.

She bolted toward the street's dead end. Her feet crunched over dry grass. An old utility shed rose before her. A small place in her brain still reserved for logic registered it as the spot Scottie Travers must have died twenty-four years ago.

As she neared the shed, Crackers shot past her. She lost her footing, stumbling on a loose rock, but righted herself and ran on. She heard Crackers bark before she saw the dark form lying on the tracks. The dog stood over a soft bundle, whining and prodding it with his nose. "Brian!" She screamed her son's name over the sound of the approaching train.

She leaped across the gravel divide and kneeled by her son. Davy dropped to his knees next to her a split second later. Brian lay, as if asleep, with his head on a rail. His body stretched across the tracks.

The grinding noise of steel on steel filled her ears. The train appeared in the distance. Davy slipped his arms under his son's torso and lifted. His progress stopped short, only inches above the ground.

"His shoelace," Olivia said.

The bright lights of the seven o'clock to Los Angeles illuminated the problem. Brian's shoelace had been wedged under one of the rails—a possible reason for the coroner to assume her son had been foolishly playing on the tracks, gotten snagged and was unable to jump out of the way. She yanked on the lace, but it wouldn't come loose. Crackers ran between them and the gravel sanctuary nearby, crying like a child. The warning clang of the safety arm dropping across the road ahead bounced through Olivia's brain like a pinball.

"Take his shoe off." Davy had to raise his voice to be heard.

Olivia yanked the heel of the sneaker she'd bought a size too large, and Brian's foot popped out. Thank God she was cheap. They dove off the tracks, falling in a heap on the gravel.

A moment later the seven o'clock barreled past them. It slowed as it drew closer to the station, but still, its blast blew the hair from Olivia's face and dried the tears streaking her cheeks. The reality of its crushing force staggered her. She sat, motionless, until the last car receded up the tracks, and she heard the screech of brakes.

MOLLY: Wow. That was intense. Close, close call. Thank god for mother's intuition and quick thinking. What a scary moment. I could almost feel the blast of the train as I reported Olivia's story.

And now you know who the mystery messenger was. It was Abby all along. And remember how I told you that there's always a victim connection between these crimes? Well, guess who is center stage in Season Three? It's Abby. Her's is a very strange story. I'll tell you more about it in the outro to this season.

Next, we're going to hear from Sage. This diary entry is a little shocking, so hold on to your steering wheel if you're driving. Or better yet, pull over.

Wednesday, October 28th, 1992

"What are you going to do?" Clarice sat on the bench with her back to the picnic table.

I rolled from my knees to a seated position in the dirt, removed a garden glove and wiped my brow. "All I ever say these days is, 'I don't know.'"

"You could sell the house."

"I've thought of it," I said. "But it's not just the house. It's the garden. It's Abuela Maria. It's our history."

"Abuela Maria would understand," Clarice said.

In the past three months since Scottie's funeral my family had been treated like pariahs. The ME declared his death accidental, but Mary had become fixated on the idea that Doug was responsible. She thought Doug had engineered the fall somehow. Although there was no evidence to support her belief, the neighborhood accepted it as fact. It proved the old axiom: If you say something long enough and loud enough people will believe it.

"Lily came home from school in tears yesterday," I said. "It's career week. The teacher went around the room asking the students what their parents did for a living. That Romano boy..."

"Rickie?"

"Right, Rickie, he asked Lily how it felt to have a murderer for a father."

"Kids are mean." Clarice leaned on her elbows and tilted her face to the sun.

I picked up my trowel and stabbed at the dirt. "It's not just kids. Mary is obsessed. Even Paul can't control her. She shows up at the police station with new evidence every week. She started a petition to have our children thrown out of Mission Basilica."

"The kids? Why is she targeting the kids?" Clarice sat up.

"She says as long as our kids are in the school, Doug will show up for events, and he's a danger to the other children.

"She's—"

"Grieving. She's grieving, Clare. I can't imagine what it would be like to lose Tomas."

"I get that, but attacking you isn't going to bring Scottie back."

"When kids die, people want something, someone, to blame. They don't want to believe it was chance, because if it was chance it could happen to them. They want to understand the risk so they can fight it, protect against it, assure themselves their children aren't going to be the next victims. Doug's an obvious choice."

"Then move. Get out of San Juan. Get a new start somewhere else." Clarice's jaw tightened. "I know you love all the heritage stuff Abuela fed you, but for God's sake, Sage, this place is killing you. You can't sacrifice your family for a patch of dirt."

"Where would we go?" I popped a starter plant out of its plastic pot and positioned it in the hole I'd just dug.

"Go to Doug's family in Michigan. His mother is worried sick about you. He has two brothers who could help. You need help, Sage."

"Doug went to Providence today. His doctor cleared him to return to work. He wants his old job."

"That's not going to happen," Clarice said with a bitter laugh.

"Why?" I said, but I knew the answer.

"Beverly Parker, the HR director at Providence, is close friends with Mary Travers's mother. Scottie's grandmother. She'll never sign off on it. I'm telling you; this area is incestuous. You've got to get out of here."

"Even if we wanted to move, we're broke. Doug hasn't worked for, what five, six months? The insurance money is almost gone. Moving is expensive."

"This house is worth a lot of money."

I patted dirt around the basil plant and stuck my trowel into the ground a foot away. I had so little left. If I lost this garden too, I was afraid I'd lose myself.

The back door to the house opened. Doug stood in the doorway. I saw Clarice stiffen and felt another pang of loss. When Doug and I started dating, Clarice was still in high school. She'd had such a crush on him, she'd turn pink and stammer over her words every time he came to pick up me for a date. As the years passed, the crush became a friendship, and then a brother-sister relationship. Now I could see Clarice was afraid of him.

"How did it go?" I asked.

"Okay. They filled my old position. Had to. I was gone so long. But Hank said they'd keep me in mind if anything opened up."

"Good. That's good," I said.

"Can't count on it, though. I'm going to have to get my resume together."

"Something will come up." I wasn't sure I believed that, but I smiled to encourage him. "There's a glass of tea and a sandwich in the fridge for you."

"Okay. Thanks." The door closed.

"Don't forget your pills." I raised my voice so he could hear me through the screen.

"I'd better get going." Clarice rose from the bench and kissed me on the top of my head. "Don't get up."

I watched my sister walk around the side of the house to her car. Going through was quicker. But Doug was inside.

I took my time planting the rest of the kitchen herbs I'd bought that morning in a small plot near the door. When I was done, I rose and stretched the stiffness from my back. I picked up my trowel and the empty black plastic pots and headed to the potting shed.

I was halfway across the yard when I heard the crash, followed a second later by Doug's bellow. I stood still for a moment, then placed my gardening things carefully on the ground, and walked toward the sound. The sight that greeted me took my breath away.

Doug was on his knees in the living room, slapping at something I couldn't see on the floor. "Watch out. They bite." His words were laced with terror.

"What bites, Doug?" I asked.

"The dogs. All the little dogs."

A chill traveled down my limbs. "There are no dogs, Doug."

He howled in pain and batted at his shins. "Stop. Stop. God, I'm bleeding."

I took a step toward him.

"Look out, Sage. The black one." Doug backed into a corner of the room and kicked his foot at an unseen animal.

"What's wrong with Daddy?" Lily had come up behind me so quietly I hadn't heard her.

"I don't know, sweetheart. Go get your brother for me. Please."

Lily disappeared down the hallway.

"Doug, honey." I moved two tentative feet in his direction. "Why don't you get up? You can sit on the couch where the dogs can't reach you."

"Are you crazy?" His eyes were wide, pupils dilated. "The gray one is on the couch. He took a chunk out of me before you got here." He held up his arm for my examination. The skin looked clear and smooth. "No, no, no." His voice escalated to a shriek, legs and arms flailing. "They're all over me. Do something, Sage. Do something!"

I reached for him, to try and soothe him. He smacked my hands away.

"Mama." Tomas's voice was quiet. Lily hid behind him.

"Tomas, call 911."

"What do I say?"

"Tell them to send an ambulance. Daddy's having hallucinations."

I never took my eyes off my husband. I heard my children's steps move toward the kitchen, the swinging door thud shut, and Lily's whimpers muffle.

Doug curled into a fetal position and covered his head with his arms. He rocked back and forth, shoulders twitching. I sat on the coffee table. I wanted to be close, but not too close. That's how I'd lived for the past five months.

Those first days after the doctors backed off the coma drugs, Doug had seen horrible images on the ceiling of his room, screamed in fear when the nurses came in to take care of him. They'd had to restrain him to change his bandages. But the delusions subsided little by little, and by the time I brought him home they'd stopped altogether. But now they'd returned.

Outside the window, I saw a mockingbird swoop and dive at a crow, defending its nest. I heard the cawing lament of the big black bird and the high chatter of the smaller one. Somebody a few houses away started up a lawn mower. The scent of dirt and basil rose from my hands and clothing. Familiar things. Familiar things that didn't belong in this strange nightmare world I'd been living in.

I thought I heard the distant sound of a siren, but it was Doug. He'd begun keening, high and quiet. Exhaustion wrapped itself around me like a boa constrictor. I felt hollow and emotionless, like there was nothing left inside me but brittle bones.

I looked at Doug, panting, eyes squeezed shut, beads of sweat on his impossibly white forehead. Why had I tried so hard to keep him at home? To defend him? A yearning for a normal life, for sanity grabbed me with such force I hugged myself to stop the pain. God help me, I didn't care what happened to him now. I only wanted him gone.

MOLLY: Hallucinations, huh? Sounds suspiciously like what happened to Brian. Could Tom have had a hand in his father's death? Could there have been a poison from the garden involved in both cases? Sage mentioned several times that she taught her children about the plants in the garden, which were curatives, and which were poisons.

We're about to hear what Olivia learned in the hospital regarding Brian's bloodwork. Maybe that will answer part of that question. Let's dive back into her story.

$2.8.4$

OLIVIA SAT on the floor in Brian's hospital room and leaned her head against Davy's knee. Once they knew Brian was okay, that the drug used to tranquilize him wouldn't cause any lasting damage, she'd dozed off. Relief and exhaustion doped her into a deep, dreamless sleep.

She woke when a nurse came in to check her son. "Sorry. I was out," she said.

"No problem." Davy smiled at her.

"How does he look?" Olivia addressed the nurse.

"Fine. He's sleeping it off. Probably have a heck of a hangover."

"Do we know what *it* is yet?" Davy said.

"Not yet, but the doc is pretty sure it's diphenhydramine—Benadryl. His vitals are good, so keeping him hydrated and letting him rest are the plan for now."

"I've given him Benadryl before. It helped him sleep, but it never knocked him out like this," Olivia said.

"You probably didn't give him as much." The nurse made a note on a tablet and left the room. Her words hit Olivia like a punch in the gut. She had trusted Tom, trusted a man who would give a child an overdose of medication then put him on a train track. Rage and guilt barreled down on her with the force of the seven o'clock to Los Angeles.

Hands gripped her shoulders. "Stop it," Davy said.

"Stop what?"

"You're punishing yourself again. He's okay. He's going to be fine. You saved him, Livvie. You did that."

"He wouldn't have needed saving if I hadn't been such an idiot."

"Yeah, well. You wouldn't have the chance to act like an idiot if I hadn't gone on a two-year drunken binge and left you both to fend for yourselves. We can't change the past. It's done."

Olivia inhaled the truth of his words, but she knew it would take time for them to permeate the thick barriers in her soul. Time for them to make their way to the cellular level that changes who you are. Grace and forgiveness weren't qualities that came easily to her. She didn't extend them to others, or to herself. For now, she would sit with the knowledge that her son was safe.

Mike and Sarah peeked through the partially opened door. "Okay to come in?" Mike asked.

"Sure. He's still sleeping," Olivia said.

"I have news."

"They found Tom?" Davy said.

"No. Not him, but the boys finally got a judge to sign a search warrant for Tom's place. They found some interesting things. Namely a bottle of liquid Benadryl, berries from a plant they're trying to identify now, and a glass jar full of some herbal tea stuff. Looks like he had his own pharmacy in the kitchen."

Olivia sat up straighter when she heard about the jar. "I was giving Brian a medicine Tom's mother made. She gave it to me in a glass mason jar."

Mike's eyes narrowed. "Did he ever do the delivering? Drop it off for you?"

"Only once. Right before I broke up with him."

"Isn't that when Brian started having problems again?" Davy said.

Olivia covered her mouth with her hand. She couldn't speak.

"You have any of that stuff left at home?" Mike asked.

She nodded.

Sarah sat on the end of Brian's bed and put a hand on Olivia's shoulder. "We do our best, sweetheart."

Tears swelled in Olivia's eyes.

"I blamed myself for a long time for what happened to you, but it didn't change anything. Beating yourself up won't fix the past."

"Mom," Olivia said, then stopped. She was having a hard time getting the words past the tightness in her throat. "I blamed you too."

"I know."

"I get it now, and I'm sorry. I'm so sorry."

"I know that too."

Olivia's head dropped onto her mother's knee. Sarah stroked her hair just as she used to when Olivia was small. They sat that way for a long time.

2.8.5

TWO DAYS AFTER CHRISTMAS, Sage sat on Olivia's green couch, sunlight glinting off the salt in her salt and pepper hair. Her face was wreathed in sadness. "It was angel's trumpet," Olivia said.

"Angel's trumpet? The flower?" Sage said.

"Yes, the crime lab identified the berries."

"I have a plant in my backyard. Tomas must have gathered some when he came to see me. Tea made from the berries will cause hallucinations. If someone is given enough of it, particularly if they are already on certain medications, they can die."

"He gave Brian a soda whenever he went for tutoring. Tom must have added some to that. The doctor believes that's why Brian was acting so strangely."

"I'm sorry," Sage spoke in the hushed tones used in a funeral parlor.

"They tested the tincture you made. The jar he dropped off. It was fine, no poison. But the jar they found in Tom's kitchen was full of the stuff."

"I should have known. Should have seen." Sage looked stricken.

Olivia hesitated, two voices in her mind were fighting for dominance. The first wanted justice, wanted to punish Sage for her blindness. The second was more circumspect. It understood the heart of a mother, the raw, aching desire for a healthy, whole child. "But you didn't know," she said, and the words cost her.

"I suspected." Tears filled Sage's eyes and splashed onto her cheeks. She wiped her face with her hands.

"Why?" Olivia said. "Why innocent children?"

Sage didn't say anything for a long moment. Then she said, "I have a plant hospital on the far side of the house. It's a sheltered area that gets morning sun but no harsh weather. I start seedlings there and sometimes, if a plant gets a disease or a parasite, I cut it back and stick it on a shelf in the hospital. Try to save it, you know?"

Olivia nodded, but didn't think Sage noticed. Her eyes were on the past.

"One day when Tomas was sixteen, I went out to check on my patients, but they were all gone. I found what was left of them in the trash, roots mangled, pots broken. I thought maybe Tomas was playing ball and knocked down the shelf by accident. I didn't say anything. But then a few weeks later, I found aphids on a potted rose. I cut it back, sprayed it, and put it on the shelf. Next morning—gone. Lily had gone to live with my sister by then, so I knew it had to be him. I asked him about it."

She paused for so long this time Olivia finally said, "What did he say?"

Sage met her eyes. "I don't like damaged things. That's it. That's all he said."

A ripple of nausea coursed through Olivia. "Are you saying Tom got rid of those boys in Idaho and Arizona because they were damaged?"

"I think in his own confused way he was trying to help their mothers."

"Why did he kill Scottie then? Scottie wasn't damaged."

"Scottie's death was an accident." Sage's face showed genuine confusion.

"Abby thinks Tom vandalized the jump and that's why it collapsed."

Sage shook her head slowly. "Mary thought that's what Doug did, but I never believed it. What are the chances of the jump breaking at exactly the right moment and in exactly the right way for Scottie to fall across the tracks and hit his head just as a train was coming? It isn't possible. No one could plan that. Not an adult. Certainly not a child. It was an accident. Tomas grieved for his friend."

Sage grabbed Olivia's hand. "You didn't know him before Doug's accident. He was a wonderful boy. I tried to protect him from his father's influence, but I'm afraid I was too late."

"Too late?"

Sage gave her a sad smile. "I've done unthinkable things for the people I love. I think Tomas loved you, Olivia."

Olivia yanked her hand away. "No. You don't show love by destroying the one thing that gives that person a reason for living. If Brian had died, I would have been right behind him."

"I think he wanted to rescue you."

"From what? From my own child?"

"From a life of pain—a life of watching the person you love leave you by inches, turn into a monster before your eyes."

A deep chill settled into Olivia's bones. That wasn't Brian's story. What was Sage trying to tell her? "I think you should leave," Olivia said. She couldn't listen, didn't want to know. Sage didn't move.

"Hear me, Olivia. I'm not excusing him any more than I'm excusing myself for the wrongs I've done. I just want you to understand."

"Brian was getting better. Tom made him worse by giving him a hallucinogen. Tom wasn't trying to save me from something. He wanted me all to himself. Brian was competition."

Sage stared at her hands for a long moment, then stood. She reached into her purse and handed Olivia a slip of paper. "The recipe," she said. "For the tincture. It's not hard to make when you have the ingredients." She moved toward the door.

Olivia let the paper flutter to the floor. "Do you know where he is?"

"He's gone." Sage never turned.

"He's dangerous, Sage. He needs to be in custody. He's killed two children. Tried to kill Brian."

"He won't kill again." Sage put her hand on the knob.

"Who's going to stop him?" Olivia's voice was edged with hysteria.

"I will." The door closed behind Sage.

MOLLY: So, Tom got rid of kids he felt were defective. Nice guy.

This entry brings up the constantly reoccurring theme of this podcast: How much of psychopathy is genetic? We know that Tom's grandfather was an unfeeling abuser. At least, according to Sage, he was. If Tom didn't have a DNA strand linking him to that kind of behavior, would he have taken the path he took? Or would he have become, say, self-destructive when his father went off the rails? Or maybe he'd have gone the other way and tried to compensate for the wrongs of his family by joining the Peace Corps, becoming a priest, or even just a phenomenal and compassionate teacher.

Science has been debating this issue for decades. We probably won't solve it in this podcast. However, I believe it's good for us and for society for us to take a long, hard look at crime and ponder its causes. Maybe, in that way, we can head a few things off at the pass. Reduce the number of victims in the future.

On another topic, what did Sage mean that she'd take care of things? How did she plan to do that? We can't know for sure, but this final diary entry from five years after Doug's death fills in some of the missing puzzle pieces.

August 8th, 1997

I heard a crash. It came from the direction of the living room. I ran toward the sound. Lily cowered on the floor by the couch. Tomas stood over her, something glinted silver in his upraised hand. His face was as red as Lily's was pale. "Tomas," I shouted.

His eyes met mine, but I don't think he saw me. Not at first. Several long seconds passed. He dropped his arm. My garden shears hit the wood floorboards with a clatter. Lily scrambled away from him and wrapped herself around my legs.

"What are you doing?" The words, aimed at my son, shot from my lips.

Tomas stared at his shoes. "She was an hour and a half late. I know how worried you get when she's late."

"You don't threaten someone with shears because they're late."

Tomas looked at me. "She's always upsetting you, Mama."

Lily had turned thirteen six months ago, and it was as if a switch had flipped inside her. She'd always been my easy child, but no longer. She was now defiant, disobedient, and disrespectful. I'd grounded her, taken away television, issued all the usual parental threats, with very little results. A month ago, Tomas decided to take matters into his own hands.

The first time he meted out discipline, he'd slapped her with an open hand after she'd spoken disrespectfully to me. The next, I found her locked in the garden shed. She'd sneaked out of the house after I'd grounded her. Today was the first time Tomas had picked up a weapon.

"You cannot touch your sister." My voice trembled. "I'm her mother. It's my job to raise her."

"You're not doing it very well." Tomas spun on his heel and walked out. A moment later I heard his bedroom door slam.

I sank onto the couch and pulled Lily into my lap. She buried her face in my neck and cried as if her heart would break. She loved her brother and didn't understand his cruelty. But I did.

When Doug was in college, he'd studied psychology. He'd planned to become a psychiatrist. By his junior year he realized he didn't have a burning desire to help people. He wanted to understand his father, and he learned everything he needed to know in his undergraduate courses. Clyde Hartman was a psychopath. Doug also learned psychopathy was influenced by genetics.

One day when Tomas was five or six, Doug found him watching a moth that had flown too close to a citronella candle in the yard. His small face was serene as he watched the moth struggle on the tabletop. After a moment, he picked up the glass jar that contained the candle and smashed the insect.

"That was kind of you," Doug said.

Tomas looked at him without understanding.

"To put the moth out of its misery."

"I don't like broken things," Tomas said.

After that, Doug kept a close eye on Tomas. And he read. He read every new study, every new report that came out on abnormal human behavior. He learned not all psychopaths were the mass murderers of movies and television. Most were CEOs and CFOs of large corporations, politicians, and highly paid salesmen. Most never resorted to violence. So, what was the deciding factor? Why did one man become ruthless on the golf course and another torture and kill his family?

Most researchers believed it had to do with the environment the person was raised in. If he was loved, protected, sheltered from violence, it was unlikely the child would grow up to be a monster. On the other hand, if he was abused or often threatened, he would learn to strike back. In a fight or flight situation, the psychopath tends to fight. If he fights often enough, he might learn to enjoy it.

I rocked my daughter now, who was almost as tall as I was, and whispered comforting endearments into her hair. She would have to go away. She wasn't safe here anymore. "Let's call your *tia*," I said.

"Why?" Lily raised her damp face.

"Let's ask her if you can stay with her for a while."

"You're sending me away?" Her mouth turned down and her chin trembled.

"No. No, *mijita*. It's Tomas. He's having a hard time right now. I can't take a chance that he'll hurt you. You're too precious to me."

Lily wiped her nose with her hand like a little girl, the red nail polish on her fingers a contradiction. "Why don't you send him away?"

"Who's going to help him get better if I do that? You're the strong one, *corazon*."

Lily's face crumpled. "I don't want to leave you, Mama."

"It's only for a little while," I said, but it wasn't true. Clarice's house had always been like a second home to Lily. She would be happy there. She would go to school, make friends, and by the time Tomas was better —if he got better—she wouldn't want to come home. Taking Lily to Clarice's was for the best, and I'd become quite proficient at doing what was best, no matter how painful it was.

I sent Lily to her room to pack and knocked on Tomas's door. He was on his bed reading a book. His feet reached the end of his mattress; he'd grown so tall. I stepped into his room. It was spotless. I could bounce a quarter off his spread, the bed was made so tightly. I knew without looking, the clothes in his closet were arranged by color. Even the books on his shelves were lined up according to size in perfect rows. It had been this way since the week I brought Doug home from the hospital.

"Tomas," I said. He didn't answer but kept his eyes on his book. "I'm taking Lily to *tia's*." Still no response. I sat on the edge of his bed. "I can't bring her back until I know you won't hurt her."

He set his book aside and looked at me without expression.

"Don't you care?" My voice broke a little.

"It'll be better without her."

"You don't mean that," I said.

He scooted into a seated position. "I do. Lily has been causing a lot of problems for you. This is a good solution."

I picked up his hand and held it in both of mine. "I'm afraid the last few months of your father's life, he wasn't a very good example."

Tomas rolled his eyes to the ceiling. "Why are we talking about Papa?"

"Just listen to what I'm saying. Before the accident, Papa was a gentle man. He never hurt anyone."

"I know." His voice filled with impatience. "You've told me this, like, a hundred times."

"Yes but," I squeezed his hand, "I'm sorry you had to see his fight with Mr. Travers. I'm sorry you knew he poisoned Pepe." Doug and I had made a pact after the moth incident to shield Tomas from violence to the best of our ability. I'd let us both down.

Tomas smiled, his right cheek dimpling. "Papa didn't poison Pepe."

My heart skipped a beat. "What do you mean?"

"Papa didn't poison Pepe. I did."

"Don't make jokes about such a serious thing."

"I'm not joking. I did it for you. Pepe made Papa angry. When Papa got angry, he yelled at you. I thought he'd stop being so mean if I got rid of the dog."

The enormity of his words rolled over me like a tidal wave. "But he told me he'd done it." As soon as I said it, I realized it wasn't true. Doug had never said he'd done it. I'd assumed he had, and he never corrected me.

"Papa knew I did it," Tomas said. "He heard Scottie yelling at me about it that day at church. The day Scottie and I got in that fight."

I struggled to comprehend what he was saying. The pieces didn't fit into the puzzle picture I'd constructed years ago. I had believed the accident turned on a faulty DNA strand somewhere inside Doug. His behavior had become so much like his father's, it was as if he'd become his father. When Paul Travers accused Doug of poisoning Pepe, I never doubted it.

"Abby saw me feeding Pepe, and she told Scottie." Tomas's smile broadened and turned my heart to liquid pain. "Boy, was he mad."

It never occurred to me Doug was protecting Tomas when he took the blame for the poisoning. I hadn't thought he was capable of self-sacrifice, or compassion.

"That's why he was so upset after church that day."

"Why?" My voice was rasp.

"He didn't want me to turn out like Grandpa Hartman. That's what he said."

Maybe Doug's anger was misguided, but he'd been trying to help Tomas. The implications of that sent ice water through my veins.

Doug had been recovering from the brain damage, but I'd been so blind I hadn't seen it. I'd seen a man afflicted with a demon, one that would never leave him. Every protective, maternal instinct in me sprang into action. I wouldn't allow that demon to infect my child. I believed it was my responsibility to stop the family curse.

"Don't feel bad, Mama. Papa was right to be mad at me. Trying to kill Pepe made everything worse, and I didn't even get the job done." Tomas withdrew his hand from mine, picked up his book, and began to read.

I stood, left his room and walked outside into the garden. Its colors were muted in the twilight. The scent of angel's trumpet struck me like an accusation. I had convinced myself Doug would've agreed with my course of action if he'd been in his right mind. My only regret until this awful moment was the method I'd used. I hadn't known *Brugmansia* poison would cause such terrifying hallucinations.

It was dark now. A sliver of the moon crested the horizon. A soft breeze kissed my cheek.

Doug's autopsy had shown traces of scopolamine, atropine, and hyoscyamine, the toxic alkaloids of that vine. No actual plant parts were found in his digestive tract, so it was believed he must have ingested the poison as tea. The tea, dangerous enough alone, interacted with his anti-depressants and the St. John's Wort I'd been giving him. He'd died within hours.

The stories about his demise were varied. Some thought Paul and Mary had killed him. Most, including the M.E., chalked his death up to suicide over guilt for what he'd done to the Travers family. Very few believed it was an accident. After all, how did someone go to all the trouble of brewing a potent tea from the seeds of *Brugmansia* by mistake?

I knew some thought I'd done it. It made the most sense when you thought about it. I had the knowledge, the opportunity, and the motive. But it was hard to prove. Besides, most of the local police wouldn't blame me if I had.

I turned and faced my home. Yellow light spilled from the windows, warm and welcoming. I'd thought I'd made it a place of peace once more. Strife and discord had never been allowed in Abuela Maria's home. She must be turning over in her grave.

MOLLY: Abuela isn't the only one. I have to say; I was shocked when I read this entry.

Looks like the apple didn't fall far from the tree. Sage kept beating the drum about Doug's father, but she, herself, was a murderer. Obviously, she believed she had a good reason for doing away with her husband. She thought she was protecting Tomas.

But, seriously, how blind can you be? There were other ways to protect Tom that didn't involve taking a human life. She could've left Doug. She could possibly even have had him committed somewhere. He was pretty fractured. The fact that this was the solution she came up with, makes me wonder if Tom's psychopathy came through her bloodline all along.

And then, there's the garden. Sage felt the presence of her ancestors in its soil, just as Gwen thought she felt a presence in the basement of the Cliff House. I see similarities between the two. Both held beauty and danger, good and evil, possibilities and poisons.

Could it be that there was a presence in both places that affected the behavior of those who lived and worked in them? I know, I'm getting out there, a little woo-woo, but I want to plant that possibility in your minds. As Shakespeare penned: "There are more things in heaven and earth, Horatio." Or as another famous philosopher once said, "We don't know what we don't know."

I won't leave you on such a somber note, however. Olivia, Brian and Davy did have a happy ending. Let's listen to Olivia's final words.

2.8.6

"CAN I HAVE ANOTHER PIECE?" Brian held out his plate.

"For you, or for Crackers?" Davy said as he slipped a slice of pizza on his son's dish.

Brian smiled. "I gave Crackers the last one. This one's for me."

Davy frowned. "Remember, that dog is sleeping in your room tonight. Pizza makes him fart."

Brian wrinkled up his nose.

"More?" Davy asked Olivia. She shook her head. She was full. Full and content. She lay, leaning on her elbows, on the old blanket he'd brought and allowed her gaze to cross the Mission's central courtyard and rest on the Serra Chapel. Spring had come early. It was late March, and the gardens were already bursting with buds. The air was fragrant with the scent of roses and citrus blossoms. She found it strange Davy had chosen this spot for a picnic. It was a place at once peaceful and anxiety producing.

Before the events of the past six months, she'd loved coming here with Brian and watching him delight in its history. As far as her son was concerned the Mission was almost as good as Disneyland, and it was certainly a lot cheaper.

But, in her mind anyway, this is where it all started. It was here she'd first had the sense someone was watching her. She'd been correct, of course. Abby had tagged along on the class field trip last October and followed Brian into the graveyard to watch over him like a guardian angel.

Maybe Davy wanted to wash away the evil memories. Replace them with pleasant ones. Whatever the reason, Olivia was glad they were here. She was done with hiding and blaming. She was ready to reclaim her life. She closed her eyes and tilted her face to the sunlight.

"I saw Gwen Bishop when I dropped Brian off at school Tuesday," Davy said. CPS had given Davy custody of Brian for the week it took to review the police report on the events of late December. Olivia had been absolved of any wrongdoing and released from the Safety Plan in January. But Brian had loved being at his father's house so much, she'd reluctantly agreed to try joint custody. Brian alternated weeks between their two homes. She missed him when he was gone, but it was working.

"She had interesting news."

Olivia hummed a question mark. The warmth and her full belly made her too lazy to talk.

"Sage's property in San Juan Capistrano just sold."

Lethargy suddenly gone; Olivia's head popped up. "Is she coming home to sign papers?"

"No. They're handling everything through lawyers. There's one on the US side and one in Mexico. She has family there. I'm sure neither of them will ever come back." Davy put a hand on Olivia's.

She'd been too busy to think much about Tom and Sage between work and the lawsuit. After Brian had almost died for the second time in his short life, Olivia realized she had to tell the court her story. Proctor may not have harmed her, but she'd felt threatened. How could she judge Sage for her actions, if she wasn't willing to do whatever it took to stop another predator?

She was making a trip to Vermont in two months to testify. Mark, Teach's son, would be taking the stand, and the Vermont prosecution team had gotten in touch with two of the other grown children from the farm. Once the trial was made public, Olivia wouldn't be surprised if victims from other states came forward. Her mother was going with her. Sarah wanted to be there to lend moral support.

Olivia knew she was doing the right thing, but some nights she woke in a cold sweat. If Brian was home, she'd go to his room, sit by his bed and watch him sleep, Crackers curled up beside him. It gave her courage and resolve.

"Brian, how many different saints do you think are in the Serra Chapel?" Olivia pointed to the entrance. He shrugged. "Would you go count them for me? I've been thinking about it since we got here."

He looked at her out of the corners of his eyes with suspicion but said, "Sure." He jogged toward the building.

Olivia lowered her voice even though Brian was out of earshot. "Aren't the Feds going to try to extradite Tom?"

"No. Are you kidding? Why would they want to open that can of worms? He was a teacher. Three different schools missed it. Doesn't look good for the administrators or the cops. Besides, I don't think there's enough evidence to get him brought home anyway." Davy stretched out his legs and leaned onto his elbows.

Benadryl was an over-the-counter medication. Angel's trumpet vines grew all over southern Orange County. It would be hard to convict someone for having its seeds in their kitchen. Brian's recollections of the day wouldn't convict Tom either.

He remembered getting more and more nauseated as the afternoon progressed. When he left his classroom, he'd run to the bathroom sure he was going to lose his lunch. But the door was too small, and it wouldn't open. Olivia was pretty sure what had actually happened was he'd tried to open the locker Crackers had fixed on, thinking it was the boy's room.

After that Brian said everything went crazy. Demons flew out of heating ducts. A cartoon Tasmanian devil chased him up a mountain. He vaguely remembered a dark-haired, green-eyed giant hiding him in some kind of cave. That was it.

"But what about the other boys? The boys Tom killed." Olivia sat up, agitated now.

"Those aren't even cold cases. As far as the police are concerned, they were accidental deaths. I don't think re-opening them would give the parents any comfort either. I'd rather believe my child had died in an accident than by violence."

"It's hard to accept he's never going to pay for what he's done."

"There's such a thing as divine retribution, Liv. People pay, one way or another."

Divine retribution. One of the lessons she'd learned through this nightmare was that she wasn't the final arbitrator of justice. The twelve steps Davy was following weren't only for addicts. Olivia struggled to admit she was powerless and needed the help of a higher power too. Her compulsion wasn't alcohol, like his, it was bitterness and anger. Wrath had often blinded her to the good in life. She'd worn the emotion like a shield, but it was false security. It hadn't protected her, hadn't protected Brian.

"Six and one more if you count Jesus." Brian's words cut across the grass. Olivia smiled. He threw himself between his parents, grabbed his abandoned juice box and sucked on the straw. His hair was damp with sweat and stuck to his forehead. Olivia reached out and brushed it back.

"Good job, buddy." Davy rubbed his knuckles on the top of Brian's head messing up the hair she'd neatened. She gave Davy a pointed look, but it was playful.

It had amazed her how easy co-parenting had been so far. She'd expected disagreements and inconveniences, but Davy had done his best to keep things amicable. So amicable, in fact, they'd gone out for dinner once or twice without Brian. She wouldn't call them dates exactly, but they had started talking about the future as if it was "theirs" and not "his" or "hers".

"Do you know what today is? Why I asked you here for this elegant and expensive repast?" Davy broke into her thoughts.

"Elegant and expensive? I saw a coupon for Enzo's pizza in the mail this week," Olivia said.

"It cost Enzo something, didn't it?"

"Why did you want to have a picnic, Dad?" Brian said.

"Six months ago today, your mother and I made a deal," Davy said. "We agreed that if I behaved myself, she'd consider a proposition I was going to make."

"Have you behaved yourself?" Brian grinned.

"Of course."

"I remember saying we'd revisit some issues in six months, but I wasn't aware you had a particular proposition in mind," Olivia said.

"Oh, yes. I did. It just wasn't the right time to spring it on you. You were a tad cranky if I recollect correctly."

"What's the proposition, Dad?" Brian said.

"I'm going to ask your mother for an annulment."

Olivia crossed her arms over her chest. "An annulment? We're already divorced."

"Exactly. I want a divorce annulment. It was a bad idea. The whole divorce thing. I'd like to pretend it never happened."

"Does that mean you'll move home?" Brian jumped and landed with one knee under him.

"I thought maybe you two would move in with me. Crackers likes my house better than yours."

A flash of irritation sprang up like a weed in the midst of the happiness growing inside Olivia. It was just like Davy to propose in front of Brian. If she said no, she'd be the bad guy. Again.

But she had no intention of saying no, and she was fairly certain Davy knew that. "How does someone go about getting a divorce annulment? I've never heard of it."

"I believe all you have to do is take a trip to Vegas, visit one of those little chapels, sign some papers, listen to an Elvis impersonator sing *Love Me Tender*, and you're good to go."

"Can Grandpa Mike and Grandma Sarah come?" Brian had both knees under him now. He was so excited he couldn't sit still.

"We do need witnesses," Davy said.

"Noah Wilson went on a zip line when he went to Las Vegas. It was in his hotel. Can we go on a zip line after we see Elvis?"

"Absolutely."

Brian leaped to his feet and raised both fists over his head. "I'm in."

Davy looked at Olivia. Her gaze traveled across the grass to the Great Stone Church. The gray ruin, once a barren monument to death, was now surrounded by a profusion of lavender, roses, and hollyhocks. Their scents perfumed the Mission grounds. Life went on. "Me too," she said.

MOLLY: Aw. Sweet, right? The family got back together, and they're doing great. In fact, you'll see Olivia again in Season Seven if you stick with me that long.

And speaking of future seasons, I promised I'd let you know what's coming up. As I mentioned, Abby Travers will be our main character in the next season, titled *The Hiding Place*. I have to say, her story is one of the strangest of the bunch. Abby is a very unique person.

We've already seen from her dealings with Brian that she's caring and compassionate, but she was also pretty broken by the events of her childhood. Her brother's death and her mother's subsequent breakdown had a huge impact on her. Consequently, she doesn't think the way most of us do. I mean, how many of us would've put newspaper articles on someone's windshield instead of walking up to them and letting them know they might be in danger?

Abby hates confrontation. She begins next season in hiding, hence the name. She sees a terrible thing happening nearby and does nothing to help. You may find yourself getting pretty angry with her.

However, one of the things I love about all seven of these stories is how redemptive they are. The women at the center of these crimes grow in strength and character. They learn about themselves as they face their foes and their fears, which is inspiring for all of us. At least, it's inspiring for me.

Abby, in particular, was very vulnerable when I interviewed her. She wasn't proud of the way she acted in the beginning, but trust me, her transformation was amazing. By the end of next season, you'll be rooting for her.

But I am getting ahead of myself.

I hope I've given you something to think about in this season. And I hope you'll join me for Season Three — *The Hiding Place*.

Be sure to check our show notes for a link to a free copy of *The Dark Room*—a prelude to all the crimes we'll be discussing. This story, documented by local author Greta Boris, takes place before the events of Season One. Some believe that what happened in that Capistrano Beach cottage actually set off a chain of events that culminated in the seven crimes we are exploring. Read it and decide for yourself.

(cue music)

VO: If you enjoyed this episode, please leave us a five-star review on your favorite podcast service—it really helps. *Murders Under the Sun* is edited by Jim Wilbourne, theme music is by Eclectic Blends, and I'm your host, Molly Shure.

Get your free digital copy of *The Dark Room* at:
https://bookhip.com/ZQMTCLP.

If you enjoyed this book, please do one or more of the following:

- Leave a review on your favorite book review site
- Tell a friend about *The Garden: An Almost True Crime Story*
- Ask your local library to put Greta Boris's work on the shelf
- Recommend Fawkes Press books to your local bookstore

VISIT US ONLINE

www.FawkesPress.com

www.GretaBoris.com

also by greta boris

An Almost True Crime Story:

The Cliff House

The Garden

The Hiding Place

The Tower

The Keep

The Manor

The Cabin

The Mortician Mysteries:

To Dye For

Mortuary School

Hair Today, Gone Tomorrow

Bald-Headed Lies

A Permanent Solution

Buzz Cut

Splitting Hairs

9 781957 529264